YUDHANJAYA WIJERATNE

Numbercaste

First edition

This book was professionally typeset on Reedsy.
Find out more at reedsy.com

Contents

PART I	1
One	3
Two	12
Three	28
Four	39
PART II	58
Five	60
Six	71
Seven	82
Eight	97
PART III	105
Nine	114
Ten	137
Eleven	154
Twelve	163
PART IV	176
Thirteen	178
Fourteen	187
Fifteen	199
Sixteen	210
PART V	224
COMMON: A HISTORY	226
COMMON: A HISTORY - II	245
COMMON: A HISTORY - III	262

Epilogue 275
Author's Note 293
Dedication 294

PART I

I have always loved being behind the camera. I love how it sets you apart in a crowd, so that you can float at the edges, pausing only occasionally to capture a moment.

In its own way it's easier than writing. As a writer, I have to know people, to talk to them, to barge into silences with a dozen of those little lighthearted quips that lead up to a conversation. And even then, they're guarded around you. Nobody wants their drunken conversation written down somewhere.

Being a photographer is different. People come to you. They smile. They flirt. They make sure you see only their best side. Nobody wants to upset the camera.

Stop.

The mind wanders. The medication. The noise. The clock by the bedside that tells me I have just hours before they follow me here.

I want to tell you a story. A true story. And I want to tell it the old fashioned way. I don't want this on Facebook, or YouTube, or Anagram; I don't want some faceless monolith of a company owning my voice and my message. I want to write about Julius Common and about NumberCorp.

PATRICK AUDOMIR UDO, Marrakesh, May 3 2071

One

My mother died on the 3rd of February, 2030. It was a bad start to a good year.

Public Health Services came for the body. Two white suits knocked apologetically on the door of our little apartment and watched as my father pressed his lips to her hand. I went outside to the balcony, where the light only reached you once the sun battled its way over the concrete forest of Chicago. When I came back in, they were gone, and so was my mother.

My father, the old journalist, had a cure for death; he cracked open the bottle of whiskey in the cabinet and poured himself a shot. There was no reason to have a funeral, but we had one anyway. Funerals are for the living, not for the dead, said my father, and opened the doors to everyone from C Block.

That was how I met Julius Common.

I still remember him as if it was yesterday. A bald man, large verging on fat. He was dressed in black, in the kind of deceptively simple clothes that you immediately know cost more than your monthly paycheck. People parted to let him pass, their little circles opening up to him like flowers turning to the sun. The conversations hushed as he passed and doubled in his wake.

Up close, I saw that the fat man wasn't really fat, but meat bordering on fat, the kind of bulk that looks harmless until you get into a fistfight or put on a tuxedo.

"Julius Common," he said with great gravity, holding out a hand. Letters marched across it in angry black strokes. *MEMENTO MORI*, they said. "Your father's an old friend of mine."

That was bullshit; my father didn't have friends. People only remembered him when they wanted stuff written up.

Nevertheless. "Patrick Udo."

"Patrick's looking for a job," my father said. "He's a writer, too. Needs to make a buck."

"So do you,' Common said. 'Does Watchmen Press pay?"

"I'm too old for your startup stuff," said my father. He was tired. It showed in his face. "Talk to my son."

Only years later did I understand what it meant that Julius Common had sought out my father. Julius never went looking for people. People came looking for him.

Common handed me a business card. Thick. Heavy. Real cardboard. An '=' symbol glimmered, woven out of marvelously intricate sketches of people and cities. NUMBERCORP, the card said. There was an address in California.

He said he needed a writer. I asked what kind. I don't remember exactly what Julius said, but he made it sounds like a corporate content gig. I didn't jump. There were enough content farms in the world: I didn't want to get sucked into writing Ten Things You Should Do Before Breakfast and Why You Should Vote For Politician X. That way lay madness.

"Give me some time to think about it," I said. "We need to see these people out."

Common looked around. For the first time he seemed to notice the people filling that sunless apartment. At the people who looked back at him, wondering who he was, what he was doing here in his expensive suit.

"These people aren't going anywhere," he said. "I am."

A couple of months later, I opened up my bank's website. I usually had no reason to check the damn thing, but I'd found a job as a lecturer's assistant and there was some money in there. It was a boring job, correcting what the computer missed, but it gave me a shot at getting a loan for my Masters. I figured I could educate myself to a better paycheck. Not many people had a Masters degree.

"Sir, we need you to authorize your Number," said the smooth-faced chatbot assistant that popped up on my laptop.

"My what?"

"Number, sir. Download the Number app -"

"Hold on," I said.

"- now log in with your United Nations Identity -"

"Downloading..."

It tapped the screen.

"Log in with your UN-ID," it repeated. I did.

"Now enter your bank account and this one-time passcode, sir. We'll send them your bank statements for the past five years. Please take a moment to read these Terms and Conditions of service and agree to them."

A number ticked into being on my screen: 3480.

"You'll have to give it your Facebook and other social media accounts, sir. You get higher scores if you're connected."

I did. Facebook. Instagram. Visual.ice, where I kept my photographs and had a bit of a following.

6032.

"Very good, sir!" said the bank, sounding much friendlier now. "What you see there is an aggregate of the traditional credit score, plus additions for your social connections, and any other information known about you."

"Like what?"

"Well, sir, I see you attended Wheaton College for your degree," it said. "Attending a university on that tier generally is a significant multiplier. Not to mention your Facebook following. So, as we were saying, your Number of 6032 entitles you to Tier III loans for personal, professional or educational use..."

Interesting, I thought. I dismissed the bankbot and started looking up this Number business.

NEW FINTECH SERVICE AIMS ADDS SOCIAL MEDIA TO CREDIT CHECKING

YOUR BANK ACCOUNT IS NOT THE ONLY THING THAT DEFINES YOU, SAYS NUMBERCORP, AND WE AGREE

FIRST THE UN, NOW YOUR BANK ACCOUNT: COMMON'S LATEST VENTURE

By the time my father came home, I had like twenty tabs open. Most of them were about NumberCorp, which turned out to six billion dollar financial tech company. The mainstream tech media didn't really talk much about it, except to note the funding coming in.

The rest were on Julius Common. Social scientist. Business tycoon. Born in 2000, at the start of a new millennium. Educated at one of the most hardcore tech universities in China. Comes back to civilization at the age of twenty one and creates the UN-ID, the global blockchain-based identification system that completely disrupted the entire passport and VISA industry. Uses that money to create an investment fund that used prediction markets to invest all across the stock market. Vanishes for years, presumably off to an early retirement, and then appears out of nowhere in Silicon Valley with NumberCorp, billions of dollars in funding, and suddenly your bank's asking for your Number.

JULIUS COMMON AND NUMBERCORP: TRANSFORMING SOCIETY ONE STEP AT A TIME

Some people have all the luck.

My father, watching me, came back with an invitation. Like the business card, it was old-fashioned cardboard, a rich luxury in our times. NUMBERCORP *INVITES YOU TO SILICON VALLEY*, it said in beautiful letters of beaten gold. *UMBER TOWER, ATHERTON, CALIFORNIA 94027.*

"They give us a bunch of these," said my father. "They don't bother filling out the names, who cares about the names of journalists. Put yours in, go see what it's like. You can hitch a ride with one of the crew."

And that was how I ended up in Silicon Valley, watching Umber Tower glow.

It was a ball - a ball in the old-fashioned sense of the world, where those with power gathered to remind themselves of each other's existence. It ran for three days and it was photographer heaven. I shot Mark Zuckerberg bumping fists with Kanye West (did he ever get that money? We'll never know). I shot John Oliver having dinner with Larry Page of Alphabet. I shot photos of the Rocket Internet brothers. The wine flowed non-stop, and the food never ran out. Actors and activists, tech barons and startup sharks and Harvard graduates; my newfound Number shot up just by checking in. They let us in through the back entrance, me holding the bulky Nikon camera that Marek carried everywhere with him.

Years later, I asked Julius Common how on earth he'd managed to put that guest list together. He just smiled and showed me the Numbers of everyone who's been there. Like his own, their Numbers were infinite. Infinite influence by implication. It was the biggest bargain he'd ever made.

But that was later. Back then, Julius didn't know me from Adam. Towards the end, he walked in,dressed in his usual black, his mouth half-cocked, as if caught between a grin and a scowl. Everyone swiveled. I lifted Marek's camera out of reflex. Just before I was jostled aside, Common looked right into my lens.

I clicked.

It came out perfect. The man who would eventually become the most powerful human alive, surrounded by an army of cameras and ecstatic, hungry faces. The bulk of his body loomed over everyone else. He looked like a shark on two feet, an apex predator in a suit.

One frame. One perfect capture.

I published it that night in a drunken stupor, posting it to Facebook and Visual.ice. When I woke up the next day, it had been viewed over a billion times. Legions of celebrities had shared it. My Number was a mind-boggling 12,000. And on my desk, in the cheap hotel room I crashed in, was a pack of hangover pills and a vaguely familiar business card.

JULIUS COMMON, it said on the front. *FOUNDER, CEO, NUMBERCORP.*

On the back: *come see me.*

America is a strange place; it's easy to live a life there, but it's hard to live a dream. Two generations before mine the world needed doctors, lawyers, software engineers. Our parents got into Fortune 100 companies, went to Silicon Valley, set up private practices - and made bank. By 2030 the system had thrown us out into a world of dumb-Ai lawyers and robosurgeons and software stacks that wrote themselves. My MBA, for example, basically just guaranteed a spot in the unemployment center. My friends joined a farming collective.

It was 2030. My choices were simple: NumberCorp or poverty.

I did what any sane man would do: I packed up my bags and went to California.

Today, almost forty years later, Julius Common is an icon. Many love him. Many hate him. Some even worship him. NumberCorp is now the biggest thing since the Holy Tetra of Facebook, Anagram, Google and Amazon.

As of the time of writing, the Number is mandatory for citizens of the Americas, Canada, the United Kingdom and the half the Eurozone. It is human connection quantified. It is everything.

Consider your bank account. Every month, money flows in. Every month, a large amount is spent. Clothes. Occasions. Shoes. Cars. Like all successful humans, you have spending power balanced on the hair trigger of impulse.

Once upon a time, you would have been judged for these things by companies called credit scorers. Now the Number does it instead. NumberCorp looks at the values of the country of the region where you live. Are your people thrifty? Do they value savings? Do they respect the man with no debt? Or do they love people who live large and spend big? Based on that, they put a Number on you.

But is money the final judge of a man? What of your social reach? How many opinions do you influence? How many speak or type your name? What is your contribution to this world? Do you have patents, music records, TED Talks, a column somewhere important? How many people do your words reach? NumberCorp crunches that, too. Do you travel? Where do you check in? What type of clothes do you buy? What concerts do you attend? What people do you hang out with? How influential are they?

And wait. Are you a good employee? Do you obey workplace regulations? Are you a criminal? Do you have a record? Fights, not reported to the police, but posted online anyway? Have you made threats? Are they online?

This is the Number. It is in the things we do, the people we meet, the ID cards that we carry. It's part of our identities, our credit cards, our social interactions. It takes our influences, our biases, morals, lifestyles and turns them into a massive alternate reality that no-one can escape from. It lives on our phones, in our televisions, in the cards we swipe to enter office. At its best, it's an exact mirror of how human society actually works - all our greatness, all our petty shallowness, all our small talk and social contacts all codified and reduced and made plain. At its worst, it's also exactly that. It's how poor and rich and famous and desirable you are. It's the backchannel given a name and dragged out into the limelight for everyone to see.

It's a state George Orwell would kill to see.

And because of this, Julius Common now has more political power than any Emperor or president who ever lived. Parliaments try not revolve around his opinions and fail. He is, depending on who you talk to, either Mark Zuckerberg and Elon Musk combined - or the next Hitler. Either way, everyone agrees on one thing: this is the man who changed the world.

Many years ago, fate - if there is such a thing - set me up right where I could watch both Julius Common and his remarkable empire from the inside. I've followed Julius Common around the world. Few people can say that. I find the man fascinating. His genius, his endless ambition - and even, in darker times, his loneliness, his depression, and the curious moral dilemmas that he finds himself in.

Other people have written about the technology behind NumberCorp - see Eva Lovelace's Inside Number webseries or Shiva Kannilingam's The Wheels That Drive Us. But very few have written about the company itself, because Julius Common prefers it that way.

This book, published after decades of exile, is my record of what happened. And I will warn you: I write from memory. There are things in here no-one can prove; you only have my word for it. This book is a story, and like all stories, it should be taken with a grain of salt.

Two

Like most tech companies back then, NumberCorp had its own campus. It was a small affair, nothing like Facebook's Menlo Village; perhaps a hundred people lived within a kilometer's radius in a bunch of Tercel flats. Even at that size, though, it had been obviously built for a much larger workforce. *WHAT'S YOUR NUMBER?* screamed the wall that marked where San Francisco ended and NumberCorp began.

"You have arrived at your destination," the taxi said. It was an ancient clunker Toyota with one of those Morgan Freeman voicejobs. "Your fare is three. Hundred. And. Forty. Two. Dollars."

WHAT'S YOUR NUMBER? screamed the wall.

I paid and got out.

The taxi left me, humming its metal song, and I was ushered in by a secguard with a menacing mechanical arm. She noticed me staring. In Chicago, people with augmentations were rare, and usually very rich.

"Two tours in Iraq and Mexico," she said.

The shuttle hummed and took us to someone who looked quite young. Don't Panic! said his T-shirt, gaudy gold splashed over black. His face was baby-smooth, topped with a neat row of curls and framed by spectacles slightly too big for his face.

"Russell Wurth," he said, extending a hand. "So you're Patrick Udo?"

His voice was a rich tenor, the voice of a man several years older than my estimate.

I shook his hand. "I'm here to meet Julius?"

He surveyed me and grinned. One of his lenses flickered.

"He's a bit busy at the moment, I'm afraid," he said. "Anyway, you'll be working for me. So did you like the invite? Card in your room, cryptic wording? My guy almost got arrested breaking into your room."

"That was you?"

"Yeah, we thought you'd like the touch, like in one of those old spy movies. Mission Impossible, what? Where the guy always gets his directives in the most we've-been-watching-you way possible?"

It took me only a short time to put Wurth's story together. Rich parents. Ivy League education. Most of the bourgee used to go for stuff like International Relations or Politics or some useless crap like that and land a UN job, but Wurth went in for double degrees in journalism and digital forensics. His mother, who had landed a UN job, eventually introduced him to her boss, who introduced him to the Special Advisor on the United Nations Global Citizen Identification project. The Special Advisor was, of course, Julius Common. As it turned out, Julius's team at the UN needed to sell a lot of government people on the idea. They needed a good pitchman. The story cleans out from there: Wurth got the job, working under Julius at all of his ventures, and eventually wound up here, at NumberCorp.

Wurth - it was always Wurth in my head, never Russell - walked me out of there as we chatted. The room opened up into a great cavern of a place; walls of different heights sneaked like a maze superstructure from the center, forming tiny partitions and giving the impression of half-formed cubicles. In the distance I could see what looked like a hundred people talking, typing, working, and the faint snatches of classical music stole through. A cathedral display made up the ceiling, showing a starry night at a resolution that was almost too perfect, overlaid with a couple of lines of plain text:

US-AVERAGE: 4043

HIGHEST: 19552

A few janitor droids stood looking up at it, as if their tiny digital minds were entranced. I did, too. It would have made a great photo; now it exists only in my mind.

Wurth asked me if I knew how the Number worked. No, I said, looking away from the scene. He led me to a glass-fronted office, all brick and carpeting; on one wall were photos - men and women, portraits in black and white.

"Time's 100 most influential," said Wurth. "Now imagine you can calculate their connections. The people they talk to the most, hang out with the most often. Second layer. Those people have other people they talk to and hang out with: follow the same reasoning. Third layer. Right?"

It seemed about right. "Can you do that?"

"Oh, easily," said Wurth. "It's a lot like Google's PageRank, but for people. Heard of that? No, that's okay, they abandoned it decades ago. Good thing is, because of how interconnected people are now, there's only three degrees of separation between any two people. Sorry, I've been in here too long. A lot of this stuff is obvious. You know someone who knows someone who knows someone. You to the King of England: there's only two other people in the way. It used to be six, but

Facebook did a study on this sometime in 2016 that showed how tightly integrated society is ... anyway. The number of layers between any two humans is quite small, so that Top 100 can be linked to every single person, and we can plot out ranks for each of these people. Voila: the Number. Every person's social worth, relative to every other person. PageRank for people."

I was impressed.

"Not exactly that simple," Wurth said. "There's a lot more stuff that goes on under the hood. But this'll do for a basic reference. The work we do here is really something we, as in we humans, you know, we've been doing this for centuries. Facebook does it. Credit card companies do it. Even we do it - you and I sit down for a chat and start figuring out who we're related to or who we know so we can put each other on a sort of mental scale. The Number is just about doing it right."

"And this is accurate?"

"Better than anything else out there, that's for sure."

I looked at the Times' 100. They looked down at me, faintly condescending in their black-and-white glory. "Interesting," I said.

So we sat down and started talking business.

"Top-of-the-line healthcare," Wurth said. "You'll have your own apartment here on campus, full room and board, three meals a day free, anything more than that, we've got a cafeteria and a restaurant you can pay at. If you want, we can offer you limited augmentation - you know, most people go for photo-optics, face resculpting, things like that. Signing bonus."

I read the salary offer. It was six times what my father made.

I could have kicked myself for not accepting earlier.

"But look, before you say yes, listen to me," Wurth said solemnly. "The idea is that someday, someday we'd be able to quantify every single thing that defines us. To take you, or me, and every single thing we do, and come up with a number that says this is what this man is worth. It's a hell of a long shot, I have to tell you, but you know the kind of people we have in here. Julius is a genius, so is everyone else at this place, and there's a lot of money in play. But it is a risk. You say no, I'll go on my way, you go on yours. You say yes, you take the red pill, and we'll get to see how far this rabbit hole goes."

What do you say to an offer like that like that?

"I'm in," I said.

"Excellent!" said Wurth. "Fingerprints here and here, please."

That evening I shelled out what was left of my cash for a flight back to Chicago. There wasn't much to take, but it felt important that I say goodbye to the old man in person.

"Go west, young man," he said. "You're too young to remember that, aren't you?"

"I think everyone's too young to remember that," I said.

"True."

He stubbed out his cigarette and we looked out over Chicago. A city of spires and cubes rose to the sky.

"Remember you work for J.C. now,' he said quietly. "Stay close to him. He'll take you further than anyone else can, but tread lightly. Whatever work he gives you, keep your head down and do it well. Jobs like this don't come easy."

I agreed.

"Good luck," said my father, the old journalist. "And stay

out of trouble."

And so I packed my bags and left for the Valley. A day or two of sorting things out with the HR bot, and I was officially a Silicon Valley employee.

NumberCorp, I soon discovered, was split into camps, like most Valley companies. On record, it went something like this: Engineering was split into three - Product, which sat right in the middle, Support, which sat one floor above, and Algorithm, which worked on the Number mechanisms and lived in a tower everyone called Orthanc. The Algorithm folk had to collect tons of data and figure out how to generate ever more accurate Numbers. The Product guys had to build the code. Bizdev had to sell the Number to as many banks as humanly possible; and Support had to back them up.

In practice, Engineering was an interchangeable army of geeks in Monotone T-shirts and jeans. Bizdev, the salesmen, were the peacocks in the zoo: they were glamorous, wore heels and faux leathers instead of rubber shoes, and had Princeton and Harvard MBAs. Engineering thought Bizdev was useful but terribly over-dressed and Bizdev thought the developers quaint but terribly uncivilized. Everyone argued day and night with everyone else and worked from ten in the morning to ten in the night. Those who had someone to show off for paid huge chunks of their salary to rent or lease out an apartment nearby; the rest of us crawled to the company apartments. Meals arrived at your desk via an app and were debited from your salary, and anyone who made the bad mistake of ordering company food three times a day, thirty days a month quickly found how little we actually made once the expenses set in.

It was, in short, your basic large startup.

Wurth, it turned out, was more or less my boss, and was basically NumberCorp's Communications arm; he floated between Bizdev and Engineering, doing everything from marketing to meetings. On Fridays he ran little webcast called Electric Sheep.

"Phillip K. Dick reference," he told me proudly. I acted like I understood and signed into my work mail. After all, this was the Valley, where everyone did something weird or crazy with exotic references involved.

Wurth had settled me in an office jutting out from a balcony. It was all synthbrick and glass. There was a pull-out desk in a corner: I tapped it twice, and the surface lit up. Good. WiFi. I switched over from my phone to the desk. There was a series of automated onboarding presentations: I plugged in my headphones and sat back, learning.

Back in the day - think 2000, 2010, 2020 - the world ran largely on a lot of invisible math. I call it invisible math, because the people who made up the variables in the equations involved had absolutely no idea what was happening to them or how. This was true of a lot of things - personal finance, the stock market, teenage pregnancy - but especially true of credit scoring.

Credit was basically an incredibly complicated way of putting a number on your financial status. How much money did you make a month? How many credit card payments did you miss? What's your mortgage? Do you have a history of credit, and if so, how long is it? All of this, and a thousand other factors, went into a very complicated mathematical models designed to predict risk.

In the US and the UK, at the time, the FICO score, as it was officially called was peddled by Equifax, Experian and TransUnion - three incredibly powerful companies that, between them, could make your life heaven or hell. A good credit score meant you were a healthy financial creature. A bad credit score meant you could be turned down at a job interview, be charged more for utilities, get turned down when you applied for a mortgage. In China, there was Sesame Credit - run by Alibaba, the ecommerce giant - and a few other players that basically did the same thing.

NumberCorp buried almost all of them.

It wasn't just the technology. Credit ratings had always been an incredibly divisive subject. The whole system relied on an incredibly complex web involving everyone from Wall Street shortchangers to the man at the local bank refusing your loan. The banks and agencies creamed billions off the system as Joe and Jane Average were kicked out of their homes and busted down to unnem status. The 2008 economic crisis should have showed the world how flaky their models were; instead, governments bailed out the whole doddering ecosystem, and the world went on ticking. The crisis was postponed to 2025, when the stock trader bots went wild and whole system went down the toilet and the activists set fire to Wall Street. No more, the governments said.

And into this darkness, Julius Common whispered. If you've ever seen him work, you'll understand why I used that strange imagery. A man's worth is not just in his bank account, he said to the right people. Let me try a different approach.

It was initially just a mathematical model, like so many of these things, a series of complex equations built out of a hacked personal finance book and a very thorough understanding of modern humanity. Unlike those who dreamed up the old credit scores, Julius knew exactly how much data each of us leaked out to the world - through our social media, through our likes, dislikes, check-ins, comments, typing syntax, causes, clicks, through the people who responded to us, even through the apps we choose to have on our phones. At any given moment a data scientist, tapping into the social web, matching it with purchasing and search data from a few other select providers - like Amazon or Google - could judge you better than your own mother could.

The first version of the Number delivered on its promise in a very humble way - unlike the scores of an earlier age, it penalized the high-spending jocks, boosted the artists, the authors, the activists, the people with voices and causes larger than their bank accounts, and made sure Mom and Pop, with their scrupulous savings habits, didn't do too badly. Julius took the result on the road, hustled it to a few major banking consortiums - the kind with trillion-dollar assets to protect - and voila: NumberCorp was truly born.

My job was to peddle it. I was paid a ton of money, right off the bat - the legendary Silicon Valley salary - and given a corner of my own. Across my screens, in an exotic orgy of tabs, flowed everything I needed to know for the job. Market research. Search engine optimization. Company profiles. Influencer analysis.

A work Request arrived. *Ping.* We had a Workbench system where any work request had on file the names of the people who were supposed to see, check and sign off on something.

Write a two-pager on our product and its implications, said the Request. The names attached to it: Ibrahim Monard, Aniston Chaudary, Russell Wurth. It was a test.

Right, I thought. Shouldn't be too difficult.

I put the pieces together and looked at it. Wurth's Time 100 explanation was still fresh in my mind. From what I could understand, a great deal of proprietary tech read your posts, figured out who you talked to, where you checked in so on. First it tried to figure out roughly where you were on the incredibly interconnected web of people online. Then it went a layer deeper. Routine misspelling, a certain percentage of re-shares to original posts; a certain type of content watched; a certain class of jobs; poor engagement on your statuses - a social model would immediately mark you down as less likely to be economically successful. Smaller Numbers, then. Proper English, a certain type of content shared, a certain amount of attention from the rest of your social web - a recipe for bigger Numbers.

In a nutshell, I scribbled, the Number looks at data and tries to put a value to who you are as a person.

The sentence gave me the sensation of looking down into a deep well.

I wrote and rewrote, hunched over the small desk. There was just not enough information out there. It was surprising at first, and infuriating later. A six billion dollar company, and not a peep from the press - only vague PR announcements of partnerships. Very soon I passed the point of what I knew and sailed right into the land of bullshit speculation.

Nevertheless, I wanted to make a good impression, so by 3 PM the thing was ready. Wurth was on his way upstairs. He pushed the door in with his head, performed an awkward wiggle, and emerged triumphant with his coffee intact. I showed him the article.

"But we don't just use Facebook," he said.

"We don't?"

"Good grief, no!" He seemed astonished. "We use everything, dude. UN-ID gives us travel records. Twitter, Anagram, Tenjin. Even geodata. We've got deals in place with almost every university, you know, so we can access education records. I mean, there is a lot, repeat a lot more than this."

I wanted to point out that I knew absolutely nothing. I'd just joined. "There's nothing on Google."

"Yeah, the public stuff is terribly simplified," he said. "There's so much we really can't put out there. Like, can you find a decent up to date explanation on how the Google algorithm works? Or the Facebook timeline?"

A bell chimed in the distance, spilling loud notes that echoed throughout the chamber. Some sort of tea break.

My desk chimed, too. A comment from Aniston.

Too generic, she had said. *Read up on the business case studies and the credit checking industry a little bit. We need to write against our competition.*

Expected better. Redo from start, Ibrahim Monard had commented simply.

Wurth looked thoughtful and sipped his coffee. "Good news is, you can write," he said. "Good hook, good summary. Bad news is, you don't know your tech. Alright. Let's try this again ..."

I have to say I got a handle on the work pretty fast at NumberCorp. I reported directly to Wurth. The next most important person, as far as I was concerned, was Aniston Chaudary, who turned out to be the Viking-blonde Harvard postdoc who ran Business.

By unspoken agreement I understood that Wurth also expected me to deal with the things he didn't want to. Things

Wurth didn't like: writing, routine, making presentations, attending meetings. Things Wurth liked: hosting meetings, research, cooking up grandiose marketing schemes. Net result: he did most of the ideating and the people stuff, I did most of the work.

Occasionally Bizdev, via Chaudary, would ask us for 'materials' - presentations, write-ups, whatever it took to convince customers. I made sure they had it. If the request was far out of my technical depth I went to Exhibit C: Ibrahim Monard.

Monard, it turned out, was the Head of Engineering. Ibrahim would usually explain it in one sentence. If he couldn't, a helpful, but slightly confused developer would show up and explain that Ibrahim was busy, could they run me through whatever I needed to know?

I got very good at writing things that very few people read. And in the meantime, I got used to life. I got used to my little faux-brick apartment and the wallscreen and the three free meals a day and the paycheck I didn't have to spend. The work that came my way was mostly market research stuff. Refinance Corp, for instance, would want to know what the Number could do for them. I'd look at their market, assemble a nice writeup full of what we called use cases, throw in some reasonably intelligent estimates about cost savings and such, and send it over to Business. Wurth would read it. Aniston would put her stamp on it. Then they'd pass it on to the CFO or CIO or whoever it was.

And Julius? I barely saw him around in those early days. But he was everywhere; in the Workbench threads, in the news, in the codebase. Sometimes, over lunch, engineers would talk of bizarre bits of code that did things that shouldn't even have been possible; often it would turn out that these bits were written by Julius years ago. They took a sort of weird pride in arguing with him; those who argued long and often with Julius were given the same sort of respect that you give a man with several bombs strapped around his chest.

I didn't quite understand it, but I didn't need to.

"How's work?" my father would ask every time I called him, which was once a week or so.

"Good," I said. "Food's good, there's a good pub nearby, apartment's not too bad."

"And the work?"

"Good."

"There's not a lot about your company on the Internet."

It was 'your company' now. "Proprietary tech, and the market is B2B," I'd explain. "Banks, finance corps, you know how it is."

"Good, good," my father would say. "Work hard."

Do I make it sound like my tale should have ended here? Perhaps it should have. In any other lifetime, it would have. I'd have put in a few years at NumberCorp, traded in my ID for a job with better pay, maybe at Google or at Facebook, where people made real money. I'd have burned out, tried doing my own startup, failed, and gotten famous off a blogpost taking myself apart. Maybe I could have denounced the whole scene and gone off to live on a yacht, like that guy who wrote Chaos Monkeys. But life, as one wise man noted, is a play, and that was not my part to act.

Instead, one fine day, Wurth asked me if I drank. Or had someone to drink with.

"Not very social, are you?" he noted after a while.

I told him I preferred staying indoors.

"I know the feeling," he said. "But if you can drink with

people, drink. It's easier to get stuff done once you've had a few beers with someone."

I don't know if it was pity that compelled him, but to this date that remains some of the most practical advice anyone's ever given me. When in doubt, drink.

The taxi arrived and took us out on a road that snaked around the arse end of the campus. In the distance, the sun shimmered off towers of glass, sprinkling itself over the city that rose in the haze. We were quite a way off.

"Pretty," I said.

"It gets prettier at night," Wurth said. "Here we are, Elkhead."

Elkhead was the pub. It was a six-tiered layer cake of a watering hole. Each floor was different. The first was just an open space with a bar; the third strobed with neon lights and the drinks glowed in the dark; and then there was the fifth, where we sat: a passable mimicry of an old English pub, with synthwood paneling and photos on the walls. Someone looking closer might have recognized these photos. Robert Noyce, Gordon Moore and Andy Grove of Intel; Steve Jobs and Steve Wozniak of Apple; Elon Musk; Mark Zuckerberg; Peter Thiel; and others, too many to count. It was a shrine to those who had made the Valley what it was.

And here were the people I was supposed to meet. The chatter of beer-time conversation drifted over us.

"Ladies, gentlemen, everyone in between," broke in Wurth with a grand flourish. "Meet Patrick."

"Wurth, you finally get a minion," said Aniston Chaudary, who was in full-on Viking goddess mode that day; she had a great mane of golden hair held in a braid: she looked like she could fit into a catwalk or a medieval warzone with equal ease.

There was a flurry of small talk as she introduced me to a few of her team; other newbies, just like me.

"Patrick Udo," I replied to each of them. "Communications."

Wurth handed me a beer.

"So go on," said a lean man who looked more like a soldier than a developer. He was reclining lazily in a corner. "How'd you end up here?"

Monard. Or, as he said: "Ibrahim, no need to be so formal."

I quickly sketched out the chain of events that led me to NumberCorp. They knew my father. Marcus Udo, it turns out, was not a celebrity - that was reserved for the CEOs and the investors - but he was known for his investigations into the stock market collapse and the Valley's part in it, and he was remembered for the postmortems he'd done on Valley companies that went bust.

They talked about him a bit.

"Damn good writer," Wurth said. "No wonder Jules tried to hire him."

"Not the kind of man who'd work for a corporate," Ibrahim said. "More the kind of man who'd write our obituary."

"Yeah, well," Wurth said, tilting his glass at me. "We got his son, didn't we?"

It seemed a point of pride with him. My father would have felt some small sense of gratification, knowing that these Valley folk, making ten times more than he ever would, still knew his name.

"So what do think of NumberCorp, Pat? Like the place?"

All eyes fell on me.

"Loving the place," I said, with all the confidence of six glasses of beer. "Lot to learn, but that's what I'm here for."

Wurth raised a glass. "That's the spirit," he said. "Welcome to NumberCorp. The product's stable, we're minting money, and all of us have damn good jobs. Can I get a toast? To NumberCorp. To beer at five dollars a glass."

"To NumberCorp," the rest of us echoed obediently.

Three

Not too long after I joined, I found myself crossing the field from my quarters to the office. It was a cold, quiet sort of morning, and I was up far earlier than normal. Which was why I was so surprised when a car thundered past me. It was a long beast, low and black, one of the few petrol ones that still ran the streets. Julius's car.

I met it again just outside the main office. Bizdev was clumped up together. Anxious chatter drifted through the air.

"What's up?" I asked someone.

He nodded up. The meeting rooms on the top floor had glass walls. In one of them we could make out Julius, Wurth and Aniston. Aniston appeared to be yelling.

Ibrahim, who was habitually late, strolled in and saw the meeting. A look of alarm crossed his face and he immediately took off like a rocket for that meeting room.

We were at war with one of the biggest tech giants in the history of humanity.

How this happened was simple. From Facebook we pulled the data of over two hundred million Americans: posts, photos, contact details, location history, the works. It had been one of our best sources of user data.

Maybe we were pulling too much data from their network,

because at some point they tried to negotiate. Julius refused. Facebook retaliated by taking the Number hooks off their network.

It wasn't the only social network we connected to - Anagram, run by Paul Moneta, was almost as large - but it was a massive loss. The engineers howled, and Julius held a council of war.

My memory of Common in those days is different to what he's like on the screens now. I remember him being taller, fatter; back then, his hair was shaved almost to his scalp, and he only wore a very severe black. All in all, he looked a bit like a fat, demented monk. He had a habit of drumming his fingers on the table when angry. The fingers drummed furiously as the list of affected users scrolled across the Pit.

There were engineers in the room. There were bizdev people in the room. There were even board members in the room. Nobody had any idea what he would say next.

"Drop them," he said.

I could see the engineers blanch.

"Jules," Aniston said. "That's a lot of people."

"I can't vouch for the algorithms," Ibrahim said. "But half our server infrastructure goes into crunching Facebook feeds. We pull the plug on this, the Number is going to go haywire. All due respect, but if there's a point, I don't see it."

"When I started building this company, we knew we'd be dependent on services like Facebook," Julius said. "But what people like this don't understand is that the larger we get, the less they can fuck with us. We have two hundred million users who come in from Facebook, right? You know what happens when two hundred million people realize their Numbers dropped?"

He drummed his fingers.

"We're going to tell these people that they dropped because Facebook dropped us. We're going to say the Number needs the data and it's their right to share it with us. And we're going to drop their Numbers again. And again. Until they riot on the Internet and make those Menlo Park motherfuckers come to us with their hats in their hands."

There was silence.

Julius swiveled to Wurth. "Can you do the letter stuff? Mail the editors, cast this around the web, the works. Hire people for social media if you have to. There's a PR nightmare coming and I want you on top of it."

Wurth nodded. "I'll call a press conference ASAP."

"Ibrahim," said Common. "Look for a method called Order 66 in the operations codebase. Read it, call it. It'll start dropping the Numbers at preset intervals. Take backups, make sure you shut down Basecalc and Prediction core before you call it - it'll break the heuristics."

Ibrahim tried again.

"No arguments," said Julius.

"Yes, sir," said Ibrahim. He looked unhappy.

Julius's gaze flicked over me without recognition and settled on Aniston.

"You make sure everyone who uses us keeps using us. Banks, financial agencies, top priority."

"That's a lot of people, Jules," Aniston repeated. "We're going to hurt their Numbers, their financial future..."

"Good," Julius Common said. "*Cuius testiculos habeas, habeas cardia et cerebellum.* When you have them by the balls, their hearts and minds will follow. Do it."

That, for better or for worse, was my first real introduction to Julius Common. Within hours we were in a state of cold war.

By every single standard on the planet it was nothing short of suicidal. Facebook was one of the Tetra - over thirty thousand employees, a veritable city within a city in the Valley, and enough influence and money in the bank to buy several small countries. We were a hundred-man outfit with a retrofitted campus.

But it worked. I never saw the effects in the world outside those walls; when you're barely a month into a new job, you don't fly off to see the world around you. Instead, I saw the battle as it unfolded inside NumberCorp.

Bizdev went into crisis mode. Within days, half of the glamorous crowd had shipped out to clients to make sure they didn't drop. They converged in hordes on the banks. Sleep with them if you have to, just make it happen, Aniston is supposed to have said. And it did. We lost just one customer; twenty thousand dollars a month, no more.

Moving at lightning speed, Wurth engineering a revolt. I have no other way of putting it. He marshaled about twenty engineers who had the kind of online reputation he wanted and put them to work. lt started on Reddit, with us profusely apologising for what just happened, and hinting that it was Facebook's fault. Facebook, we alleged, was using its monopolistic control of the market to ruin companies like ours, and there was nothing we could do about it.

We redid the website. *WHAT'S YOUR NUMBER?* it said at the top. There was a collage of some pretty famous people and their Numbers.

It looked good. We came up with the most bait-worthy taglines we could think of. We made sure that whoever looked for NumberCorp would find something fancy to read - and we started hitting out left, right and center. We split out to rant about it on Facebook, Anagram, ReadNet. We conducted violent verbal warfare over mail threads. We started Change.org campaigns. We reached out to rival social networks and users with ridiculously high Numbers alike and urged them to bitch about it on every single channel they could.

Meanwhile, the banks started calling. They wanted their Numbers back to being reliable.

STARTUP POINTS FINGERS AT FACEBOOK, said the headlines.

And, on the heels of that, because people were now paying attention:

WHAT IS NUMBER?

'The Number,' we wrote grandly, 'is the measure of your value as a human being.'

There were some who laughed at us. *KLOUT ON STEROIDS*, the New York Times called it. *DOES SILICON VALLEY HAVE NOTHING BETTER TO DO?*

Wurth laughed when I showed him this.

"Have you seen that old movie where these guys capture a pirate and tell him that he's the worst pirate they've ever heard of? 'But ah,' says the pirate, 'at least you have heard of me.'"

"I have no idea what you mean," I said patiently, as I always did when Wurth pulled out one of his obsolete pop culture references.

"Marketing 101," he said. "All publicity is good publicity. The only thing worse than being talked about is not being talked about."

He was right; three months ago we couldn't have gotten us on NYT even if we wanted to. For the next ten days we worked at a tremendous pace, barely taking time to eat and sleep. We had gone from from being a small, exclusive business to being the poster child for the Silicon Valley underdogs.

I have to say those few days gave me a real appreciation for how Wurth did his job. He played the media game like a chessboard: he'd set up one Valley webcaster to talk about Facebook's monopoly (and how stupid that was), and in a flash he'd get someone from Vice to write about how the Number had completely changed how the banks viewed people. We hinted that we might sue. I was on call with every second-tier editor from here to India. The top-tier ones were handled with exquisite care by Wurth.

INSIDE ONE STARTUP'S FIGHT AGAINST THE FACEBOOK EMPIRE, wrote the Watchmen Press.

CALCULATING THE VALUE OF A HUMAN, wrote Ars Technica, *CHINA'S DREAM EMERGES IN THE VALLEY.* It referenced an old Chinese project where the government had tried to provide people with scores based on political leanings. *The old Chinese utopian dream*, it said, *is being rewritten by Julius Common, the reclusive billionaire. For now, this is simply a website, unlike the Sesame Credit system that Beijing launched in 2015; while that system became a way of life, this remains a toy that exists on our smartphones. Nevertheless, let us not forget that once you could talk about Tiananmen Square or go bankrupt and watch your most essential privileges being cut off by a state.*

"What's this?" said Wurth when I sent them the link. "Sounds serious. Did you follow up?"

OLD CHINA STATE PROJECT, replied @IBRAHIM_M.

My WorkChat buzzed with links. Old websites. *CHINA HAS MADE OBEDIENCE TO THE STATE A GAME*, said the Independent. Samuel Osbourne, December, 2016. Years before I was done with uni.

We had a Workspace where we posted ideas. I posted a summary there and put it out of my mind. It was too old and China was the furthest thing from my mind.

Julius came by once. It was almost midnight; I had lost track of time. Wurth was asleep in a corner. The big man glided into our hastily converted war office like a cat.

"How goes it?" he asked, surveying the wallscreens that surrounded us.

"We're ... making progress," I said. I think I was too tired to be too polite. I gestured at the feeds that wrote and rewrote themselves on the screens. Everything the Internet was saying about NumberCorp. "A lot of people are talking about us."

Julius's great, bald face surveyed the scene. "Good," he said. "Good, good, good."

He gripped me by the shoulder.

"Win this for me," he said. It was both a plea and an order.

Within two weeks, the Menlo Park motherfuckers were calling. Still Wurth held out; three weeks and they were ready to bargain proper.

To celebrate, Ibrahim brought twenty bottles of tequila to the office and gave us all shot glasses. Someone printed Korporal Havoc's latest work of art: a thirty-foot poster of the Facebook logo and a young Zuckerberg standing on a deserted road. On the sides, from the lamp posts, hung the corpses of dead social networks. At the far end was Hi5, MySpace and Yahoo! 360. Right in front Twitter. NumberCorp and Anagram peered out from behind the foremost posts, staring intently at Zuckerberg with pale eyes, one clutching a gun, the other a knife.

A Facebook delegation visited us and blanched visibly when they saw this in the foyer. They were neat and good-looking and geeky in their blue-and-white T-shirts; we looked like hell and felt like hell.

When it was all done, and the Facebook-NumberCorp negotiations had officially begun, we crashed. I went back to my tiny faux-brick apartment, turned off the wallscreen, and slept.

The Great Facebook War, as we called it thereafter, left us changed ever so slightly.

First, it won us a great deal of respect - from everyone else, but also, surprisingly, from Facebook itself. Word was that Zuckerberg had actually wanted to buy NumberCorp, but Julius had flipped him the bird and walked out. All of a sudden, it seemed we were being courted by every company worth mentioning. Now that Facebook was paying attention to us, everyone wanted in.

Second, it catapaulted us right into the eyes of the media - and the world in general. Aniston was very happy with this: apparently we were receiving inquiries from banks all over Europe. Hordes of economists were lured our way by this strange new startup that was making waves everywhere.

"For once," as Ibrahim put it. "We don't have to beg for attention."

He was right. TechCrunch, the website that was news central for Silicon Valley, ran pieces on us. Forbes, Business Insider and Wired did in-depth profiles of the company and of Julius. MIT's Technology Review named him one of their 35 innovators under 35. Conferences began to invite us to speak.

Part of the magic was the technology. But part was also the story that we had spun during the brief digital tussle - the story of the valiant underdog startup fighting Facebook itself. We lived in an age where the supercorporations were this close to godhood.

Everyone liked seeing a god bleed.

Things had changed inside the company, too. They say soldiers fighting in the trenches grow almost brotherly bonds towards each other. For the first time, I saw some version of that between people from Bizdev and people from Engineering. People had war stories now, and they bore those stories with pride.

Because we won.

And because it had been a war of words and messages, and it was Wurth's game, Communications won, too. Sometimes respect is as hard a currency as money is; we now had it. Previously we had been looked at as glorified copywriters; now we were the hermits who had fought off Facebook. Wurth was, if not a hero, at least the man right out there on the front line; it was exhilarating.

"People like a show," my father used to say. "You be careful. The same people clapping for you today will be the first to throw stones when it's your time in the spotlight."

I mentioned this to Wurth, who, one evening, took me to Julius's main office in Algorithm. We had, on our grounds, a tower that stood slightly apart from the main building, a dark and looming creation that everyone called Orthanc, after the wizard's tower from the Lord of the Rings. Orthanc was the territory of Algorithm, and unofficially ruled by Ezra Miller, the recluse who ran that division. Julius's office was a dark cave all the way at the top of the tower; Ezra herself had the office just below him, insulating him from the world.

Two secguards in gleaming white armor showed us in. The last time I had been in this room, it had been a war room, full of people arguing about the Facebook deal. Julius had towered above them all then. Now it was an office, large and empty, polished wood shaded by a sort of twilight gloom that hung over it. Julius looked much smaller, cut in sharp lines before the matte black of a single inactive wallscreen.

"Sit," he ordered. "Well done, both of you."

We made appropriate noises of thanks and sat down. The wallscreen hummed to life.

"Do you understand why we won?"

Wurth and I gave a whole bunch of reasons. Clever use of social media. Et cetera. Facebook's monopolistic self-portrait. Et cetera, et cetera.

Julius Common listened to us with a vague smile playing on his features, and began to draw on his desk. On the screen behind him, a shape formed. *MONEY*, it said.

"Go on," he said when we stopped. Again, that half-smile.

"I think the whole underdog angle really worked for us," Wurth said. "We got everyone on our side."

Julius swiveled in his chair and pointed back at the screen, where the word *MONEY* was now circled.

"This is why we won," Julius said.

Silence hung in the air between us.

"In all civilizations before us, those who controlled access to wealth came to control almost everything," said Julius. An arrow sprouted from *MONEY* and grew a question mark. "Our little catfight was no different. Now the question is, what do we do next?"

We stared at the diagram.

"So many possibilities," said Julius, almost to himself. Then he saw our expressions.

"You still don't see it?"

No, we didn't.

"Yeah," he said. He sounded disappointed. "For now, let's just say the underdog angle really worked for us."

Four

My second brush with Common came in 2031.

It was some time after the Facebook incident, and I was really warming up to work. There was a particular kind of energy in those early days, something I've only really found in startups. The regulars - the boring 9-to-5 people - haven't invaded the world yet. All around you are people who practically buzz with mental adrenaline - the kind of people who sneer at words like *policy* and *dress code* and fill the office at nights with pizza and bad jokes and the relentless tip-tack-clack of keyboards. They push boundaries, turn small ideas into game-changers and small arguments into fistfights.

No company can last forever this way: it's a bit like being in a cage. Eventually the strange ones move out and give way to order and conformity and all the things that make for a smoothly operating machine. But that brief chaos is what really gives a company its soul.

Whatever the press thought, though, we weren't making money- not back then. On paper, we were worth billions, but in reality NumberCorp ran off a colossal amount of private funding at a truly alarming burn rate. I asked Julius about this once. We were just a hundred million short of everyone in the US at the time. I know I throw these numbers around like they're nothing, but that's what they were to me at the time: just numbers on a screen. I pointed out that we should be looking at advertising, perhaps bigger service fees.

"We don't need the money," Wurth said. "Not yet."

"But the business model -"

Wurth leaned over in his chair. "We have every piece of data on 200 million people," he said, ticking off his fingers. "We have their bank accounts. We know how much they make and how much they spend and where. We have their social media. We know what they talk about, who they influence and how much. We know exactly how important each and everyone one of them is. There'll come a time when what we make off this balances against what we spend getting there. For now, we need to make it grow."

"Typical Valley," said my father. "Valuation, not money coming in the door. Remember Uber?"

I remembered Uber. Like Uber, we soared forward, leaving a trail of expense in our wake.

There came a day when everyone agreed that we had "captured" America. I wasn't the one making these decisions, but here's how I understood it: after years of careful wrangling with essential services companies, we'd made about three hundred million and thirty people - the population of the United States of America - dependent on the Number, at least as far as financial services went. You could no longer get a loan from any bank without first signing up to a Number check. That was the first big milestone.

We threw a massive party to celebrate. I have very vague memories of this time, but there are a few things that stand out in the memory like snapshots, and that party was one of them. Aniston Chaudary glimmered in gold. Those who had made it through Business with her beamed and hid their exhaustion under makeup. We booked the entirety of Umber Tower and the party lit up half the city. Late into the night Julius Common appeared, large and forbidding. Aniston met him at the door, silhouetted against his vast bulk like a comet against the blackness of his suit. She gave him her hand. He bowed and took it, and as the crowd roared in applause they walked through it, the king and queen of NumberCorp.

In celebration, I guess, Wurth wrote a blogpost, which I still have recorded:

My name is Russell Wurth, and I am an ambassador for Number-Corp.

If you're reading this in a country without the Number, that might sound like a subtle way of saying I'm unemployed. Don't worry: I'm not. This is not a donation request.

NumberCorp is the next big thing. What we do is provide a platform that integrates social networking into every aspect of life - from government to paying the bills to education to fame and fortune. Everything. We've turned political power into measurable metrics, scaled a human's social reach to match their output, and basically linked everyone on the planet to everyone else.

Well, maybe not everyone. At that point, I'll be out of a job.

It's easy enough to explain. Picture a social network. Every person signed into that network has an ID. This ID is unique. Well, make that ID the default identification system for a country. Now consider things like reach and followers - all staples of those first and second-gen social networks. Throw that in there.

Now give people points for working, for interacting, for sharing, for producing content, for reaching out to people and influencing thought and opinion. Bingo: we've just quantified fame, fortune and influence. Then we take all the services we already run and tie them into NumberCorp. Police records? That's tied in. Yes. Instagram? Yes. Facebook? Yes. YouTube? Yes. Birth records, travel, credit history? All of it.

The rest is easy. You get points for doing a good job at work. You get points for influencing people. You get points for what you do on Facebook. You get points for everything you do that marks you as a healthy, productive member of NumberCorp. We have analytics for everything - popularity, work performance, civic duty, you name it, so you know exactly where you stand in NumberCorp at any given point. We have equated your life's performance with your actual life. No more fakes. No more unsung heroes. With NumberCorp, you know exactly what you're worth - and so does the rest of the world. NumberCorp is the true measure of how humans interact.

We've overthrown the Fake. We're ushering in the Real.

If you're interested in finding out more, drop me a message.

He interspersed it with photos I'd shot: photos that showed powerful people talking to each other, gesturing, their Numbers digitally superimposed above their heads, showing the power that they wielded in real life.

It went viral. Mark Zuckerberg himself commented on it.

I'd never seen Wurth get wasted, but we had a rather elaborate lunch that day with the bigwigs of Facebook, I saw him passed out while Julius and Zuckerberg shook hands with each other and talked world domination. The next day, when I got to work, there was a PortaCooler and a bottle of the finest wine on Wurth's desk.

"To the Number," said Wurth, in the half-darkness of our

office-cave.

You have to take your victories where you can.

"To us," I said, and we drank.

A few days later, my phone buzzed with a message from Julius. *Come to Sri Lanka*, it said unfolding a flight plan, hotel stay and the works. I sent it to Samantha, our @HRprocess bot, who congratulated me and sorted out my place tickets. Before I knew it, I was on a plane, and that plane was soon skidding onto the runway at the Bandaranaike International Airport, Sri Lanka.

Sri Lanka is a beautiful little island nation parked perilously close to India; a little too hot, a little too humid, and perhaps too expensive, but to its credit are fantastic beaches, strangely melancholy hills, and the ruins of kingdoms past. Common was on pilgrimage there, I was told.

Just as I blundered out of the packed doors and into what felt like a heatwave, a car rolled up to us and an alarmingly fat man poked his head out of the passenger window.

"Mister Patrick Udo?" he rumbled in a fantastic bass voice.

"Hey. Yeah, that's me." I said, hoisting up my backpack.

The man flapped a hand imperiously.

"Get in, Mister Udo," he said, "we've a long ride ahead."

I got in.

The fat man turned out to be right. Transport in Sri Lanka is largely reliant on a series of highways snaking over and around a spiderweb of old roads - narrow, winding things constructed with the sole intent of making it as difficult as possible to get from point A to B. The Colombo-Kandy highway was closed that day, shoving hundred of thousands of cars onto these winding roads. We spent hours trapped in that car, trying to travel a little over a hundred kilometers through sixteen lanes of traffic squeezed into four.

The fat man, as it turned out, was Amarasinghe. ('Amara-sing-her, Mister Udo. Amarasinghe.') Amarasinghe was in his fifties, grossly overweight, but one of those people who wear their weight regally; it lent him a fantastic gravitas, and his presence was often enough to send officials scurrying for their papers. A combination of butler and security chief, he did everything for Common - from arranging meals to laundry to escorting high-value guests.

In the time we have known each other he has refused to called me anything but 'Mister Udo', delivered in the sort of tone that makes your inner schoolboy want to hoof it with all haste.

Amarasinghe had a great fondness for tea ('Tis what makes the world go around, Mister Udo!') and made it a point to stop at odd little places ferreted away in the hills.

At each of these places, he would casually question me over tea and biscuits; about my work, my relationships ('Confirmed bachelor, eh?'), what I thought of Julius Common, et cetera, et cetera. I answered without fuss. Part of me wonders whether this was intentional: after all, Common could have airlifted me out of that place anytime he wanted.

Finally, it seemed Amarasinghe was satisfied; the car, after wrapping itself around a steep hill, rolled to a final stop. Outside, I could see green hills touched by a hint of cloud, an unpolluted, almost pristine skyline; a bell tolled gently in the distance. It was a beautiful place.

"Good luck, Mister Udo," said Amarasinghe.

I got out, leaving the fat man behind, and saw Julius Common's home in Sri Lanka.

Someone - perhaps it was Wurth or Aniston - had mentioned, in passing, that Julius owned the most eccentric house they'd ever seen. And here it was: a massive, snub-nosed aircraft, with great wings and a strangely whale-like look to it. It had been cut up mounted on top of an almost flower-like construction of synthwood and glass: it looked almost as if the flower had spread its petals to offer up the plane to the world.

And on this plane, the founder of NumberCorp, sitting cross-legged with a cigarette in hand. He jumped down from the wing and stuck out a hand. In the humid weather of Sri Lanka he wore black-and-white batik. Strange designs crawled all over his bulk. It was the first time I had ever seen Julius at anything resembling leisure.

I complimented him on the aeroplane. A faint smile twitched across Julius's features.

"I got bored with normal houses," he said. "Come on. Bring his bags," he said to the guard. "Patrick is going to be here for a while."

I was ushered into the semi-lit darkness of the plane. Inside, it was surprisingly homely: softly lit, with couches along the sides, and every so often there was a corner with a table in it. An aide showed me to my room, a cabin-like construction in the middle. Julius, of course, had a room up front, with the best view.

When I woke it was time for dinner. Julius did not say much. Three phones sat beside him at the table. Two constantly blinked with the light of incoming notifications. The other rang just once. Julius answered.

"Is it live?" he asked. There was a pause. Then: "Okay. Call me on this number when it is."

He put the phone down.

"What's happening? If you don't mind me asking?"

"Oh. Events," said Julius. "We're retooling the network to detect and understand things that are happening to our users around the world. It's taking some work."

What network? I thought. Then I decided I didn't want to sound stupid.

Perhaps he saw my look of befuddlement. "The kind of events you go to say a lot about you as a person," he explained. "The problem is that you need large amounts of data to identify patterns. Does opera make you intelligent? We don't know, but we do know it means you have money or move in certain social circles."

"Are we releasing it soon?"

"Oh, no," he said dismissively. "Like I said. Not enough data, not even close. Maybe in five years. For now we're using what we have to set up a little side project. Remember Twitter?"

I remembered Twitter.

"Dead now," he said. "People used hashtags, a hundred and forty characters, and you send a message out, and people who follow you could read it. Same mechanic we have now on most social networks. Stripped down. It was all the rage back then."

"It was pretty useful for getting news out," I said, remembering a lifetime of impromptu journalism lessons from my father.

"What we're building is something like that. Not quite, but similar. The plan is you're in the area, and people are talking about it, then you know it. It could be anything from a revolution to armed robbery to a party happening two lanes away. It doesn't matter. If it's something you can benefit from, something you might enjoy, we'll point you that way. NumberCorp's got you covered."

I took this in, pretty sure that I had already heard of something like this.

Julius grinned. Briefly. "Yes, it's not very original," he said. "But it's the start of our own social network. We're filling in where Twitter left off. Plus Ibrahim insists on giving the interns something to do."

"Is it a permanent project?"

"Facebook and Anagram and Totem are doing a damn good job of it, but if I can I'd like all of them squashed under our boots. But if we have a shot, I'll settle with taking the news. We've got, what, almost three hundred million people with a Number?"

"Three hundred and thirty."

"Okay, now scale that to billions. Say we grow ten-ex to three point one billion. Taking out China, that's half the world population. What happens when you control the news for three point one billion people? We're not just delivering Number update notes - if we play our cards right, we control what three billion see in the morning, so we control what three billion people think. It's an interesting side project."

As you can see, Julius Common deals in large numbers. Even for his side projects. The next thirty minutes of our conversation was only broken by the clink of forks and the images in my head of cities full of people looking down at their phones in the morning and seeing our green and gold logo.

"By the way," I said, trying to keep the conversation going. "You still haven't told me why I'm here."

"There's a party tomorrow," he said. "We're launching the Number in South-East Asia, starting with this place. You know how the Number tallies behavior with cultural norms?"

I didn't know that, but I nodded. Julius saw right through it.

"Every single time your Number is adjusted, there's a mechanism in there that looks at your activity and tries to determine whether this is considered good behavior for wherever it is you live," he said. "Spending a lot on a mortgage, taking out a student loan, being politically active, going to a good college - that's considered good stuff in the US. Having a car is nothing. Here the game is slightly different. Here people don't like being in debt, but apparently having an expensive vehicle is a good thing. Being political is apparently dirty. We need a sort of guinea pig to test this stuff. A small population that we can monitor and test and retest the bulk of our SEA algorithms on. You see why we're here?"

I nodded.

"This place is perfect," he continued, cutting into his steak. "Highly connected, almost everyone's online, and the government will let us do whatever the hell we want as long as their ministers are happy. I want you to come with me tomorrow. Take photos. Make it look like the most important event since the first moon landing. I'm told the President wants to feel like he's involved, so he may be there as well. Do you have everything you need? Equipment?"

My ocular surgery was still a month away, but I could very well make do.

"Anything I can get you? The only things I can't offer you are children and politicians: the first is illegal and the second is expensive."

That threw me off: then I saw that he was joking. Or at least, trying to.

"Alright, then," Julius Common said. He must have sensed the awkwardness, because he raised a glass of wine. "To a good launch tomorrow."

"To a good launch," I mumbled. We ate the rest of the meal in silence.

The next day I laid out my best suit and tie. Into the eye went the Wireframe Optics 300. Into the bag went my battered Nikon.

The 300, at the time, was on every professional photographer's utility list. It was Google Glass done right and fitted into a contact lens. Snapshot, video, zoom capability. It was the only truly expensive thing I owned, mostly because of the license. It was uncomfortable, but it packed an iPhone's worth of camerawork into an eye. The Nikon was a different beast. Bulky. Imposing. A thing of metal and lenses. Heavy in the hand. High-power optics designed for high-resolution photography. A sensor large enough that it could make even dark club lighting look like daylight. Light field tech for manipulating camera angles after a photo was shot. I still have it.

Amarasinghe's crew had polite, smiling faces: they ushered me into a hotel filled with light and the sound of money and power. Women in extraordinarily beautiful sarees swept past with diamonds in their hair. Ornately dressed waiters floated by with trays of canapés and wine. Julius was nowhere to be seen.

I quickly downed a glass and set to work.

There are two ways a society photographer becomes famous. The first is to take lots of photographs of very beautiful women. Beautiful women have a following all their own. If that sounds misogynistic, I'm sorry, that's the way the world works. Homer said the Greeks went to war over a woman. I can't get a battle, but I can get a few hundred thousand views with the right face in a skirt.

The other option? Take very few photographs of the most important people in the room. Catch them when they don't know they're being watched.

So I watched and I waited. It was easy to sort out the wolves from the sheep. That thin, skeletal-looking man in gray clinking glasses with a bland-faced man in white. The Minister of Energy and the head of one of the island's largest telecom providers. Important. Probably some kind of deal happening there. The fit, well-dressed young man charming the life out of a retinue of fit, well-dressed young men. A Minister's son. Not important. The very pretty woman who seemed to know everyone in the room. No career of any effect; no publications; no online reach. Not important.

Two people walked in and everything changed. One was the President of Sri Lanka. The other was Julius Common. You could see the social circles splintering as they approach. The President nodded and shook his way in, briefly becoming part of every circle in his wake, leaving a trail of erect spines and self-important smiles. Common swept in like a shark, acknowledging no-one. The two men met in the middle and shook hands. The world closed around them.

For the next hour and a half, Julius Common became the perfect guest. He had eyes for no-one but the President. He laughed with genuine mirth. He listened with grave seriousness. He nodded with understanding. I'm pretty sure that whatever advice he offered (and he could never resist offering advice) was delivered with the utmost modesty and humility.

I took one photo of that conversation: Common leaning forward, showing his phone screen to the President. The President's face, gently illuminated by the screen, is a mixture of wonder, admiration and awe. Common is smiling - a charming, quirky smile in a face unused to it - but if you know him well, you know that's the smile he makes when he's winning.

That night we all congregated at a hotel, drunk on alcohol and success. Sri Lanka was ours. Of course, the actual work had just begun – legions of Bizdev people would be hired, set to work: cultural experts and anthropologists bought and paid for both their insight and their silence: an entire operation set up to support the fifteen million people who called this place home (people have pointed out to me since then that Sri Lanka once was home to over twenty five million people; the TRS-81 superbug, which hit Asia hardest, had done in millions of people, and the country's tax base almost collapsed).

But the board had been set: the pieces were moving. The most important part of a NumberCorp deal was always that first giant seduction.

Amarasinghe picked me up from the hotel they had set for me, looked vaguely disapproving at the outfit, and drove me to Common's airplane home in silence. It seemed that something was on the portly man's mind.

Inside the plane were the power circle: Julius, Aniston, Russell, Ibrahim – and a few others whose stories you may have heard: Hatsuko Temada, Ray Kawasaki, Aaron Kotalawala.

Temada committed suicide after the 2050 Boston Riots, after a glitch in the system dropped her Social Number to almost nothing: the first of the NumberCorp celebrity suicides. Kawasaki built the infamous Paradise Islands, where the uber-rich and the uber-famous go to have their bodies restored to youth. Kotalawala, today, runs Atlantis: his empire of custom-designed minicities are the most exclusive living spaces in the world – places that only those with the highest Social Numbers can dream of calling home.

And here they were, future icons all, raising their glasses as I walked in. The noise hit me like a grenade.

"Patrick!" shouted Julius, staggering drunkenly to his feet. "Everyone, you know Patrick?"

They did, apparently.

"Have a drink!" ordered Julius, gripping my shoulder with a drunk man's strength.

I did my level best to melt into the background, but he was having none of it. For some reason, he introduced me to every person in that room; Temada, Kotalawala, the lot.

"And this fatass over here is Elya,' he said, shoving me at a dark woman sitting in a corner. "She's an investor. We need her money."

Elya seemed as unsurprised as I was mortified. Thankfully, Wurth arrived at that moment, and Julius was distracted. I was left awkwardly facing Elya, who seemed unfazed.

"Had a lot to drink?" she asked.

"No, I just came here," I said.

"Do yourself a favor, get some more alcohol," she said. "You're going to need it tonight."

I saw the sense in this and found a corner I could hide in.

It was interesting, to say the least. Elya and Wurth went out for a smoke. Ibrahim Monard, and Aniston Chaudary, who I could swear never spoke two words to each other at office, drew closer and closer together, until his hand was on her hip, and she was holding a wineglass in one hand and playing with his hair with the other. Hatsuko, diamonds gleaming in her hair, drew women like a magnet. Kotalawala shifted from businessman to businessman, working the crowd even as his steps grew clumsier and his laugh louder. A motley crew of people floated in and out.

And Julius drank. I have never seen anyone drink like he did. To say he drank with a vengeance is almost understating it: it was almost as if there was a thirst there, a deep and insatiable craving that made the man keep going back for more and more until he sat down in one corner with a bottle. I expected him to hold court, but he didn't. People congratulated him, shook his hand, took selfies with him: Aaron Kotalawala brought him one VIP after another to bedazzle: he shook them away and drank. I watched Aniston gently put a hand on his shoulder and try to take away the bottle: he let her go and simply called for another. I watched him until Wurth appeared out of nowhere and clapped me on the shoulder.

Wurth was stone cold sober and tense. "We need to take care of the crowd," he said. "You keep an eye on Jules."

I don't recall the next bit: I know Julius and I fell into conversation, one way or the other. It's easy enough to have wonderful conversations when drunk and not remember any of it the next day: that's the point of it all. What I remember was that Julius kept getting more and more intense, and at some point, when I was sobering up enough to remember what I was drinking, he pointed behind me and asked: "What do you see?"

I looked. It took a while, because my head felt like it was on overlubricated bearings: it swung this way and that until I finally managed to control it. I saw Wurth charming a minister and his wife in corner: Aniston dancing with Ibrahim: two bronze-skinned men kissing: and a crew of would-be-celebrities and models and political creatures bickering, laughing, flirting...

"What you see," said Julius, his voice slurred with the drink. "Is all the bullshit that follows a win. All the small fucking bigwigs in a small fucking pond sensing big money to be made, so they're here to bend the knee and kiss the arse and flash enough leg to get a piece of the action. Sharks, Patrick, sharks. These people sense money like a fucking shark senses blood. Look at them in their fucking costumes and perfume! That's how you know you've won, Pat: when the sharks come looking for you. Your father understood, Patrick, do you understand?"

I didn't: I was too drunk to understand anything.

Somehow this seemed to anger him.

"Do you understand?" he shouted suddenly, leaning over the table. "Why do you not understand, you half-wit?"

I started, sending my chair – and the tiny drinks table just behind me - crashing to the ground. A hush fell over the party.

Parts of this are blurry. Someone helped me to my feet, but what I remember was Julius. "Why do you not understand?" Julius Common bellowed into the silence. He struggled to his feet. "Do you not understand what you signed up for?"

Silence. They looked at him, their attention now entirely on the man who stood weaving; and he was trapped like a deer in the headlights of their attention.

"Jules-" said Aniston.

"No, fuck off, don't shut me up," said Julius Common. "Ten years from now, we're going to be in a different fucking world, alright? A world where you can name a man and I can tell you exactly how much he means to us, to fucking humanity. Not just the money in his bank, but his actual fucking worth, as a member of this fucking species, and you can't hide that shit or make it up. Fuck your consumerism. Fuck your generational wealth. You can drive your shitty expensive cars and roll our your stupid makeup but in ten years time none of that will matter. I'm going to take this world and I'm going to goddamn grind it into something more real."

"Jules!"

Julius weaved. "We're going to throw out the fake," he promised them, echoing Wurth's blogpost. "We're going to bring in the real. We're going to fucking change the world."

A stunned silence followed these words. And then they started to clap.

Someone shouted from the back "Throw out the Fake! Bring in the Real!"

That did it. "Throw out the Fake!" they chanted, whooping. "Bring in the Real!" They faced Julius Common and gave us a standing ovation. "Throw out the Fake! Bring in the Real!"

I didn't understand it. Julius didn't, either. He just looked at them, drunk and confused. He looked to me, as if for an answer, and all I could to was stagger away as Aniston and Wurth ushered him back to his room. As they passed, Wurth glared at me.

It's funny how life sets us up with people, because Julius called me the next day.

"I'm told I insulted you last night." he said.

"You were drunk."

"Yes, yes, I was," he said. There was an embarrassed silence.

"No problem, Julius," I said. "I was completely out of it, too."

"I have just now come from a party where I was its life and soul; witticisms streamed from my lips, everyone laughed and admired me, but I went away and wanted to shoot myself," he said.

My phone - bless Google - tagged the quote instantly. "Kirkegaard?"

"Exactly," he said. "Are you free today? Lunch at my place?"

That was his way of saying sorry.

That drunken night began what you might call my friendship with Julius Common.

How do I tell you the rest of the story? You see, NumberCorp today is so intricately tied up with Julius Common – like Amazon with Jeff Bezos, or Facebook with Mark Zuckerberg – that I find it impossible to separate the two. Over the next ten years, as I tried to put together the pieces of the puzzle, I came to one realization: that to tell the story of NumberCorp, I had to tell the story of Julius himself. To truly understand Creation, as a man called Lars Koenig once put it, one must first understand God.

But as a storyteller, I understand that this story flows in one direction, and to divert you now would break it. And therefore, at the end of this book you will find one of the more enduring monuments of our friendship - an exclusive profile of his life, written with detail he has never given to anyone else, and first published on the Watchmen Press. As time passed, and my relationship with Julius and NumberCorp changed, the article was updated, much of it with material he was profoundly unhappy with. Read it at your own discretion.

And understand, dear reader, that Julius Common today is the most powerful man on the planet, and certainly one of the most reclusive; today, he has no friends. But there was a time when I knew him enough to share his food, drink and company;

there was a time when he let me tell his tale.

PART II

In 2012, [Michal] Kosinski proved that on the basis of an average of 68 Facebook "likes" by a user, it was possible to predict their skin color (with 95 percent accuracy), their sexual orientation (88 percent accuracy), and their affiliation to the Democratic or Republican party (85 percent). But it didn't stop there. Intelligence, religious affiliation, as well as alcohol, cigarette and drug use, could all be determined. From the data it was even possible to deduce whether someone's parents were divorced.

The strength of their modeling was illustrated by how well it could predict a subject's answers. Kosinski continued to work on the models incessantly: before long, he was able to evaluate a person better than the average work colleague, merely on the basis of ten Facebook "likes." Seventy "likes" were enough to outdo what a person's friends knew, 150 what their parents knew, and 300 "likes" what their partner knew. More "likes" could even surpass what a person thought they knew about themselves. On the day that Kosinski published these findings, he received two phone calls. The threat of a lawsuit and a job offer. Both from Facebook.

- from ***The Data That Turned the World Upside Down***
by **Hannes Grassegger** and **Mikael Krogerus**, reporting for Vice.com

Five

The Sri Lanka coverage, when it finally came out, was a roaring success. I've never been able to confirm this, but I'm told the then-President of Sri Lanka kept, in his office, a print of my photo of him with Julius.

The rest of the photos and videos didn't do too badly, either. Paired with Wurth's text, it made quite the ripple in South Asia. ReachMap, our tool of choice for analyzing our work, showed it spreading like wildfire through online communities in India, Pakistan, Malaysia, Thailand. Ibrahim, using a new batch of interns, knocked out an internal tool that rated the content we put out in the same way that we rated people, judging its influence and power. Everything concurred: Asia knew we were coming.

Thus began my first big break. I was a storyteller, said Julius. When not making NumberCorp events look like something out of the Great Gatsby, it was my task to document how people used the Number. Use cases, in engineer terms. We would hire people to do the press relations stuff I did: I would be able to put those photo skills to good use. It was obviously a promotion, even if a little bit hazy on the job description.

I suspect Wurth knew I got the job because of my friendship with Julius. Nevertheless, he took it in stride and, I think, made good use of my enthusiasm. "Bizdev knows who the biggest kids on the block are," he said, and so we arranged another meeting of the Elkhead gang: myself, Wurth, Aniston, Ibrahim ... except this time, we pored over Aniston's complex lists of organizations and targets-to-hit.

The first, most obvious pick was to hit the Valley itself. The first place most people encountered the Number was when they went to the bank. But Silicon Valley, back in those days, was a beast entirely of its own. The race to hire and retain tech talent had grown to the point where the company you worked for would handle all your banking needs for you: if you took out a loan, you'd take it from the company, which would in turn take it from the bank at better interest rates. Nor did most companies care about the human influence scoring; most of them either had their own internal systems for tracking the numbers they deemed necessary - like Amazon - or never intended to rate people in the first place. Tech utopia had no need for our product.

So I went to New York, the only place that could make overpopulation glamorous.

Every New Yorker thinks they're automatically better than everyone else in every other city on the planet: even their unnems were a better class of beggars. I landed to a riot of experiences. There was a community march in Long Island protesting 5 Pointz being torn down. Hudson Yards, where our NYC branch was, was new, glistening office space - and almost entirely empty, because everyone had gone to see the protest. Someone attacked an AirRail line and the riot police were called in, an ominous wave of dark blue with their sedative mortars and mechanized limbs. The crowd heaved in a schizophrenic frenzy; one half lay down and slept or smiled at each other, shaking the arresting officers by their hands; the other half hurled angry insults and paint. I lost two drones trying to film it.

Something had happened in New York. A handful of media companies had started using the Number as a metric for hiring their photojournalists and writers and presenters. Clarice Starling (American Information, now heading World Broadcast) met me, gave me the grand tour, and the bottom line: advertisers had always wanted views, the editors had always wanted social media shares. It made perfect sense to hire people who had tons of sharing potential – the Number just happened to make it so much easier.

"After all," she said, "Isn't that how you got hired?"

No, it wasn't, but I chose to keep mum on that. I went back to our diagram, the one that said *MONEY* and the question mark next to it. Julius called a short meeting. *INFLUENCE*, I added. *EMPLOYMENT*, added Julius, drawing lines that circled them. *COMMUNICATION*. He smiled.

A week later, a company-wide message rang in our inboxes. Julius.

Small announcement. Just heard back from Facebook: their next algorithm update is going to use the Number. For @engineering, in-depth explanation here, go read ASAP.

For others: from October, higher Number means (subtly) higher engagement. Facebook isn't entirely sold on what we have, mostly because Zuck thinks they can do better. Fun fact: what they have is nowhere even close to ours. Theirs is Echo Valley. Ours for the first time bridges the real world with the social network.

Going forward: use case: if you were successful in real-life, now that success will automatically transfer to Facebook. No need update your Instagram ten times a day with #travel pictures to be popular. Basically popularity.

Congrats to @Algorithm and @Communications. Now we need to sell this and sell it hard.

And shortly on the heels of that:

Small announcement (2): Goog is also on-board. For media sites they will be linking Google account with our Number profile. People with higher Numbers get ranked higher. We just made it into SEO essentials, people. @Patrick tells me the newscorps have been hiring for Numbers for some time now but NOW IT'S OFFICIAL.

Russell called, deliriously happy: apparently my replacement had arrived.

On his desk was a cardboard box.

"It's a box," I said.

"Take a look," said Wurth.

I did. SmartPerson by Kissing Labs, it said. Inside was a set of gray cubes that looked like they had been made by a color-blind Rubix. They slotted together smoothly, and, once the whole thing was done, Wurth reverentially plugged it in to his workstation. The gray cubes blinked at us.

"Hey," they said. They had a curiously feminine voice, with slightly hoarse overtones. "Are you Julius Common?"

"My name's Russell Wurth, and this is Patrick Udo," said Wurth, gesturing at us in turn.

"Russell Wurth, Patrick Udo, registered sub-licensees, primary owner: Julius Common, NumberCorp LLC," it hummed, and brightened. "So. What are we working on?"

Wurth grinned and rubbed his hands in glee.

That was how we ended up with Minerva, arguably the hardest working employee that Communications ever hired. After a couple of weeks of analyzing our responses, the little machine learning system she ran inside had our language and messaging nailed. She was ready.

From then on Minerva ran our social media channels, and, once we got around to buying the Hover module, doubled as the most expensive coffee tray in the company. She became a favorite among the engineers, especially Monard, who fitted her a little hat (seriously: he actually knitted) and a tiny electric shock module in case anyone decided to punch her.

I have to confess that I didn't take to her: I wasn't quite sure whether to be flattered because Julius thought replacing me really did cost this much, or whether to be unhappy, because I was so obviously and irrevocably replaced. Artificially Intelligent systems were, under Turing Law, illegal for exactly this reason. Not because of some science fiction fear that robots might declare war on us, but because once, near-AI had displaced millions of jobs, almost triggering a total collapse of the job market and the worldwide economy. The United Nations were terribly strict on the subject; Kissling skirted a very fine and expensive line in developing Minerva. Just smart enough to be useful, just dumb enough to not need a human handler around.

Sometimes we would get drunk and debate whether she was sentient.

"Looks like you're minting," my father would say on one of our infrequent lunches.

The money suited him. I had moved him out of Block C to a place not far from Oak Street Beach. He had taken to playing chess and teaching young journalists how to do their jobs.

He was doing good. The money was useless, but being able to pay for his own lunch made him feel better.

"It's alright," I said, and moved a piece on the chessboard between us. King G6. I was playing black and losing badly.

"You know," he said. "It's good that you're getting out a bit more. Being stuck in that campus of yours is the worst thing you could do to yourself."

Queen G8, check.

"How so?"

King F5.

"It's what we called Valley mania," he said. His knight, white, took F3 and my black pawn. "Bunch of people go out to the Valley, create something new. Us out here in the world go hmm, that's interesting, and start using it. Meanwhile the Valley guys are convinced they're the second coming of Christ and start overhyping and doing all sorts of things that aren't even useful anymore. The tech press clap and clap until it's time to write the obituary. Seen it happen too many times."

"This isn't like that," I said confidently. I then told him about Minerva.

"Interesting," said my father. "By the way, you've got nowhere to go."

We looked at the chessboard.

"Knight takes E1, Rook takes F7 and Queen to D5," he pointed out.

He was right. We stood up and shook hands.

"Remember that Kasparov lost," said my father. "And Sedol and Nakamura and Watts all became famous for losing to a machine. Whatever this Minerva thing is, make sure you don't lose to it."

My father was echoing the fears of a generation that had seen their jobs go to the machines. Gary Kasparov, chess grandmaster, played IBM's Deep Blue and lost in 1997. It was a historic day. In 2016 - just after I was born, actually - Lee Sedol, 18-time world Go champion, lost to Google's AlphaGo. Tetsuo Nakamura, in 2021, one of the most gifted neurosurgeons in the world, famously pitted his career against a SurgeonBot and killed himself when it did his job better than he could. And Watts, 2024 - how could anyone forget the woman who lost thirty billion dollars in a day to a bot trader?

"I, being poor, have only my dreams," said my father, half to himself. "Tread softly, because you tread on my dreams."

I waited, but he said no more. "I'm not a grandmaster, dad," I reminded the old man. "I've got nothing to lose."

But my father had a point. I didn't fight Minerva: I let the little bot gradually go about the task of becoming more competent than I was.

Instead, I did what only I could in our little understaffed Communications department: I looked out at the world. In Sri Lanka, a cabal of writers had got together and published a 50,000 word review of NumberCorp's ID system, its potential, its use to the nation, and how we were actually collecting more data than we needed for the simple task of servicing banks. We tentatively tested out Thailand, and the media hated on us. Then the king extended his approval, and everybody swung in a smooth 180-degree circle and said this way, Mr Udo, this way to the party. Hong Kong embraced us with open arms. The

Hong Kong police wanted to know if the Number could track criminals. Yes? No?

I was sent to the suited folken of J.P. Morgan and Chase, who thanked me for coming. They'd been considering the Number for a while, they said, testing their own system against it. It turned out the Number was better. Hats off, they said. And how was Julius these days?

BNY Mellon, which had once helped finance the Union Army during the American Civil War, wanted to know if we'd considered applying the Number to business rankings? Just a thought.

2031 whipped by in a blur and became 2032.

I found myself in Ecstasy. (Have I explained Ecstasy? If not, let me give you the short version. A bunch of nightclubs banded together and built a social network. And were acquired. Soon an entire clubbers' network built up – one single place to see which clubs were packed, which were not, what was playing, who was seen where, and to summon a driver to whizz you off to wherever you needed to be. To date I still think it was the weirdest thing to come out of that era).

Jared Kopper, Ecstasy's transgender, body-modding enthusiast of a CEO, rambled enthusiastically. They told me how different clubs wanted different Numbers to get in. That way, they said, they could maintain exclusivity and really address market segments. They complained about the costs of NumberCorp's APIs and complained some more about Julius's morbid dress sense. Then Jared offered me some A-grade Dopamide and offered to send me to Ooze, their underwater VIP tripper haven.

I accepted, but not before I'd made one last round to the Socrates Foundation. "It's Klout, just Klout v2," said Kathyusha Balasubramaniam, the harried-looking CEO of Socrates. "It's nice, but we aren't building anything with it."

That was ironic, because a decade after NumberCorp announced that corporations would have their own Number, Socrates had such high standing that even the famously bloody Boston Mechanical Riots paused to let Socrates Medical Aid trucks through. Nobody wanted to attack anything with a 300K Number. Kathyusha had, of course, been forgotten by then.

We were making history, and I was getting paid to document it.

I went to Julius and Wurth with each new use case I found, and we'd pull up our diagram. It was now a company-wide project. *EMPLOYMENT*, we confirmed, submitting everything I had seen and recorded and thought. Ibrahim Monard and Ezra Miller owned that space.

And Wurth spun the marketing machine.

"What do you know of a man you hire?" he'd ask a business conference in London. "Do you know if he's a good man? An honest man? A leader? A follower? A social reject who'll affect how people around the world see your business? Of course you could - given enough time. Well, we're going to make it easier for you, ladies and gentlemen. Soon one glance, one search, will be all you need. You'll know exactly how much a person is worth to you, to your company, to your business."

I knew the speech by heart right now, because I had written it for him on Julius's explicit orders. He had told us exactly what to put in. Now we watched the audience for a reaction.

"What are we going to call it?" said Ibrahim Monard, watching Wurth's performance on the screen.

"Number for Work," said Julius Common. He seemed satisfied. "How soon can we have the basic functionality running?"

Ibrahim thought a bit. "Ezra's already done with most of the algorithm stuff," he said.

"And I've already given you the architecture. How long?"

"Say a month?" Ibrahim said. "At this stage it's mostly data visualization. Two with testing. We'll need authorization, I'm pretty sure this might be violation of privacy..."

"Why would you trust a celebrity?" Wurth was asking another crowd in Tokyo, with the translation software turning his English into flawless Japanese. "Just because they make music? Shouldn't you be looking at if this person is a good human being? If she has a police record? If she's in debt? All the hot selfies in the world don't make you a good human being. What if we gave you a way to find out with one search? With one number? What if we gave you a metric you could absolutely trust?"

"Weak," said Julius. "Make sure we never push that angle again. Next?"

The next video opened. It was Wurth in the Valley.

We had yet to become what we be. There would come a time when, in - good old America - you couldn't even buy a car now without the dealer checking your Number. There would come a time when the rich and the famous discreetly bought access to look up the Numbers of people they wanted to keep in their circles or keep out. All of that was still in the future, but you could see the seeds of it here, if you looked closely enough. The way law firms checked up on the Numbers of people they represented and the Numbers of those they went up against. The way people who managed celebrities had started obsessing with their client's Numbers. These were things in the cracks.

I missed those things, distracted by the lights, the flashing, the posturing. Because it was the Age of Google and Facebook, and we despaired of ever owning the world the way they did. Google, that all-powerful city that sprawled across Mountain View, saw all, knew all. It lived in your watch, diagnosed you before you even knew you had symptoms. It asked you what you wanted from your politicians and then tell you who to vote for. It managed everything from taxis to the daily commutes of those very few people who still had private vehicles.

And Facebook? If Google controlled facts, Facebook controlled opinion. One knew what people did; the other understood what people thought. What they talked about. What they shared. One company owned the first core aspect of the web - information. The other owned social connections. Without the prodigious amount of data that they gave us, we were nothing; we literally paid through the nose for the privilege of analyzing searches and statuses.

Julius used to say that we stood on the shoulders of giants. To me it always seemed like we were in their shadow. It never occurred to me that we were the shadow that they projected, and that one day we would rise up and overwhelm them.

Six

By mid-2033 we were doing spectacularly well: we were in France, we were in Spain, we were in Italy, we were in Germany. Even the News project was working out: a little subdivision of Ibrahim's engineers were demo'ing the thing: there was talk of spinning it off into a separate company altogether, drawing in some new investment, setting it up as our own social network of sorts.

NumberCorp was moving like greased lightening, and if I wasn't the tip of the spear, I was at least riding close to it.

There are many things that I could mention, but on the whole, I think, it would be a waste of your time to read them. Let's just say that after the Facebook Deal was announced, things accelerated. There were few things in the Valley more powerful than an investment from one of the Big Four. It was a lot like having a Mars V rocket strapped to our necks.

For our main body of work, Aniston had set precise targets: we were to execute with relentless precision the methods we had perfected on the United States - banks first; then whatever relied on exclusivity as a selling point. We were moving cautiously through these waters, it was true, but the first stage of the siege had begun. All told, we had about 600 million users on board.

In the office Wurth and I used there was a copy of the diagram Julius had once drawn for us. *MONEY. INFLUENCE. ENTERTAINMENT. EMPLOYMENT. EXCLUSIVITY.* We had a list pinned next to it.

Washington, it said. *Banks; most first and second-tier entertainment; most first and second-tier restaurants; large corporate tenders and contracts*

New York. Banks; all first and second-tier entertainment; all first and second-tier restaurants; large corporate tenders and contracts; testbed, social connection

San Francisco. Total as per spec. Waiting on (experimental): startup scoring, investor scoring, venture / trust integration and penalties

And it would amble around all the cities we were in, all the ideas that were slowly washing up on our shores. *Bangkok,* it would say: *sex worker scoring??? Colombo,* it would say, *implementing politician / demagogue trust? London: police departments? Parliament ratings?*

Word had it that Harvard and the other Ivy League universities were offering scholarships: except now instead of low-income, they called them small-Number students.

Was I blind? It is often difficult to see your company for what it is from the inside. At some point it goes from XCorp, makers of this, this, and this, valued at this many billion, to XCorp, where I sit right across from this, this, and this guy and do this, this, and this to pass the day. It's the same with people: we have a terrible time knowing exactly what we're like, because we've been on the inside of our skins so long that we can never be objective. Familiarity may breed contempt; but perhaps it would be more truthful to say that familiarity breeds blindness. For a year, this list buzzed past the pit, and I was really too blind to sit and take it in.

I tell myself that I should have kept this in my head. I should have understood what it meant when Ibrahim and his Integration team shipped out and returned three, six months later to resounding cheers. These were entire cities we were dealing with; millions of lives that we were changing in small ways.

Perhaps it helps to understand why we paid so little attention. The 2030s were complicated, to say the least. We evangelized, but it was also the closest we'd been to a second cold war. A couple of jets flying over the South China sea had turned into threats. Threats, in the hands of politicians, turned into rhetoric and embargoes. China, very pleasantly and politely, hinted at economic sanctions and a complete halt of all major shipping lines to the US.

The tech industry was minting. Defense contracts - especially government cyberdefense - started flowing our way. SpaceX and NASA were going to send another colony mission to Mars, and figure out what went wrong with the first one. The Turing Act, which made it illegal to employ an Ai if a human could do the job, was being re-examined. Silicon Valley had high hopes for the future. Glamorous hopes.

And among all this noise, there was us. We were not a sexy thing. People opened the Facebook app thirty times a day. The Number? No. The Number existed in the background. It was, as Julius once explained, a toothbrush; everyone needed it, but you only wanted it twice a day. We went ignored in the middle of all this upheaval. All we could do was throw out feelers and keep learning, always learning, like an amoeba slowly oozing into the fabric of the world.

One day, we sat in Elkhead, thinking and drinking.

"Why is he obsessed with China?" Wurth asked. We were, of course, discussing Julius.

"I don't know," said Aniston.

"Are we expanding there?'

"No, it's a code thing," Ibrahim said gloomily, lighting up. "Some part of the core codebase was written by a Chinese guy. I think Jules is trying to track him down."

We thought about this. "But why?"

"It's messing up the Numbers," Ibrahim said. "Emergent effects. Nothing obvious. Religion module isn't running properly. System's running some kind of political calculation, but we don't know what the hell it is."

"Can't you take it apart?"

But neural networks don't work like that. You have to build the model anew, retrain, retest. One small misstep can lead to one giant fall.

"Bad time be looking for a Chinese guy," Ibrahim remarked to no-one in particular.

We agreed and drank.

"What's happening on your end?" Ibrahim said.

"Restaurants," Wurth said.

"Restaurants?"

"They've started using the Number," Wurth said. "First a few big chains, up-market, five star gigs. Remember Ceasar's?"

We remembered Ceasar's.

"Now they won't let you reserve a table unless you have, like, an 8K Number," Wurth said.

"That's morbid," Ibrahim said. "Can't even eat now unless

you're a celebrity, eh?"

"Exclusivity has always been a thing for these establishments," said Wurth. "We're selling like mad now."

"And clubs," I said.

"And clubs," Wurth agreed. "Anything exclusive."

I was blind.

Life had settled into a comfortable rhythm. Every day, I would wake up in my quarters. Faux-brick walls, a decidedly Japanese mountain on the wallscreen, me zipping up. Google Home would play me my music as I hopped around. My clothes were uniform: jeans, shoes, NumberCorp T-shirt. I had been issued T-shirts in five different colors; I cycled them religiously. Black I kept for Fridays, just in case we went out.

Our new apartments were built into the circular wall around the compound; they had knocked down the Tercel flats and rebuilt everything. The running joke was that they'd been too cheap for concrete core, so they decided to use humans. I lived in the West circle - Edison complex; my route took me halfway through Tesla, where the lighting was quaint mock-vintage bulbs that glowed as you approached. There were shuttles, but very few of us took them: most of us walked, cycled or jogged. We must have looked like an army of NumberCorp Ants, converging on the main tower in the morning. Most of us came back at night, to sleep; our apartments were empty - more glorified hotel rooms than anything else.

Occasionally Julius's black car would roar past. If it was a good week, we'd chase it, flushed and breathless and grinning.

I'd get to my office at five, maybe six in the morning. Programmers usually came in at ten; Wurth and I didn't have that excuse. We had to be the first message in everyone's inboxes, and by the time the tech world came online - which was also at about ten - we had to be firing on all cylinders. To compensate, we stopped all work at lunch and resumed only after six. Dinners were spent eating in the glow of screens, typing one-handed over burgers and coffee.

"Hey Udo," Wurth would occasionally say. "How do you break up with your Japanese girlfriend?"

"What?"

"You drop the bomb on her ... twice!" he'd chortle into the darkness. My WorkChat would buzz with the context, and I'd grin. Always in spectacularly bad taste, we were, digging old puns and memes out of the dark corners of the Internet. On long days the humor became particularly dark.

What strange and thoughtless creatures we were, back in those days. We would go up to the rooftops to smoke, Wurth and I; and there in the company of other insomniac souls we would look out at the vast expanse of lights and glamour. We watched the towers as they climbed higher, and higher, as humanity reached for the skies. We saw the apartments and rooftops that glinted like diamonds against the night sky.

We would sneer sometimes at how pointless it all was, all those bourgeois souls wrapping themselves in luxury, isolating themselves from the raw edges of the word; and in between puffs, we would smile, and dream of owning those streets, dreaming the same dreams that we scorned others for.

You could say I grew to love the Valley, despite its quirks and oddities. There was a level of crazy there that, in any other society, would have been cast aside and discarded; here it was celebrated, venerated, funded. I went to a Google party, for instance (and man, the Googlers knew how to party) where

Dennis Rybak was the guest of honour. Rybak founded AirRail, which back then almost crushed private transport with their Rail network and the Google's driverless public buses. Julius was a huge fan, which meant we were automatically huge fans as well.

We went for the talk, but got drunk, took a wrong turn somewhere and ended up with a bunch of equally drunk Russians claiming they could resurrect anyone as a chatbot. They asked Wurth for his messages and tweets, hooked the stream up to their pads, and I'll be damned if we didn't end up chatting (on text) with something that thought it was Russell Wurth and sounded a hell of a lot like the man, too. Then a bunch of passing Googlers picked us up, took us to another party, and the resurrection winos ended up wooing a bunch of investors in a corner.

Today you'll know those people as the Lazarus Cult, aka the Speakers to the Dead. www.speaktothedead.org lets you talk to a reanimated, digital, text-only version of your loved ones. The Church, the Caliphate and Congress want to outlaw them. If someone knocks on your door and promises you eternal life as an AI, remember: Wurth and I nearly ran over them once. If it hadn't been for drive assist, your afterlife would never have existed.

These kinds of things came and went in sporadic waves. It was the Valley, after all; this was where strange things came to live and die.

Slowly, our creeping climb to ubiquity became noticed - mostly because we were raising funding and Wurth wanted us noticed. A handful of wary journalists demanded to know what Common had in store for them. Julius grinned his shark grin and sent Wurth.

When you have them by the balls, their hearts and minds will follow, he had once said. We'd hint at overseas expansion. Where? The United Kingdom, of course. Europe. So many more world to conquer.

Which brings us, in a neatly roundabout fashion to the United Kingdom. The UK meant very little for user numbers - another 60 million people or so - but where others saw arts and culture, we saw something much more valuable - the vast network of banking and finance operations rooted at the heart of England, spreading out to grasp the rest of the world in a complex spiderweb older than some countries. Granted, it was a shadow of what it had once been, but you still couldn't own the world's banks without owning Britannia.

We were a bit short-staffed those days, so I was temporarily attached to the UK office; I, and a bunch of Aniston's underlings, were shipped over the pond to gloomy London, where security cameras watched us from every corner and light and theater lit up the streets at night.

The good news was that the UK wanted us. The economy was failing and the sterling pound had yet to recover from Britain's historic exit from the EU. The average Briton was forty thousand pounds in debt and businesses were leaving wholesale. The government and the employment agencies welcomed us with open arms: the UK office swelled from thirty to three hundred in almost no time at all.

The bad news is that we screwed it up.

One of the UK's largest industries is education. Every year, millions of students would arrive on British shores, paying through the nose for the all-important British degree. Most of them were from Asia. And the moment they finished fighting their way through Britain's notoriously difficult Immigration, our algorithm chewed up their bank accounts - some of which were with banks we hadn't integrated with. It looked at their nonexistent financial history in this country, and non-existent friend networks. And it marked them as being practically worthless.

Entire legions of students began life in the UK with Numbers in the low 2000s. They might as well have been marked as sex offenders or drug dealers. Bars and clubs refused to admit them. Banks refused them credit cards. Companies that farmed out student housing refused to lease out their apartments. Phone companies dragged their feet.

The police came calling. Why, they would ask, were you being denied these services? Ah. Why was your Number so low? Who did you owe money to?

And it didn't help that almost all of these students were Chinese and Indian.

I can't say, even now, that we were racist. It was statistics, pure and simple. We simply didn't realize it until it was far too late. This was a country that for years had both welcomed and spurned people of many nationalities, embracing their diversity, and at the same time managed to harbor a deep unease about their own culture; the classic Britishness that had once held empires together was, if not a flag to rally around, a rock to fall back on.

It was here the hammer stroke fell the hardest. When the drums began beating, and someone stood up and shouted 'racist!', they met passion coming the other way. And thus the London Ethnic March happened.

On the 4th of August 2032, in a protest near the South Bank of the Thames, near Newington, a young Indian student was shot by the police. She recovered - but not before the whole disaster kicked off violent clashes across the country. Students spilled out across university borders.

They said later that the army had been involved. They said that conservationist politicians armed the mods. They said that media coverage touched off waves of copycat violence across the city; some fought for England, some fought against. At the end of a week twelve people were dead and a hospital had been set on fire.

We rose to the challenge. By 3AM that day Wurth and I were at battle stations. By 6 AM we had a scripted, rehearsed clip of Julius live and on air. We were absolutely stunned, he said. Racists and unreasonable, violent men still existed. At NumberCorp, he said, we were still trying to come to grips with the fact that our work was used as a basis for oppress people.

"Every technology that humanity has ever created has also been used to oppress, to destroy, to divide," he said, staring straight into the camera. "Worldwide communications were used to co-ordinate worldwide war. The Internet was used to promote the causes of terrorism. Perhaps we forgot that our technology, too, might be used this way. On behalf of NumberCorp, I'd like to say that we will do our absolute best to make sure that this never, ever happens again. Stay strong."

He waited until we were done, then dialed. "Ibrahim, Ezra? My office, five minutes. People like this should be kept off the streets."

In a week's time, we quietly introduced a new update. We couldn't account for under-the-counter relationships, but if you were open friends with people marked as violent or having racist tendencies, your Number took a hit. Julius, in a closed briefing, showed us a series of detailed predictions: over time, anyone with an history of hate would be pushed further and further down the scoring ladder.

And if tech press was starting to raise the eyebrow at us, what of it? What did journalists know of tech, anyway? Who gave a damn about the press? We were the Good Guys. Changing the World. Doing the Important Stuff.

Most in the company felt that it was terribly smart.

Seven

But old Britannia wasn't done with us yet. At least, not myself and Wurth; it took our message on the Ethnic Marches and gave us Lars Koenig.

Koenig was a university man. Professor of Abrahamic Religion at one of the colleges that made up the University of London, born to German immigrants. Old, immaculately dressed, educated at Eton and Oxford: the kind of man who held the door open for his date. He had a lifetime of studying a subject that no-one wanted to learn about; not in this century; it gave him a gentle, slightly stooped air and a salt-and-pepper beard a little longer than it should have been.

His daughter was caught up in the March. Nobody knows what happened, but word was that someone had thrown acid, or set her on fire. She was left disfigured.

Koenig was a patient man. Over the next year, he went around methodically interviewing the students who were caught up in the Marches, assembling proof. He followed the trail of violence all the way to the powder keg: the lowered Number. And then he must have had his epiphany, because he started following the Number outward.

If this Number can cause a barman to refuse to serve a student, he wrote on his blog, if it can cause riots and marches and corpses, what else can it do?

Initially, only a handful of academics and a few people in government read him. But the views started racking up, and he took to producing videos. Videos showing people being refused service at restaurants. Of students unable to enroll at universities because their parents and friends were from small-Number backgrounds. Of copywriters with low Numbers fired from Internet content farms for not being influential enough. He made gentle comparisons to older times, when one could only get in if one came from a certain type of family and spoke with a certain type of accent, or, even worse, was born with a certain shade of skin.

The Number, he said, was bringing back those times.

He was smart. He didn't sue us; he didn't threaten; whatever he proposed he backed up with long interviews and disclaimers. But the tongue, like a sharp knife, kills without drawing blood, and before we knew it it was exploding across the Internet.

"No doubt this is a fascinating problem for Mr Common and his entourage of brilliant Silicon Valley people," he said on webcast. "But I feel one has to consider the repercussions. Our societies were built on the ideals that a man could rise to any position regardless of where he started out; in fact, any child can name a leader or two who rose from the meanest position to the highest. Yet here comes Mr Common and his Number, telling us that if you were born into poverty, or if you were born into poor social connections, someone will come and put a number on your head that prevents you from going any further up the ladder. No doubt this is legal; but is it ethical? Who is Mr Common, that we should consent to be judged by him? Who are these programmers locked away in a closet, that we should bow down to them? Are we not free?"

To say it went viral was an understatement. Before we knew it, hundreds of people had uploaded their own chatter; videos, webcasts, articles in the media. Even worse: hacktivist groups started to prowl the waters. We were staring down the barrel of a gun held by some very angry Brits. We shifted once again into damage control mode. Wurth was tasked with keeping the story out of the US media. I was still attached to the UK Project; I had to sort out this mess.

I had my work cut out for me.

"Yes, yes, it's all terribly tragic," said the harried-looking Member of Parliament who was our liaison. "The point is, Mr. Udo, the government can't help you. We can't even be seen helping you. I agree with you that the underlying social problems caused this, but as of today I'm afraid it's your mess. Please tell Julius that if you can't sort it out, it's on you."

Julius listened to this with an impassive face. Then he made a couple of calls.

"Talk to her again," he said.

This time, the MP was much more obliging. "Perhaps, Mr Udo, I can ask the main outlets not to go ahead with the story until you've had time to formulate a response," she said, looking doubly harried now. "Please tell Julius this is all I can do. I'm sorry."

Next I tried to see Koenig. He refused. I went so far as to stalk him to the campus. Amarasinghe, who Julius had apparently shipped to the UK to look after his estate there, hired two detectives for me ('Not Sherlock Holmes, Mr Udo, but close enough') and we set them to dig out Koenig's motivations. It was then that we discovered the daughter. I received a letter from him; an old-fashioned letter, written on paper.

"My dear Mr Udo," it read. "Thank you for your offer of

payment for my daughter's medical bills. A university salary does not cover what it once would have, but I assure you we can manage.

"As to our debate: I have called you out in a public forum. Therefore please do me the courtesy of responding in kind. Battles of ideas should not be confined to private phone calls and agreements."

"To respond," Wurth said. He was calling from Washington, DC, "is to legitimize him."

"He's pretty legit already."

"He's still one guy," Wurth said. "If we go after him, it makes us look like we're trying to bully him. That's never going to work."

I was stumped, to say the least. I went and sat down in Piccadilly square on one particularly cold evening, wondering what the hell I was supposed to do. We'd already done the blanket statement of denial, we'd already refused to comment on the subject; we'd done everything short of calling the man a crackpot.

As I sat there, a group of students cavorted past me. One of them stood up and gave a rousing speech. He was pretending to be King Lear, the mad king of the Shakespearean tragedy.

Pretend

Mad

It hit me. I threw away my coffee and raced back to the office, where I dialed Wurth.

"You want to make fake Koenig videos?"

"If we paint him as a madman," I said.

Long ago they made spy movies where a character perfectly mimicked someone's voice, thanks to technology that only a few elite agencies possessed. By our time you could pay a hundred dollars and buy something that could not just do audio, but video, as well. By law this stuff was supposed to include something - perhaps a waveform or a watermark - that would let a careful investigator know the video was fake; and all the big software corps complied. But there was always bootleg stuff that could do the trick without the signatures

Wurth got it. "Take the next flight back to Cali," he said. "Let's do this." He and I got those investigators of ours to photograph Koenig from all angles; we wrote up a script; and we fed the whole thing into Minerva.

"This isn't exactly ethical, is it?" Wurth said quietly as we waited in the semi-darkness.

I think I made a preposterous crack about how all was fair in love and war.

On-screen, a fake Koenig ranted, rendered frame-by-frame.

"Once we questioned Google becoming evil," Koenig said into his microphone. "Now, we must question something new: NumberCorp. They say they have understood a way to put a value to the trust you can place on a man or woman; to their worth to our human species. No doubt America is fascinated with this project. But one has to remember this is first and foremost a company, a capitalist instrument. Behind this "trust" facade is a more sinister mechanism. Global identity, government accountability, scoring humanity . . . but behind it comes something else. What?

"The Bible speaks of the mythical Tower of Babel - a tower that the humans built as a testament to their glory, so high that even God came to realize that the humans were becoming powerful indeed. And thus He smote down the Tower and scattered humanity, dividing them forever.

"Whether this story is true or not, you must understand

that here is this Number. It purports to bring us all together again. What happens when the Tower is complete? What happens when NumberCorp is truly everywhere? Are we talking about the death of trust? Will we someday meet on the road, strangers, and have to check a machine because we have forgotten how to trust each other, how to let someone into our lives, without giving them a number? Of course Mr Common and his band will say they are changing the world for the better, but should we not pause and think what kind of world will result?"

It was a carefully written composite; we had deliberately included trigger phases that might make some of the wilder channels to pick it up. At the same time . . .

"It's drivel," said Wurth, running it over and over again. "It's perfect."

. . . there was a core of truth in it, because the best lies are all woven around a half-truth.

We sent it out. Fox News pounced on it, probably because it had God somewhere in it. The Internet took it, absorbed it and sent it out. #WhatHappens began trending on NumberCorp News. And thus mainstream America's first introduction to Lars Koenig, the erudite Oxford man, was that of a British madman drooling philosophy from his lips. In vain did he rebut and denounce that video.

When my father called, I was exhausted.

"I saw Koenig's videos," he said without preamble.

I jolted upright in my seat.

"Journalists talk to each other," he said. "Something doesn't add up. Why'd he go off the rails towards the end?"

"I don't know," I said, keeping my voice as even as possible. "He was a religious guy, wasn't he? Anyway, we kept it out of the courts."

My father grunted. There was silence.

"Whatever you're doing," he said at last. "Be very bloody careful, my son."

That evening, Ibrahim was waiting for us outside the office. He had his own car, which was surprising; a very stately grey machine that waited patiently as he finished his smoke. Aniston was in the front seat.

"You boys look like you could use a drink," he said. "Want a ride?"

"Elkhead?" Wurth said.

"Elkhead."

Dusk was falling. Around us, a steady horde of NumberCorpers streamed out of the great revolving doors, heading for their little cubby holes in the Walls. Hundreds of them, faceless, nameless. They looked at us as they went by, in the wordless salutes of underlings. No doubt some of them wanted to be where we were someday.

Inside the car, Aniston twisted to look at us and gave us a little nod, as if she was satisfied with what she was seeing.

"You did what you had to do," she said.

I'll share something else that I remember that perfectly explains the post-Koenig mood of the company. Back then it was common practice in the Valley to host weekly company meetings. TGIF, as they called it, began with Google, and with increasing numbers of ex-Googlers setting up their own companies, it quickly became Valley tradition. Whoever was leading the company was supposed to field any question that was asked. An open forum of sorts.

At NumberCorp it was the opposite. Julius perfected the black box approach, as Wurth called it. Each part of the company ran more of less by itself. Each business unit had one or two people whose job it was to interface with the other parts of the company. He liked it that way. But I suppose #WhatHappens shook us all up a bit, because there came a day when Wurth knocked on our door. He looked exhausted.

"You're not answering your phone," he said.

"I was editing," I said, blinking. I disconnected myself from the terminal and waited for the buzzing in my optics to go away. "What's up?"

"Come on down," said Wurth.

I went down. The Pit had been cleared; it was bare space, with a bar set up in the corner. Wurth was chivvying around. The display that showed the US and EU averages now showed the NumberCorp logo. It looked empty, almost cave-like. We waited, watching the people file in.

It was the first time I had seen all of NumberCorp assembled in full force. What a motley crew they were. Up front was Aniston and her acolytes. She was stunning in white; they were less radiant, but an air of glamor hung around them nonetheless. They had their own crazy fashion thing going on; this month it was braids and faux-leather boots. Behind them were the Product crew - a bizarre zoo of people in everything from 2010-era sneakers and button-downs to Swarovski suits. Here and there were pockets of cyberpunk aesthetics, especially among the ones with mechanical body parts. There were one or two that even looked like sexbots, but every so often they moved and I was sure I was mistaken.

In one corner were the Integration team; Ibrahim's crew. The ones who actually spent most of their lives outside, and it showed: they looked more weather-beaten somehow, and carried themselves with a sort of dangerous confidence. People gave way to them as if they were tigers prowling among the sheep.

"Five hundred people," said Wurth's voice in my earphone.

"Where do they come from?"

"Beats me," said Wurth.

Julius walked in. Suddenly the tigers looked like sheep again.

"Hey, everyone," he said without preamble. Silence fell.

"A mathematician and a engineer agree to a psychological experiment. They're both put in opposite corners of the room, and right between them is a bed with a beautiful, naked woman on it. The psychologist says, 'Every five minutes, you both are allowed to halve the distance between you and the bed.'

"The mathematician is pissed. He gets up and storms out. The engineer, on the other hand, is all good to go. So the mathematician is a bit confused. 'Don't you realize that you'll never reach her?'

"The engineer smiles and says, 'Yeah, but I'll get close enough for all practical purposes!'"

Titters, laughs. Common grinned. "Old joke, and my apologies to those who aren't into beautiful naked women. Now - some time back, all of you saw this man going ham on us with that webcast of his, right?"

The background changed to a giant photo of Lars Koenig.

"So I want to clear something up," said Julius. "Firstly, this guy is right. Everything we do here - in as simple a way as I can say it - is about building a diverse set of algorithms that can use data to understand, to quantify, human trust and connections.

"The two pillars of society are money and influence. We all know this. The two are often tied together, but it's not a direct one to one relationship. Our Number is a measure of both of these. Facebook was definitely doing something like this a while ago, but not the way we do. Ours is better. Which is why they use us."

Cheers, clapping.

"A shout out to Russell for making that happen!" said Julius. The cheers and clapping intensified: people whistled. Wurth, grinning and surprised, sketched out a bow.

"Now regardless of what anyone says, everyone sizes each other up when they meet: we've just made it so much more accurate. Now mapping money is easy; but influence there is a lot of work into making that accuracy really work. When you take societies, what you actually get is a series of microcosms interacting in their own little bubbles. What's considered hip in New York is not going to fly in Tokyo. So we actually need to tailor algorithms to every one of these identified microsocieties. We've gone a long way since just Pagerank for people. This is the Algorithm team, people. They're a really diverse bunch -" and at this, a really diverse bunch did stand up - "and they make this happen."

"The really amazing part about this is that this brings up so many opportunities. For hiring people, for instance, you need a different algorithm there; you need something that. in addition to your usual Number. will look up the people working in a company and generally determine whether this new girl will work well or not. That's what our Product team does: they figure out how this fits into a larger picture. Bizdev - Aniston -

identifies customers and helps them understand what we can do for them.

"And I have to say: we've got tentative signups for Number for Work by. . . About twenty five percent of the Fortune 500 companies; we're selling Number for Governments in Sri Lanka, Indonesia, Thailand, Maldives - and Washington is doing a trial right now. With every push we make, we get closer to exploring more and more possibilities. We're not really where we want to be right now, but we have roadmaps that stretch five, ten years into the future. We're going to make them happen. To quote that engineer, soon we're going to be close enough for practical purpose."

Laughs, applause.

Julius began to pace. "Now some of you came to me before this and asked me to address a few elephants in the room. One - and this is something people will always throw at us - bribery allegations, being evil, all that. Apparently we whisper in politicians' ears - and all that. To which I really have to say - the way things get done in this world is money and influence. If you want that, go rewrite ten thousand years worth of human history, and then come talk to me.

"Second - Google. Google has a massive amount of data. To be honest, no other organization in the world has the kind of data and processing they do. But we have a different hook, a different problem we're solving, and our algorithm right now is far superior. They can't move into our space without some serious anti-monopoly action kicking in. Same goes for Circle. I know, for a fact, that they have skunkworks projects doing what we do, but we moved first and we're winning this. We know this because Google is working with us.

"So what can I say? We're taking over the world. An old-world economist called Adam Smith used to write about the Invisible Hand that governed markets. That's us. Our job is to be the Invisible Hand that governs a part of social interaction that no-one's really thought about yet. Lars Koenig is right; we're everywhere, and we will be everywhere, because we're doing a damn good job."

Thundering applause. The cheering was so loud we barely heard him call for questions. I, standing back, was reminded of that first photo I took of Jules. I've heard that powerful leaders have a reality distortion field that makes them able to sway anyone to their cause. Julius had it out in full force. As the speaker pods moved through the audience, seeking questions, he took their hearts, their minds.

Someone in vivid dynapunk colors stood up. "Anjou, from Support," she said. "So I have a question - in terms of Product, what's the next big thing on the horizon? What are we working on?"

"Ibrahim," said Julius from on stage.

Pepperwater nodded out a subordinate, a wiry man with a slow drawl. "Well, you know, Number for Government is huge. We initially wanted to focus on politicians, but that context was too fuzzy, you might remember our discussions. What we're working on now is the Number for Law and Order, which we call Number Police, so what that does is integrate with police and federal and all sorts of criminal databases and use that data to modify Numbers of suspects and identify potential, uh, links. Certain Number patterns, once you put them together with criminal data, make it possible to, say, dig out the rest of a drug ring. We're also looking at prediction - has anyone seen Minority Report? Ours is a bit more boring but success rate is almost at 90% right now. Very few false positives."

Anjou wasn't done. "I ask because we really have no visibility here as to, you know, what's happening," she said. "Like we hear stuff, we get a use case, and that's it. Five months later we see stuff in the media and go oh, there's that thing we were working on. And then we have to support it. Sometimes it's frustrating."

One of Aniston's people took the mic next and addressed Common directly. "Maybe we need to have a freer flow of information among us,' she said. 'I know this system works right now, but more meetings, more communication, I'm sure would be better."

I'm pretty sure the sentiment came from Aniston, but she was too smart to criticize the boss publicly.

"Transparency," said Julius. "We need to work on that. Just to be clear - I don't believe in meetings, I believe meetings are a massive waste of time - if you're an engineer, you'll understand - so we have to figure out a way of improving on how we do things asynchronously. Does every department have a chatbot set up that people can talk to? Yes? No? Why not? What is this, 2010? Ezra, can you have that done by next Friday? Right? Excellent. We're doing this."

Someone else stood up.

"I really want to point out that people with augmentations are treated differently," he said. "My wife lost an arm in an accident, and ever since we got her a replacement, people don't interact with her, like they, um, used to. Her Number's dropped. I've - I've spoken to a lot of people in the augmented communities -"

A shout of 'hear, hear!' and clapping from those who were augmented.

"-And I think this thing is something we have a responsibility to look into," the man finished. "Discrimination, is, is not just racial now. It's also about the kind of body parts you have."

Silence fell as they waited for Julius's answer. The augmented ones stood almost rigid.

"I'm really sorry about your wife," said Julius. 'Vaas? Vaas, if you submit your wife's medical bills, we'll add her to our insurance plan."

Then he raised his voice. "Goes to anyone with a significant other who's had to have some limb replaced. Actually, just tell us the hospital, we'll integrate with them right away. We work pretty closely with Kissling Labs, which means we can give them the best equipment in the country. Right away. Your families, they're part of our journey. We're not going to leave anyone behind."

"Fucking hell," grinned Wurth, and wolf-whistled.

"Regarding the Number drop. That is a very valid point - and the good news is Algorithm is working on it. In fact, we're not just looking at mecha limbs. We're looking at inequality, period: race, religion, even things as stupid as geographical biases. This is wildly out there, I wasn't going to talk about this today, but trust me: over the next few updates, I promise you, we'll be ironing out inequality. If you're Muslim and brown-skinned you should not have to work twice as hard to get to where you are -"

The sound was a low murmur: a cross between admiration and astonishment.

"If you are black; if you are white, if you're Asian, if you're Hispanic, if you are a human-" said Common above the noise, and then he stopped and he waited. We slowly fell silent, looking at him like an army of children looking up at their father.

"Ironing. Out. Inequality," said Julius Common into the pindrop silence. "Might take a year, might take two, might take five. But we're going to change this world. Now if anyone wants to come and say that we're evil, well -" he grinned his shark grin, hands up, palms up. His arms were bare; that strange lettering coiled around one. MEMENTO MORI. "You tell them, you tell them we're going to make the world a better place, whether they want to or not."

Eight

Over the years, many people have asked me when it started feeling like we were heading down the wrong path.

The thing is, it never did. It never does. There is something we all learned in college called the tipping point. It has many names - Cascade theory, avalanche moment - but everyone agreed on the definition: it's a moment of critical mass, a point that everything leads up to, subtly, the point at which everything just breaks.

The thing about the tipping point is that you never see it coming. In fact, I'm not entirely convinced that we are on the wrong path, even now.

Look around you. The world I grew up in was a brutal one. The murder rate was once seven people for every hundred thousand. The average American on minimum wage could barely afford to keep themselves alive on canned food. Millions died over private oil fortunes. Wealthy men and women ran the world for profit. Fools and charlatans got into our Parliaments and set the world on fire. We had everything on paper - checks, balances, freedom, democracy - and yet to live was to be a slave.

Look at society today. Government agents held accountable. Almost non-existent crime rates. A guaranteed basic income, education and a home for every human on the system. Even schoolyard bullying is dead, thanks to immediate socioeconomic repercussion algorithms.

Karma.

Is it right? No. On paper, a digital kingdom is still a kingdom. Julius is - at least in my book - a tyrant. But you have to admit: it works. This is no utopia, but it's the best we have.

Back in 2033, Wurth plopped on my chair.

"The UN is in," he announced.

"The UN? What UN? How are they in?" I asked, poring over our roadmaps / battleplans document.

For years, the United Nations, that grand failure of an institution, had been putting out 'objectives' lists that become vaguer and more useless with each passing decade - hopeful pleas to 'end world hunger' and 'prevent racial crime' while behind closed doors, America and China threatened to blow the roofs off each other and large tracts of the Middle East continued chopping the heads off infidels. Apparently some small part of the whole thing had been keeping an eye on us ever since the whole UK/Koenig mess. Julius's newest list of additions to the Number was hot news, and they wanted to work with us.

"What are we getting out of it?"

Wurth looked over his list. "A century of data? Legitimacy? Access to every major politician out there? We get to be the poster boy for one of their little development goals, and they get to say something worked for a change."

"This sounds like a Julius deal," I said. We had our own lingo for the kind of political stunts Julius could pull.

"It is a Julius deal," Wurth said.

"Alright," I said, and off we went to meet the UN reps. Most of them were faceless, interchangeable, but hugely enthusiastic. We explained to them a lot of what we had going on, and they explained back that Mr. Common had mentioned all sorts of ways they could fit in. Right, we said, and flew a couple of them down to the Valley, because things were getting complicated.

The Inequality Update hit with the force of a nuclear bomb.

Let me give you a snapshot of where we were just pre-Inqueality. We stood at a little over 800 million users; we had branches in the United States, in London, in Paris, even in Geneva. People who had been with us at the start were running teams of their own.

In the US, Alicia Random's team had perfected the system for university admissions. Now it was no longer enough to have Numbers low enough to earn a scholarship; universities like Harvard gave their own criteria, calculations that we layered on top of our own. Among those criteria were requirements for erudition and intelligence percentile. Every single day, tens of thousands of students were mined for their social media output and judged accordingly; there were studies that tentatively proved that the constant intellectual stimulus might actually create a smarter generation of students.

In the United Kingdom, Basil Ignarsson's team was building a version of the Number for government employees. Studies had long since proven links between nationalism and economic progress, and the inverse between nationalism and freedom of thought. Careful rules were set in place, scripted to adjust dynamically during interviews. We piggybacked on the public demand for open data and did the legwork: here were hiring statistics for every department; here was what they did; here was who worked there and why. Top public servants, suddenly thrown into the spotlight, either went offline or became minor celebrities. There was talk of the US government buying the system off us. I heard Algorithm had expanded threefold to accommodate, and there was talk of a Department of Rules under Random.

In Singapore, in Vietnam, in Venezuela, Aaron Kotalawala, the hospitality mogul, was building what would eventually become Atlantis: a series of walled city-states that only admitted the rich, the affluent, the high scorers. I've heard since then that Julius wanted Aaron back because of their university affiliations; I've also heard that Aaron bought his way in.

But in truth Aaron Kotalawala is the reason the doors opened for our expansion in Asia. The downside to being noticed is that people start gunning for you, and back then, lots of governments were very, very cautious about this new thing called NumberCorp; they'd seen what happened in the UK. We wanted a smart way in.

Inequality took all of this, strapped rockets onto us, and threw us right out into the stars.

Dating sites called, wanting to integrate the Number. Japan wanted the Number At Work group to debut there - a whole new branch of the tech that we hadn't even thought about yet. The stamp of the United Nations threw us into every possible sphere of usage. Even News, Julius's errant skunkworks social network, was taking off: like Twitter before it, it would never, ever become profitable, but major news networks were taking it seriously. Lars Koenig, it seemed, had inadvertently done us a favour: he had turned News into a must-watch network for every single journalist out there. The tech press was in love. We provided them with endless material. Julius Common was compared to Elon Musk and came off favorably.

I was laid, offered book deals, webcast space, even positions in other companies; but I was already drawing a salary three times larger than anything I would have made elsewhere, and I carefully excused myself and went looking for the wine. When Wurth and I went to the mandatory party or meetup we were introduced as experts in whatever field we happened to be talking about at the moment.

And we grew.

Our deployments took on a pattern, a kind of clockwork that Wurth, Aniston, Ibrahim and I perfected one country at a time. The first into the breach was NumberCorp Credit. We needed the finance sector for initial setup; Credit had to go in flashy; we had to make an entrance. Sometimes this could take a year, but soon, the majority of the banks would be using our system.

Then we'd roll out NumberCorp Records. Records took another year, maybe two, because it required major government legislation to be passed. Once everything was ready, we'd launch Number for Work and woo the private sector businesses to implement Number integration - employee records, ratings, that sort of thing, in exchange for the most accurate employee ratings and rewards system in history.

Then came Influence. Influence, connecting to the UN-ID blockchain, would neatly tie everything together. The Number would be presented. And updated. This man - does he travel? Where does he check in? What type of clothes does he buy? What concerts does he attend? What people does he hang out with? How are their preferences? How are their Numbers? NumberCorp would know who you are and what to do with you.

I understand this caused a whole lot of overtime code-crunching for Ibrahim's people, because they had to separate the bits and pieces of the Algorithm to the point where you could launch separately. There was an entire hardware team whose whole job it was to fly all over the world and build the most cost-effective datacenters so Aniston could do her dance. But it worked, and it worked as smoothly as greased silk. Soon we had more Minervas, some of them so smart that we were on the brink of violating Turing Law. Cog. Dahli. Hegel. Each ran a country, dispensing orders to a core of about a hundred well-paid people in a local office.

That's the beauty of software: it scales. I was reminded of that first job I had - playing assistant to a grading machine, dealing with what the machine could not. Most our employees overseas lived life this way. Wurth and I watched with a kind of detached fascination as the numbers grew; by our count, Aniston had a small army under her command.

And finally, when it was all set up, we'd send Wurth.

"We don't just look at how much money a man is making," he'd say, pacing the stage. "That would be wrong. We look at how that person behaves. Who they influence. Is he respected? Is he a good guy? Does his lifestyle suit the kind of behavior you'd want your kids looking up to? Based on that, we make a calculation: here is how much this person is worth to this society. Here is his Number."

"NUMBERCORP: A BETTER WAY OF DOING BUSINESS," we said. And on our heels, the IMF and the World Bank nodded gently. There were rumors in the background about replacing the GDP as a measure of growth with an aggregate of a country's Gross Domestic Number. It was better, they said. Adam Smith's 17th century math was done, they said. It was time for a new system.

And whenever someone said something about a private Silicon Valley company wielding this kind of power, we came back and said look, we're being vetted by the collective governments of the entire world.

"We're committed to transparency," Julius Common boomed at microphones."Yes, we are a private company, yes, we do this for money. At the same time, we're aware that every piece of technology has great potential for both good and bad, so we're working with the highest authorities to make sure that our vision for the world - and our part in it - plays in with what the elected leadership of the world is trying to achieve.

"This leads us to some spectacular collaborations. In Singapore, for example, we're working with social services to identify small-Number individuals and help them. Maybe they could be fraternizing with criminals - or maybe they have poor personal finance or interpersonal skills. We can identify something like that and the state can offer subsidized support services. Of course, you've heard rumors about our Inequality Update: we're working with the finest sociologists in the world to reverse-engineer racial discrimination by boosting minority groups we find being discriminated against. Over time, we're going to normalize things to a level where, say, a black Muslim woman with an artificial arm is truly the social equal of a white Jewish man at the prime of his health. For the first time in the world, we have the data and the technology to tackle these problems instantly, at scale. Questions?"

Nobody thought to ask us how we had gotten the police to start using the Number. Or how Fortune 500 corps now asked for the Numbers of whoever was signing contracts. These weren't our plays: they were Julius's. I had caught a glimpse of his game in Sri Lanka; I had seen it being played out across America, Hong Kong, across Japan. The people who met behind closed doors, over expensive dinners, and would shake Julius's hand and politely ask that I turn over all my footage before leaving the room.

And when people like Koenig tried pointing things out, we hurt them.

There were other moments, minor Koenigs that send us scrambling to the news editors. Some of them I can mention. Cedric Roseworthy died in Berlin in a spectacular orgy involving five women and a heart attack. Prartana Singh, an otherwise unremarkable lawyer on our team, went through her third divorce and ended up beating her ex to death in her Bangalore home. An engineer's son shot himself in Texas. Everyone has skeletons in the closet.

But we were superstars. We were overthrowing the Fake, ushering in the Real. Someone set up a giant display charting the entire world and what we controlled of it; on some days it felt like we owned the Earth, and the only place left to expand to was the next planet down the line.

PART III

Watchmen Press Archives

Content type: transcript

Channel: Watchmen Tech Episode 322, 'Numbers that guide us'

> ***SS:*** *Hey there! I'm Steven Starmind, and you're watching Watchmen Tech, where we cover the tech stories that really matter.*
>
> *Today's episode is a double-special. We have Stephanie Vayner of Rector [audience cheers], talking to us about how the HARNESS Alliance is solving one of the most pressing concerns we have right now - the energy crisis. As you might remember, HARNESS hit a deep pocket of controversy recently when they set three Class I artificial intelligences to design, in a simulation, an energy network servicing the entire planet . . . while a lot of us think it was revolutionary and should have*

been done ages ago, the government is not so happy about this violation of Turing Law. We'll be getting to that debate soon.

But first up, we have another controversy to discuss. I'm sure that a lot of you are aware of a company called NumberCorp - NumberCorp's led what we here call a silent revolution, which means they've sort of snuck up on everyone and it's actually become part of our lives. It's this really interesting service that lets you immediately tell how important a person is. A lot of banks used to use it, but as the prices dropped, we're even seeing people, not Joe Average, but people like celebrities, using apps that tap into the Number data to really help them understand who they should network with, and who they shouldn't.

Here in the studio we have Patrick Udo, a Director of Communications at NumberCorp, and Alicia Random, an economist who works on .. the -

Alicia Random: on the algorithms behind the Number.

***SS:** That's right. Welcome to the show.*

***Patrick Udo:** Thanks, Steven, good to be here.*

***SS:** So let me just as, right out of the bat, how DOES the Number work, really? We all know it, we even use it, but it's a bit like Facebook Newsfeeds, nobody seems to know what goes into it.*

***PU:** Right. So... firstly, you have to understand, Number - the software, and to some extent the entire company - is a solution. Like all solutions it answers a question - in this case the question is 'how do we understand the value of a given human being?'*

So how we approach it is, we have lots of modules working together. The three biggest ones are Records, Credit, Influence.

Records is simple to explain. A program pulls up police records and looks for criminal activity. Feed it a UN-ID number and it'd look through the police and Fed databases, assign a ranking based on the record, and throw it back out.

***SS:** So like if you're a criminal -*

***PU:** Yeah, if you have a record, it'll indicate that. You won't be hitting as high as a perfectly normal guy who's paid all his taxes and never got a parking ticket. I mean, we don't want - or really trust - criminals, do we?*

***SS:** Absolutely right.*

***PU:** So the next is Credit, which I think Alicia should explain -*

***Alicia Random:** Thanks, Pat. Well, Steven...Credit is really more complicated. The moment you authorize it, it would analyze your income, expenditure and spending* *patterns, and then it'd run some very heavy math.*

SS: *What kind of math, is that, are you able to share?*

AR: *Well, not the present math, really, but I'll give you an example of an older version of it. If your net worth was equal to something like one-tenth of your age multiplied by your current annual pre-tax income from all sources, you'd be flagged as average.*

If your net worth was more than that figure, you'd be on your way to the top. You'd have great financial sense. Credit would flag you under several different grades on the good scale.

If your net worth was less, you could have it all - the BMW, the apartment in Times Square, the Pradas, but the car could be on a ten-year lease, the apartment could be paid for by your rich parents, the Pradas could be a friend's, and you could probably be knee-deep in debt and front a lifestyle far beyond sanity. You would be flagged as a risk.

SS: *Hyperconsumerism.*

AR: *I call it humanity.*

SS: *So this is an old version -*

AR: *Yeah, the new one's even more accurate. I used to spend hours looking at that data, you know. You* *know the strange part? Most people on the good side of the scale don't look like they're rich. They look like boring people - bankers, maybe developers, teachers. They drive secondhand Pruises and live in decent homes. They've got the same, er, basic financial instincts as the ultrabillionaires and the investors.*

The people flagged as risks? We have drug addicts, broke celebrities and ... all the people who look rich. The guys who have two cars and a house on lease. The people who spend thousands on dinner and clubs and end up too broke at the end of the month to pay their phone bills on time. We see the money flowing out. It's amazing what money can tell you if you listen.

PU: *Credit was Alicia's baby when I started working at NumberCorp. She knew it inside out.*

AR: *Yeah, like back when I joined, it was really based off an old book called the Millionaire Next Door; Julius wrote the thing when he was in college. Made it open source, put it out there on Github, caused this huge drama in Wall Street circles.*

SS: *Hashtag disrupt, what?*

AR: <Chuckles> *Yeah. So, somewhere around 2024, I and - well, like a handful of us - started mucking around in the codebase, updating it, because it just didn't seem accurate enough. And then one day, boom! We get an invite from this mysterious Julius Common guy, who* *turns around and basically says 'would you like a job?'*

SS: *Surreal. And did you ever get to run the Credit, uh, code on him?*

AR: *Yeah. He turned out to have broken it years ago, you know. He basically wrote a program that told him what to spend where and he followed that to the letter. So that is one of the services we offer banks, really. If you're a customer of most banks in the world the app will tell you how to manage your finances.*

SS: *Hence the popularity.*

AR: *Hence the popularity.*

PU: *Well, one of the reasons <laughs>. So component number three: Influence.*

SS: *The big one.*

PU: *Influence was what looked at what we called the human connection web. It takes the criminal ranking – negligible for most people – the Credit ranking, and then crawls through a user's social media and search profiles, trying to compute everything under the sun. Where on Google do they show up? What do they look like on LinkedIn, who are they connected to? How about their Facebook and Instagram? Who do they check in with? How many – and who – comments, follows, likes? How important are they? It adds in the criminal record* *and the credit score. How powerful are they? Can we represent that in a Number?*

SS: *And you can get all that? All of that's available?*

PU: *Oh yeah, totally. The data's been there, the idea's been out there even longer.*

SS: *I was reading this old book recently, 1984, where this fictional government sort of spied on what every single person was doing, you know, cameras in every corner ...*

PU: *Oh no, we don't need that crap. It's – it's like George Orwell's wet dream, really.*

So as it turns out, if you run this calculation enough times you end up with roughly three layers of people. Layer one are the heavyweights. They get Numbers between 10K and 16K. Presidents, international celebrities, activists, the Pope, people like that. Julius is a 16K.

Layer two is a loose band between 7K and 10K. People who're doing well, but not necessarily famous.

SS: *Such as?*

PU: *Well, I'm there.*

AR: *Middle class, really.*

PU: *That's the middle class. Yeah.*

SS: *Layer three. Bottom of the ladder?*

PU: *Someone loses, someone wins, right? The thing is, we don't just slap a number on you and tell you you're stuck with this, right. That's inhumane. On the app, we give you a pretty detailed breakdown of why you have this Number. Maybe you're hanging out with a convicted felon. Maybe all that sharing memes or fake news isn't really working out. Whatever it is, we explain why.*

SS: *And that's had a lot of effect, hasn't it? There are studies showing that people are sharing less, how do we say, like rehashed content –*

PU: *And actually, you know, hostility, hostility on the Internet, it's actually gone down quite a lot. Now we don't conclusively know that's it's because of us, but it's likely the Number is one of the biggest causes.*

SS: *What about the allegations that a sort of social discrimination is forming around the Number? For example, convicted felons finding it hard to dine at restaurants, or get into clubs, things like that –*

PU: *Well, they're convicted felons, aren't they? We locked them up for a reason, didn't we?*

<laughter from the audience>

PU: *I mean, not to be rude, and all that. But Steven, can* *you honestly say that dining next to, say, a thief doesn't make you nervous? It would, right?*

SS: *It would, yeah.*

PU: *So we're not creating discrimination. We're just making sure people are safe and that businesses really have a way of maintaining the kind of culture and people they want for their clientele. In fact, again, going back to this example of a convicted felon, the same tools that are available to you are given to them as well. The Number app will sort of show them what parts of their life they can improve. Isn't that a great thing? We're saying yes, here are these hurdles, and society has always held them here, but now we're giving people the tools to transcend them.*

SS: *That is incredible, actually, yeah.*

PU: *So basically, I can tell you the most important person in this room right now and the least important. You can decide how you want to treat them.*

Nine

Soon there came a time when we had two ways to expand: towards what we called Asia Minor - Malaysia, Singapore and so on – or towards Asia Major: India.

I know everyone was for Singapore and Malaysia, especially Wurth and Ibrahim Monard. Aniston wanted India: it was big game, she pointed out, and would let us steamroll every other country so much faster. Maybe she wanted to prove to Common that she could do better than Kotalawala. Word around our little Elkhead gang was that Aaron Kotalawala, too, was pushing Julius for bigger and better conquests.

And thus, blinded by all of our success, we blundered into the second biggest mistake NumberCorp ever made.

India, post-2035, was essentially China in 2020: a looming economic giant with its own technology, a country that could flip the bird to the United Nations and get away with it. It had two of the six billion people in the world and one of the most hyperactive tech ecosystems on the planet. Most companies that went in there faced stiff competition. Some of them, like Facebook's Internet.org, ended up being run out on a rail by the public.

The spearhead – was myself, Ibrahim – because he understood the practical tech problems – and Aniston with a dozen people from Bizdev. Wurth had been rerouted to Japan to oversee the Number at Work marketing

"You'll be there for a year, maybe more," Julius said, right at the start. "I'll give you Amarasinghe. Official title, Director of Communications."

I took the job.

My first impression of India was of a Bombay, or Mumbai, to use the right world. I saw vast hills teeming with uncountable millions in their prefabricated homes, roads cutting through them like broad black brush strokes. The skyline was one hotel after another, apartments piling on top of each other, linking bridge-arms for support, reaching almost to the sky in a desperate attempt to accommodate the population. Taxis blared up and down the sides of buildings, jetting above freeways where every car was locked in a vicious battle for survival. Crowds ebbed and flowed under holograms of Kali and Vishnu that floated above night stalls. Amarasinghe, the Sri Lankan valet, had spent a good decade in India; within seconds of our landing he had summoned a small army of personal servants and ushered us into our hotels.

"Holden, Nagata, Burton, Kamal?" queried the bespectacled young man behind the counter of the Himalaya Hotel, Bombay.

"Ag, no, sir, next batch," said one of Amarasinghe's suited flunkies, chivvying a bunch of valets around.

"Are those actual spectacles?" said Aniston, staring at the man.

We were to move into some space rented at a nearby tower,

one of those spaces that catered exclusively to foreign tech companies; but there was some sort of delay, some documentation to be processed, and so for twenty four hours I had absolutely nothing to do. Ibrahim, having disposed of the bags, came down and offered me a smoke. We stepped out into the sweltering heat, just beyond reach of the doormen.

It's funny how, of all traditions, smoking has survived the decades. Decades of lobbying and even a global ban on nicotine has yet to change the fact that we stick paper cylinders in our mouths and set them on fire. Granted, we've replaced tobacco with marijuana, but the habit itself is curious. I think people smoke not for the material but for the social license it gives: the freedom to be standing right there, next to someone, and still not have to socialize: a freedom to meditate without being disturbed.

We meditated a bit.

"You know," said Ibrahim, as we puffed smoke into the noisy night. "There was a time when jet lag was a thing? I used to get to hotels like these feeling like I'd just dug my way out of a grave."

"Yeah, my dad used to tell me," I said. Then, because it hit me. "How old are you, if you don't mind me asking?"

"How old do you reckon?"

I looked at him. Tall, fit, he looked no older than thirty, maybe thirty-five. I told him as much.

Ibrahim grinned, pulled down his collar. On his neck was a slim tattoo, like an old-fashioned QR code surmounted by five letters. I'd heard of these.

"My parents wanted a kid who was pretty smart, so they decided a bit of modification wasn't below them. Worked. I hit my prime way before everyone else did and I'll pretty much stay this way until I die. Brain's running full steam ahead all the time."

"Weren't there – I read there were side effects? Wasn't that why they banned it?"

"Cancer," he said agreeably. "Rapid cell mutation. You look twenty five for thirty years and then you look thirty five and then forty and you're dead. Doctors tell I'll be hitting the bucket soon myself, God willing."

"Shit, Monard," I said, because I had absolutely no idea what to say.

He shrugged. "I have a job, I have food, I get to travel," he said. "You know there aren't many people who'd hire folks like us - not even in the Valley? Jules, he doesn't care where you come from, you know. There's a reason I put up with all his shit."

He puffed meditatively. "Let me ask you a strange question, Pat. Where do you see yourself in five years?"

I'd honestly never given it much thought. At school we were repeatedly told to think of what we'd consider a good life – and follow the smartest path to getting there. Everyone else pictured women, cars, expensive hotels. I just had a blank. Over time, the blank had changed; now it was me with a camera, but everything else was gray. I wanted to capture moments; to freeze them and own them; I wanted little else.

I told this to him.

He lit another cigarette and was silent for a while. "Do yourself a favor," he said. "Whatever it is you want to do, get away from NumberCorp."

He must have seen my reaction.

"Just between us," he said.

"Of course," I said. "But why?"

"Let's just say I've seen the future. It's not one any of us want to be part of," he said.

Just then, a black car eased off the street and glided to a halt in front of us, spilling out Amarasinghe and the newest additions to NumberCorp.

"Isn't that your team? First time managing this lot?" asked Ibrahim.

"Pretty much," I confessed. As part of the assignment I'd been handed a pre-hired team of raw recruits. At least some of them Indian, and well-connected - nieces and nephews of politicians and celebrities, the kind of people who were fresh out of university but had the network a thirty-year-old would envy. Ibrahim surveyed them despondently.

"Do yourself a favor," he said. "Don't get too attached."

He excused himself and walked off into the darkness, puffing his cigarette, disappearing into the noise and light of the Bombay night.

Our goal in any country was simple: get to the people that mattered.

My tools for the job: a painfully fresh team full of that half-awed, half-nervous preppiness you get in recent college graduates. Only one didn't have that terrible freshness, and that was Parvati Singh, who we had headhunted from NextBigThing. Parvati was calm and composed and immediately took charge as my second-in-command, handling the admin stuff while leaving me to teach the newbies the ropes of marketing the Number.

Marketing is a curious science. While it's nowhere near as complicated as, say, solid-state physics, it's an intermarriage of pattern recognition, psychology and art. Claude Hopkins, the guy who literally wrote the book on the subject, pointed out the first two: you figure out a trigger – or a cue. Then you sell your product as a reward for that cue. MBAs call this stuff 'pain points' and talk about how companies address them, but that's not really the trick. The real trick is not solving a pain point, but creating one, and then figuring out the reward cycle. The rest is just execution.

Our cycle was ironclad. Trigger: basic financial activities – opening a loan, claiming insurance, getting a loan. Reward: a Number that you could increase by being social, without having to earn pots of money. And that was the snowball that set off the avalanche. I made sure my new minions had it down to the last letter, and off we went. We had done this in countries around the globe, and it always worked.

Except in India.

The first screw-up was with the press. We were used to the Valley, where everyone knew everyone and a few phone calls from a major corp – even something as small as ours – gave us control over when our story went public. Journalists in America were hungry and could be made to dance.

Not so in India. Bombay blew our operation wide open. NUMBERCORP IS HERE, blared headlines. NUMBERCORPS'S NEW GAMBIT: MUMBAI. COMMON MOVES INTO INDIA.

The initial stories said stuff that we were okay with – NumberCorp, the Silicon Valley based company etc, etc, were now in Mumbai initiating a launch of their new product, Number, etc, etc. America was now using the Number for almost all aspects of their etc, etc. Stay tuned, etc, etc.

The second wave was not that great.

NUMBERCORP'S INVASION OF OUR LAND, shouted a webcast by a journalist called Amali De Saram. "Big Brother is in Mumbai," she proclaimed, in a cultured British-Indian accent. "Here is a Silicon Valley company saying" that in exchange for everything we say and do on the Internet it will give us a number, and that number will show the world how valuable we are. Is it just me or does this sound a little off to you? What about privacy? What if we don't want to share?"

Shades of Lars Koenig. It went viral on the Indian Internet. One of the new team showed it to me. I took it upwards.

"Oh shit," said Wurth when he saw it in Japan.

"Oh shit," said Aniston when I showed it to her.

Ibrahim watched it intently. "Has Julius seen this?" he asked.

So I took it to Julius.

The message arrived fast: meet her.

"Unofficial visit. If anyone asks, you're not authorized to make any kind of statement," added Aniston. "Find out who this woman thinks she is."

And so I did. As it was, Amali de Saram had a reputation for a specific line on things. I still have some of those old articles saved. The Problem of the West, said one: 'As the so-called 'Third World' that once produced many of the world's primary resources grows up, the West's economies are forced to grind us back into poverty to keep their own economies stable. How do we fight back?' Global Village? Global Pudding, cried another - 'the melting pot is robbing entire nations of their quirks and cultures, and we need to stop it.'

Rich stuff, very chip-on-the-shoulder. You get the picture.

Two days later, on the rooftop of one fine hotel, I sat down and waited.

She arrived on time. Not too shapely, but flawless, golden-brown skin. Expensive-looking dress. Heavy silver jewelery. A hand. In a glove. I shook it gingerly. It was strange to see someone wearing gloves back then, even though it's become fashion (and perhaps necessity) now.

She looked me up and down. "So you're the mysterious Patrick Udo? I was expecting someone... whiter."

I was taken aback. "How so?"

"Well, Mr Udo, the world is still run by white people." She smiled and sat down in a rustle of silk and silver. "But let's change the subject. I've seen your photography, it's wonderful."

More famous people have used better words, but you take what you can. I returned the compliment about her writing, not meaning it one bit, and asked her how she got into webcasting. Again, I didn't care. I was just probing. Despite the articles, I saw no obvious bias. Not a nationalist. Not Luddite.

"So I take it you don't like NumberCorp," I said.

She smiled. She had a beautiful smile; a slender parting of the lips and a glow in the eyes that hit you like a tramcar. "May I ask you about NumberCorp, Mr Udo?"

"Of course. Though you understand I'm not representing NumberCorp today. This is purely a personal visit and all I can give you is my opinion."

A red light came on near her cheekbone. REC. "I hope you don't mind me recording this. I'll send you a copy of the audio afterwards, of course."

I didn't mind: I had no grand statements to make. I made a joke about it.

"One of the many dangers of having dinner with a journalist,' she said. 'So, Patrick - can I call you Patrick? - in your opinion, of course - why is NumberCorp here?"

I explained that the whole point was to be everywhere in the world, and that the time was ripe for an India launch.

"I'm curious," she said. "How is your perception of India, as a market for the Number?"

"Well, we're done our research, and we believe we have value to add here," I said. Standard line.

"Does that research tell you that much of the Indian public doesn't trust NumberCorp? Do they tell you that we believe our politicians have sold out to your Mr Julius Common?"

I made a guarded comment about not being able to talk about our research, but this was supposed to be a personal conversation: "Personally, I haven't seen anything of the sort on social media or the news," I said, rather truthfully. I hadn't. All I'd seen was PR.

"Ah, social media. Patrick – may I call you Patrick? Who owns the social media that you use? Are they Indians based in India, or are they American billionaires with vested interests in NumberCorp?"

"What are you implying?"

"2016," she said. "Off the top of my head. Videos of cop shootings started going viral in America. Facebook blocked the videos. In some cases they banned accounts. Even better: also in 2016, WikiLeaks started posting hacked emails from politicians. Facebook censored that. And here in India, Patrick, Facebook has been keeping word of the Kashmiri conflict buried for decades. You've never heard of the Kashmiri conflict?"

I confessed that I had not.

"Now you know why you haven't," she said.

"I'm sure they have their reasons," I said. "Either way, I'm not sure I can answer for Facebook. Especially not for events from 2016, I mean, in tech terms, you're talking ancient history."

Our plates arrived. Her next question was what our roadmap was like.

This one was safe. I had read the brief; I knew, not all, but enough to answer. I gave her a brief ramble about business readiness, service adoption, government approval, et cetera, et cetera. In my head I was taking notes. Public distrust. A possible bias in our data, though I didn't believe it for a second, because if something like that existed the media would have picked up on it. I mentioned this.

"You are aware of the allegations of bribery?" said Amali De Saram.

"What allegations?"

"Several local papers have run stories about NumberCorp bribing political figures in Sri Lanka," she said. "You know, Pat, we wondered why most mainstream media aren't running these stories, but it turns out most of those sites have investors that seem connected to NumberCorp somehow. It's almost as if someone with very deep pockets bought off a lot of people."

"This sounds like a conspiracy theory," I said, slightly annoyed now.

"Does NumberCorp have anything to say about this conspiracy theory?" she asked sweetly.

"She's a conspiracy nut," I reported when I got back to the hotel. There was a three-way call between me, Wurth and Julius, who was keeping uncharacteristically silent.

"If she's accusing us of bribery and corruption, we can sue," said Wurth.

"Don't," said Julius. "I'll deal with it."

By breakfast the next day I had a message from Julius. A link: a news item barely three minutes old. *LOCAL JOURNALIST SUSPENDED FOR ETHICS BREACH, SUSPECTED NEWS FABRICATION.* In India, with its rising unemployment, losing your job meant you were screwed: there were a thousand others standing in every other line. Amali de Saram would never be able to afford silver again.

"Okay," said Wurth, looking like a distracted mess on video. "So I've been putting out feelers, and the bloody verdict is the same. You can't sneak up on them. While Aniston works, you have to try and get Homo Commonus Indianus on our side –"

"That's racist," remarked Parvati, the second-in-command.

Nobody cared. "The journalists knocked us back a few paces," said Wurth. "Let's try this again."

We tried.

India knew there was money to be made. They saw the future. We set up meetings and dinners and little soirees, slowly plying Aniston and Ibrahim into the upper circles, and pointed out the obvious: the Number worked. It was fast, it was accurate, and the sheer amount of stuff we could offer them now was mind-boggling. Did they want the best data on earth on spending habits? We had it. Did they want to separate the important from the not-so-important, so that they could have VIP queues and service delivered exactly to the people they wanted to get at? We could do that, too. Did they want to, say, try and simulate how one specific social class might react to something they put out? We had so much data we could do that blindfolded.

Yes, it sounds mundane, but this is what sells. A bank making billions will pay through the nose for even a 1% increase in efficiency.

Except they didn't. I'm sorry, Mr Udo. The bankers came with politicians, and the politicians came with journalists. Amali De Saram was a minor incident, one person against a company, but that one person had set off an avalanche of distrust. India was going through a powerful Open Government phase, and the more people leaned against us, the less the government wanted to do with us. I remember us going to see the Minister of Communications and Information Technology. She was a lean and lanky lady with a neurodrip perpetually hooked to her computer and sharp, barking voice.

"Yes?" she said the moment we stepped in. "Don't bother with introductions, I know who you are. What do you want?"

Aniston, spectacularly polite in front of a target, explained.

"Did you open a support ticket with the Ministry?"

We had. The request had been denied.

"There's your response."

Indians can be quite rude to people they don't have a use for.

Aniston tried again.

A screen opened behind the minister. On it played a YouTube video: a young man with a reddish beard and very smart clothes. I remembered this one. Vaguely. "If you wanna grow your Number, keep growing your social network reach," said the man enthusiastically. Add people. Meet them. Check in with them. Make sure you post stuff that they'll like and share. The more famous your friends are, the better you will be. Remember you have a life outside of your bank account: use that to your full advantage."

The video shrunk. Twelve others popped up. Advice. Optimization. Social SEO. Hacking the system. A restaurant being hated on because it turned away a reviewer for having a low Number. I groaned inwardly. I'd seen this one before.

"You have a life outside your bank account, use that to your advantage," mimicked the Minister. "Now I don't have a problem with social media networks, we have enough here. But speaking quite frankly I don't want anything that forces people to game their lives setting up shop here. You can pack your bags and keep this stuff in the Valley where it belongs.'

"Minister, we don't condone-" began Aniston.

Another video opened, skipped to one point: it was a pregnant woman – barely a girl, with dirty blond hair - ranting about how her bank refusing her a loan because she didn't have enough of a Number. "I don't use Anagram," she sobbed into the camera. "I have...I have like 30 friends on Facebook. They say that's not enough. Oh God, help me, I can't do this anymore."

"You don't condone what, Miss Chaudary? You don't condone banks using your software? You don't condone being the judge of whether or not some woman has a future or not?" the Minister said. "I see your company as nothing less than a governance risk. Not in India, Miss Chaudary, not on my watch."

"That woman would not have gotten a loan anyway," said Ibrahim. He generally kept silent on these exchanges. "She looks like a junkie. Definitely a teenage pregnancy. Any bank would have taken one look at her and refused anyway.

We're not changing humans, we're just making things more transparent."

The Minister gave him a look. "You may leave," she said.

Julius listened to our report. He did so in person. Then he started making calls. Within an hour, a helicopter showed up, and Julius got in. When the helicopter showed up again, he climbed out slowly, looking dog-tired.

"She won't be a problem anymore," he said. "Patrick?"

"Julius?"

"Bottom up, bottom up," he said. "Top down is hard here. Figure out how to get the public on our side."

"Yes, Julius," we said.

"Now I need to be in Cali. Aaron just gave me a brilliant idea. We're going to start scoring governments."

Aniston he ignored completely.

It shouldn't have affected me, but it did. I knew there were people who didn't like the Number, but in the same way that people hadn't liked Facebook or Tinder or Pokemon Go when they came out: you couldn't please everyone. Politicians - promises - jobs - all of this was new to me. This kind of thing never happens in the Valley.

I suppose I'd never really thought about the actual effect we had on people.

That night, I went to bed and thought about what happened over a glass of wine.

Well, a bottle. Bottle and a half, really.

Fuck Amali and her British accent. I called my father.

He answered. "Jesus. Are you drunk?"

"A little bit," I said.

"What's wrong?"

"Look up a Times video by a girl called Amali De Saram."

"Spell that?"

I did. There was silence for a while.

"Hmm," he said at last.

"We also kind of screwed over a minister today," I said, and explained about the Iron Lady.

"Hmm," he said again. "Do you see mobs on the street? Pitchforks? Torches?"

"Don't be ridiculous."

"Get out before it comes to that."

Silence. I could hear a sigh on the other end. "You know, if you ever get tired of making millions, drop by the house sometime."

"Thanks, dad," I said. "I'll keep that in mind."

By August, things in India were going south, and everyone knew it. It was bad enough that this was the first time we'd been beaten out of a country; it was worse that it had to be the biggest market outside China. As Europe picked up the Number, as it spread towards Latin America, as Japan put down the pitchfork and started adapting it, India refused to budge.

The blow came not just to NumberCorp, but also to those of us involved. Time after time I saw Aniston hang up on a call with Julius, looking utterly defeated. NumberCorp Credit India was bleeding red ink: a shell with a hundred eager-eyed Indians with nothing to do. None of the banks would do business with us.

In the US, we held a conference - the next Utopia Con. Functioning in tech positively demands that you host a conference every now and then - that's where you announce your plans, remind people that you're making them money, and lure in future clients. I took a long, hard look at India and shipped out my little team to California. They'd suffered valiantly, and deserved to have some success to their name. We opened up our entire campus, turned every dorm into a hotel; we filled the foyers and lined the sides of the wall with bizdev; we had an exhibit hangar where we demo'd the other stuff with the data. Could we, for example, predict how happy a person was? Or a nation? Could that be linked to crime rate? Well, we didn't have all the data, we'd say, and this was only a demo, but it turns out we sort of could...we usually did this for the engineers and businessmen the governments and the Valley crowd; the kind of people who built on top of our stuff.

We invited a great many journalists and data scientists and sociologists and futurists to spin vague dreams of the future. There would be celebrities to gawk at; anyone above a certain Number was invited. The parties, of course, were wild and would probably last well beyond the actual event. Utopia was, well, Utopian.

"One massive photo op, eh?" said Wurth enthusiastically. He had come down from Tokyo for the conference.

I, keeping a careful eye on my team, was relieved. The photo op mattered less than giving those kids a break. Every other major Valley company had gone after India and won big. Facebook, for instance; despite that early, violent rejection of its Internet.org package (which I think was over three decades ago), its user base had grown exponentially over the years - to the point where the Newsfeed had all but killed off

India's mainstream media and politicians took out Facebook ads instead of trying to bribe journalists. Uber and Uberclones owned transport. Amazon, FarmersMarket and Tindr held strong. The investors held us up to those standards.

The next day the headlines re-emerged: *NUMBERCORP CELEBRATES LOSS* and *UTOPIA: AN INSIDE LOOK AT THE FUTURE INDIA DOESN'T WANT*. It was salt in a wound that was already infected.

"Tata just threw in the towel," reported Aniston. She sounded utterly defeated.

"Just one more Indian company," Wurth said, dialing in.

"Tata," Julius said, more for the benefit of Wurth than anyone else, "is a trillion-dollar company that does everything from cars to satellites to nuclear energy. Half of Asia's data goes through cables that Tata owns. If they're on the other side, we're fucked."

We said nothing.

"Two hundred million dollars and this is what I get," Julius said. "Utter fucking incompetence. There's so much bad press some of it is even going viral in the UK. Whose idea was it to take India in the first place?"

Aniston said nothing.

"Who else have we lost?"

Aniston rattled off a string of companies. Julius let out a string of obscenities.

"Aaron Kotalawala will take over," he said when they were both done. "You're off India."

"Let me try again," she said. "We can fix-"

"You clearly can't fix shit," Julius said. "All that money, all those strings I pulled, and this is what you give me? Failure? I'm putting Aaron in charge."

Aniston's fists clenched.

"I've done everything you wanted me to," she said. Her voice shook a little. "Every country, every sale, from the beginning. You're all here because of what I've done for this company. You're letting this new guy just waltz in because we couldn't break a market? You're giving him the red carpet because you fucked around at uni together?"

Wurth and I looked away, embarrassed. We didn't want to see her like this.

Julius didn't flinch. "What's your Number, Aniston? Eight thousand? Ten thousand?"

"Nine," said Aniston.

"Aaron is at twelve," Julius said. "In India he hits thirteen thousand. He has more connections than you, he has more power than you. Our own system tells me who I should go for. Or did you forget what we're selling here?"

"It's one market."

"It's two billion people," said Julius. "It's one big fucking market. Get out of my office."

Aniston got up. For a second we both thought she was going to hit him.

"Whatever happened to loyalty?" she said. "Whatever happened to giving people a chance?"

"When did those become more important than winning?"

We sat in silence for a while after she was gone. The only sound was Julius's fingers drumming on the table-top.

"I'm told that certain individuals from the Indian government have been to China," said a voice from the wallscreen. I hadn't realized someone else was connecting in. It was a harsh drone. Anonymized. Fake.

"Is China selling?"

"I'm afraid I can't say," said the voice.

"Who is that?" asked Wurth.

"People are starting to see the endgame," said Julius, ignoring us.

"The vision, as I have told you many times, must be delivered in full now, not piecemeal," said the voice.

"It's not ready yet," said Julius.

"Then wait,' said the voice. "All things come to those who wait."

Julius said nothing. His fingers tapped relentlessly on the tabletop, beating out an ominous monotone, like a war drum marking time.

There's an old saying that defeat isn't bitter if you don't swallow it. Whoever said it must have lived in simpler times, when people forgot your humiliation - when people could forget. In our age, in the age of the Internet, you don't have a choice.

In September, 2040, I called it quits. After three years we had a hundred million users - the hundred million Indians who used foreign banks - and the effort had taken the life out of me. Out of all of us, actually. I was pretty sure my reputation as a rockstar marketer was shot. The book deal dropped. I was bone-tired, and I wanted nothing more than to escape for a while; escape the Number, escape the hubris, the way people looked, smelled, talked. I wanted to be a stranger again.

I called Julius, gave him an hour-long explanation, and asked for six months off from the job. I'll be honest: when I made that call, I was thinking of quitting outright, not just taking a break. India was stressful. And I had enough in the bank to retire to the kind of middle-class comfort that my parents had slaved for throughout their lives.

But I didn't. I don't know. I had been NumberCorp's man, through and through; I barely had an identity outside it. As long as I was Patrick Udo, Director of Communications, NumberCorp, I was someone. As just Patrick Udo? Almost nothing. So I asked Julius for leave, nothing more.

"Alright, everyone," I told my team. They looked as exhausted as I felt. "Take three days off. You'll each be staying in a house down there in a different neighborhood. Walk around, live the life, try to forget this for a while. When you get back, we'll be in business. Okay?"

"Got it," they chorused, and packed themselves off with zombie-like jerkiness. I didn't blame them.

"We're up shit creek," Wurth said when they were gone. He was taking over for me for a while.

"Well, yeah," I said. He looked exhausted. I poured him a whiskey. "So how's Japan?"

He made a face as he drank. "Let's just say the India clusterfuck's cut down my ad budgets. We're reviewing everything - I've cut down six major deals, people aren't too happy. They're quitting."

He looked at me, his eyes drawn, his face sallow. "We need to sell this goddamn thing in India, man. Without the government's plus one, we're just a fancy number on a fucking phone screen.'

"Did Julius say anything? Any way we might work it out?"

"Jules? No," he said darkly. "Julius likes to keep things to himself." Something struck him. "You ever wonder if you made a mistake? Joining this clusterfuck, I mean?"

I thought about it. "No," I said. "I'm tired, I'm getting out for a while, but I've still - you know." I waved a hand at the room we were in. "I wouldn't be here."

He gave me an odd look. "Must be nice to be you. Shikata ga nai, huh?"

"What's that mean?"

"Nothing," He gulped down the last of his whiskey. "I'm going to head back, then. Thanks for the drink."

"I'll see you in like six months, then."

"See you, Udo," he said, floating away.

And so the next day, I found myself in a penthouse overlooking the teeming city of Bombay. From this height, it looked like a wave of people ebbing in and out of the buildings, poetry in motion. Beautiful place. Except we'd been so tired and rushed none of us had actually even paused to take it in. I put Deja and Dmitry (our bots for India) on autopilot, packed my bag and booked my flight.

I came home, tiptoeing in like a thief. My father was in his study, writing - the old fashioned way, with paper and a glass of whiskey. He gave a shout of joy and held me close before complaining that my shirts should fit me better.

I recounted my adventures, just as I recount them to you now. I told him about Bombay, which glowed in the night like a lamp. I told him about Bangalore, about the beaches of Goa, of Pune, where elaborate retirement homes and ashrams ringed India's ferociously competitive colleges, and liberals went to experience transcendence without getting their feet dirty. I told him of places you could expand your mind and still be within walking distance of the nearest McDonalds.

My father shook his head. "You shoulda been writing travel," he said.

Ah, yes, but it was thanks to NumberCorp that I got around,

dad.

So much for the big plan.

And then something magical happened. I got on a bus. I had taken to riding them around the city, switching whenever I felt like it; there's a lot you can see and understand from a window seat.

There was a young woman in the bus. She was seated. Navy blue hoodie and white Youtube headphones.

I remember thinking what a good photo she would make - white headphones on dark skin, crisp blue over black hair. I remember I was watching Survivor: Chernobyl on my phone.

The bus stopped.

An old woman got on. She was bent over; hands trembling. Immediately the woman in the blue hoodie jumped up and helped her to her seat. The old woman pulled out a phone with arthritic hands and tapped twice. Maybe it was unintentional that the phone was pointed at the young woman.

+100 Number, I thought.

That was it. I had it. I don't know how the hell I had it, but suddenly I had this idea, this germ, so fragile that it felt like if I didn't write it down now, it would be lost. I shot out of that bus like a missile. On the way I saw a billboard. Survivor: Chernobyl blinked on it.

I whooped in triumph and called Russell.

"Remember that blogpost of yours? Usher in the Real?"

"Yes?"

"There was a photo in there. One of mine. You took it and put numbers above everyone's head. Remember?"

"Yes?"In my mind, numbers blinked on top of people's heads, shifting, changing. "What would Jules say," I asked, "If we said we'll make a webseries about the Number?"

"A webseries?"

"If we can create a show that shows people how the Number works," I said. "If it's a show with a a good storyline, if it can showcase what we can do, in their daily lives, and still keep them hooked? Go public marketing instead of just talking to the banks?"

"Interesting," said Julius, when I sent him my sketches a few weeks later. "For India? But have you figured out what kinds of scenarios you're going to show them? Do you know to market this thing?"

"Let's do some research," I said. "Let me go on the road. Minimal staff. Let's do some principal photography and figure out what kind of scenarios we can build. We can launch this right with the Inequality Update. It'll change the game."

"How much money do you need?"

I quoted what I thought was a reasonable sum.

Julius thought about it. "Take Amarasinghe," he said at last. "Russell, you keep running Comms as is. No disruptions. Work with Aaron and find someone to take on the repetitive stuff from India. I assume you're going to take that leave later?"

Ten

Thus began a new chapter in my life.

For the first time, in a long time, I ditched the titles, locked up my Valley-style apartments, and, with the help of my father, packed a very capable bag. I wrote an email to all my staff. I was going on the road, I said. I was going to take one last shot at marketing India to the masses, and if I failed, I wouldn't come back. I was cutting myself off from the rest of NumberCorp.

It was the fabled Grand Escape, the hiatus, the pilgrimage; it was also the biggest marketing stunt I've ever pulled.

Aniston probably hated me for that move, and even Wurth was unimpressed. I can understand that; it looked like I was abandoning both of them, gallivanting around the country while they tried to hold things together. I tell myself that all I wanted to do was to tell a story.

In the next few months, I sketched out more rough drafts. Ideas.

I had pitched a webseries to Julius, a standard 10-episode-per-season format. I knew we could easily get any of the major channels to distribute it - Netflix would jump, and if they didn't, others would. The problem was that I needed a story, and to write a story for India I needed to know more about the place itself. I wanted to go north, to Rajasthan and

Uttar Pradesh and Odisha. Parvati and Amarasinghe argued. That was the warzone, they said. That was precisely my point. There was an interesting story there. Pakistan was backed (at least on paper) by China and the Saud, and the Hindustan Front was getting their best arms from Russia now. That, I felt, had a narrative that could capture not just India, but the imaginations of the world.

Fortunately, sense prevailed: we decided to go south instead. The south was where peace and the cities were.

So here was I, Parvati and the ever-serviceable Amarasinghe, speeding away from Bombay, leaving behind the skyscrapers and artificial land of India's west coast. I remember looking back at it fondly. Call it what you will, but Bombay, like London or New York, was one of the last true human cities of the world. Everything else is owned by the corporates.

If this failed, I had promised myself and everyone else, I would quit.

"Beautiful, isn't it?" said Parvati, the lights of the city gleaming in her eyes. She had been born and raised in those skyscraper complexes.

"Beautiful," I echoed, more caught up in my own thoughts than anything else.

For the next six months, I went back to the old me: I moved, I framed, I shot.

I shot the GlaxoSmithKline village. GSK is one of the biggest pharmaceutical companies in the world, and GSK India was a city-state on its own. Politically, it was more or less a separate state, anyway: so much money flowed in and out that the only restriction placed on the company was to employ humans instead of robots. Five hundred thousand people lived in an intricate and almost completely sterile city that shot up like a white fortress surrounded by a sick, sprawling slum. They had never heard of NumberCorp.

"Don't go there," said our guide, when I asked about the slum. She took us to the wall. Outside was a moat that went on for miles, an artificial river in which flowed an ugly yellow-black ooze. As we watched, the darkness on the other side extended arms, and legs, and suddenly there were gangs of feral children filling buckets from the ooze. I sent out my drones and they stopped me. The guide said something to Parvati in Hindi. I heard the word parangi several times.

"She says you don't have their permission," she translated.

"We spoke to GSK before we came here."

"Not GSK," said Parvati. "Them."

I understood. And I packed my drones. India was a strange place. They would let people starve, but still respect their rights.

I moved, I shot, I sent photos to Julius and Wurth. I knew they had sociologists and activists and coffee-shop liberals and every other type of person already telling them what these places were like, but it didn't matter. This was my work. Somewhere on the road I began to edit these photos, trying to do a before Number, after Number thing, trying to get a feel for the kind of story we could do. We had brainstorm sessions every Wednesday with Wurth, where I'd share a few videos I'd shot and everyone would pitch in on how that picture would change post-Number.

And for the first time in my life I saw a different world. I had had a long run behind Silicon Valley walls. My world was more or less NumberCorp and the Valley; my friends were from

NumberCorp and the Valley; everything I did, responded to, was as a Valley person.

It changes you. The world becomes a revolving door of offices, company housing, hotels, events. People talk about the next big thing, about disruption, about the bleeding edge, about product-and-market fits. I traded that in for the road, for the hot sun, for a world where people spoke my language, but not the language I'd been speaking for the past ten years or so. And while I explored this world, like a strange alien from Utopia-land, the wheels turned and the world of tech went on.

Perhaps it was August: one fine August in the Valley, which meant everything was doing so well. The banks were paying us pots of money to use NumberCorp APIs, crunching through millions and millions of people with our math. Employment agencies got in on the action; so did practically every single marketing firm that knew what it was doing. Did you want to know who in Washington had a Number of over 12,000, and thus could (and wanted) that next-generation Rolex? Sure. No problem: we could give you people, Numbers, their demographics, where they ate, where they hung out, where they banked.

I remember waking up at 3 o'clock one morning, restless, and reading the messages to the NumberCorp @battleplans channel:

@JULIUS: *Think possibilities*

@JULIUS*: Ffs people*

@JULIUS: *Imagine what we could do with this*

@JULIUS*: Build an app that not just tells people what their Number is*

@JULIUS: *Shows them where to go to get laid / make friends*

@JULIUS: *Where the people in their circles / other circles hang out*

@JULIUS: *Imagine if your phone could show you where you needed to be next*

It was part of a much larger message thread. Interesting, I thought, and went back to sleep. When I woke up, it was almost noon, and there were over seven hundred unread messages on @battleplans.

@SINNATHAMBY: *not limit to relationships? Wb career progress?*

@SINNATHAMBY: *Anything up your Number and get ++ fame*

@KURTZMANN: *if we can map all events, people that potentially*

@KURTZMANN: *increase a user's Number*

@KURTZMANN: *and present it to them*

@BONIKER: *Holy shit, +1*

@MONARD: *Wait, back it up, this is violation of privacy with a capital P.*

@WURTH: @JULIUS @BENNET @KOH @BABYLON @MONARD

@WURTH: *Can we meet offline?*

@MONARD: *Suggest we meet on this and take discussions further*

If there is word for that strange, sinking feeling that you get, that feeling of butterflies in your stomach mixed with dread, I felt it that day. I scrolled down and down and down. From the looks of it, several people had just threatened to quit.

I called Wurth. No response. I called Ibrahim. Again, the same. I called Alicia Random, who was still grinding her way up in Algorithm and was equally thunderstruck. Over the next two hours we stayed on line, reading out the replies to each other. The seven hundred messages became a thousand. Then two thousand.

"Holy shit," I remember saying to Random. Julius had waded back into the discussion. "This is actually happening."

Two weeks later, we were called to a meeting.

"We can't do something like this without thinking about it," said Ibrahim.

"I have thought about it," said Julius.

"It's not ethical, Jules."

"It's not ethical?" repeated Julius. "It's not ethical to give people information on stuff that might improve their lives? You want to go repeat that to every advertising company out there, even Google, tell them it's not ethical?"

"The point is that we'll be taking over people's lives," said Ibrahim. "I mean, leave aside the tech problems. Imagine we do make this work and there's a glitch. Imagine some ... algorithm on your phone telling you to do something completely crazy because it'll raise your Number a hundred points. You saw what happened with those students in London -"

"I'm not saying we go around telling people what to do," said Julius, putting up his hands for silence. "I'm saying we make the information available if they want it. Have you seen what everyone else is doing?"

He tapped. A screen opened behind him. On it played a very familiar YouTube video: a young man with a reddish beard and very smart clothes explaining how to game the Number. "Remember," advised the man enthusiastically. "If you wanna grow your Number, keep growing your social network reach. Add people. Meet them. Check in with them. Make sure you post stuff that they'll like and share. The more famous your friends are, the better you will be. Remember you have a life outside of your bank account: use that to your full advantage."

The video shrank. Others popped up.

"Do you really want to trust our product, our users, to kooks like this?" said Julius.

No, we did not. That was unanimous.

"Better us than them," said Julius into the silence. "If we're judging them, which we are, I'm saying it's damned unfair that we're also not teaching them to be better."

"Do we have the right to teach anyone to be better?" Ibrahim asked.

"Don't we?" said Julius. "Don't we have the data? Ezra? Do we not know what people get sent to jail for? Or what they should do to basically get ahead?"

"We do, Jules," said the disembodied voice that was Ezra. She never moved out of Orthanc.

"Well, then," Julius said. "People - we're not doing this because of skin color or religion or money or that bullshit. This isn't faith. We're doing this because we, absolutely, know. It's our duty."

I, outside the system and yet inside, squashed the hint of wrongness that I felt and scribbled this down as something we could add to the story. It seemed so logical, so natural. Of course we knew better. Of course it was our duty.

"You wouldn't need any of that stuff," said Wurth, looking at a clip where someone signed a contract to lease a vehicle. "Contracts, no."

"Why not?"

"Finance Update, remember. If that guy doesn't pay on time,

his Number's going to drop. Pretty soon he won't be able to park that car without being pulled over."

"We have that functionality?'

"Yeah, Contracts is coming out in the next update. Every single financial service provider will be able to enforce digital punishment if people don't cough up.'

I noted that down.

Wurth flicked to another. This one showed two shabbily-dressed men bargaining with a bouncer with metal arms. "They definitely wouldn't be let into this club," he said.

Those two shabby men ran a startup called MoneyWiser. Personal finance stuff: very effective: they made a couple of millionaires a year and made a huge fuss about it. The two had a lot of goodwill and clout. "I think the takeaway here is that if that bouncer was checking their Numbers, he'd have realized how important they were," I said.

"Done," said Wurth.

I moved to Hyderabad, once called the City of Pearls. This was before the Boston Mechanical Riots: most of India's automated systems were run by a distributed intelligence that they called RAMA. Hyderabad was where RAMA was built.

I was never a lawyer, but I knew enough from hanging around with Pepperwater that RAMA was a controversial project in Ai circles: half the world was convinced it was a true Ai and ought to be banned under Turing Law; the other half believed India when it said that all of those...really interesting decisions the system took were the result of emergent behavior. Yes, the system effectively governed most of the country. Yes, it seemed to predict and react to economic threats. No, the U.N.

could not order it dismantled.

Either way, it was a big thing in Hyderabad. Data scientists and analysts patrolled the streets and cafés of the city with metal prayer beads around their modern suits: students from the hundreds of universities that had relocated there pored over India's datastream with lesser systems at their command; a literal army of technicians rose to keep these systems in repair, much like in the days of old IBM. Acolytes of RAMA. Old gods reincarnated in the new flesh of technology. India had achieved what the West only dreamed of.

Julius was fascinated. "There's a hierarchy in a microcosm here," he said, poring over my videos. "Looks like technicians, then academics and the data scientists, then software engineers."

"Notice how they don't wear mech parts at all? Is there stigma associated with having a metal arm?"

"Won't we need to adapt the system for all of these communities?" said Wurth. "Different algorithms based on where we are in the country?"

Julius grinned. "Exactly," he said. "Patrick, keep documenting. This is going to be so much fun."

Usually, a webseries starts with one episode – one pilot being funded upfront and pushed by a studio. I sat down and hammered out a story document; a detailed outline of what the show would be and what it would touch on. This took three months and many, many discussions with Wurth and Ibrahim. Aniston, weighing in from afar, gave me one last contact, one last piece of advice: Arundhati Khatri.

Khatri was arguably the second-best screenwriter in the

world at the time - and the only reason she wasn't the best was because she was as reportedly as stubborn as donkey and routinely refused even the slightest changes from networks. She ran her own studio with her partner, Nassim Khalil, headquartered out of Bangalore. Our agreement was simple: I'd set the theme for each show, sketch the outline of the plot, and she'd fill it in; I'd then take that script and direct it.

I didn't like her at the start, to be honest: too brash, overwhelmingly critical. But that exterior, as it turned out, hid one of the most talented and empathetic writers I've ever worked with. And Khalil, the only editor Khatri would ever accept, was as gentle and organized as she was brusque and chaotic, and kept the rougher edges of the diamond out of sight. It was she who had the brilliant idea of having a cameo of Julius in every episode – everyone else thought it was a waste of Julius's time, but in reality, it cemented him to the Number like never before. Within a month we had a whole bunch of test scripts: before and after NumberCorp.

That was a good time for me. Six months on the road does wonders for your soul; it also did wonders for my relationship with Julius. He began to rely on me not just as a marketer, but more as a friend, and even more as his eyes. Soon I had the ideas out, typed, awaiting review. In my head I saw police officers and soldiers and firemen being rewarded for doing their jobs. I pictured charity workers being rewarded for being decent human beings. I sketched ideas for politicians being socially punished for playing the fool. I imagined entrepreneurs, lawyers, engineers, statesmen, artists and philosophers getting the respect they deserve, not just in vague soon-to-be-forgotten newspaper articles, but in cold, hard Numbers that would stay with you forever. Everything adjusted by state, a fluid system that took into account all the differences of India and all the vast communities that made it utterly unlike any other country. And they all came true, in one way or the other, which is why my little webseries went down in history as being prophetic.

The problem was those scenarios were all good. They improved lives. Throw contracts away, we said. You don't have to dress up for people to know who and what you are, we said. I painted a mental picture of modern Renaissance, a new chapter in history that truly brought out the best in us, in humanity. Even Julius fell in love with it.

He dropped by once, I think, in those years: perhaps to check if I really was making progress, or perhaps to talk. I'm not quite sure.

"Shit," I mumbled when I saw him at the airport restaurant. I couldn't help it. Julius's eyes were bloodshot. His hair was longer and framed his face in darkness. It was a menacing, almost sinister look.

"You've gotten fatter, Mister Udo," he said, mimicking Amarasinghe's rolling Sinhala dialect.

"You shouldn't pay me so much," I retorted, pouring myself a glass of water and waving the waiter away. "Anyway, you look like hell yourself."

"You know how it's been," he said. "Smoke?"

I took it. We lit up.

"How're things?"

The news was short. Aaron Kotalawala was officially replacing Aniston at NumberCorp India, he said. Aniston would henceforth be involved in an 'advisory role'. I had no illusions as to what that meant.

"There's a few rumblings going on at the UN," he said.

"People have accused us of bribing government officials before. I've been accused of buying the President of Sri Lanka at his dinner table. I'm just going to say this: if we have to walk that path to make this work, we will. We'll buy all the Parliaments in the world if we have to. Whatever it takes to get those users. The next generation of the Number gets nothing less than our full commitment."

"Did you hide the bodies?" I joked.

"Very deep," said Julius. He looked down at his plate. "Twelve years, six billion dollars spent, not a single cent of profit, and two of the world's largest nations don't want what I'm selling.'

I didn't know what to say, but I tried. 'We'll get through."

"Drop the consolation crap. I'm not going to cut your pay check because you failed to butter up the CEO. Kudos for trying, though. Hey, waiter? Wine."

We ate in silence. The wine was dry, sharp. It mellowed us both a little bit.

"By the way, did you check your messages?"

I thumbed out my phone.

"There was a time when you'd have stayed awake for days for a message from me," he said. "Those days are gone, eh?"

"I've kept myself on cutoff," I said. "Too many distractions. Ended up missing it back in Cali. We have work here."

Julius nodded, picked up his tab and began typing. A photo popped up: it showed Wurth, wunderkind, shaking hands and gesturing wildly with a glass of champagne and a wonderful, almost electric grin on his face. Behind him, in the shadows, loomed the face of Aniston Chaudary. It held no emotion whatsoever.

I recognized it. It was one that I had taken and never

published.

"Russell's a good guy," Julius said thoughtfully. He handed the tab to me. "Publish this," he said. "Russell is now the face of NumberCorp."

I nodded and asked the question that had been on everyone's lips before the alcohol hit. 'Aniston?'

"She failed," Julius said.

"I don't think it was her fault."

"She failed," Julius repeated. "Now, how about you show me the place? I want to see what you've been up to."

By January, we were casting. Both Arundati Khatri and I wanted talent that nobody else had seen before. Fortunately – and this is the great thing about India – talent was never in short supply. We wrote and wrote; and when she stepped in to polish the lines, I would step back and send everything we had to Julius, to Ezra, to Wurth and Monard. They would ping back, sometimes asking for clarification, sometimes pointing out that such-and-such a feature was patently impossible. Someone from Algorithm would get on a call with us, and we'd hastily rewrite. Sometimes this happened just hours before shooting.

At this stage, if this was a network show, I'd still have been jumping over hoops. But this was NumberCorp, and by February, Wurth had spun off Number Imaging as an entirely separate sub-division, with me as the COO and Julius as the CEO; and I was rolling out the cameras, making the actors rehearse their lines, my eyes split among feeds from six DeepRed drones with every single ounce of visual finesse I could muster, half-stoned on the Nootonium and Lucile mix all the image people use when controlling cameras for extended periods. Ibrahim pitched in as the producer: he knew how to make people keep their deadlines.

"Bloody hell," I remember Wurth saying once. "How many people do you have working for you?"

I waved a hand distractedly. "Fifty maybe, if you count the actors."

In truth, that was a small number: we had the advantage of tech on our side. We shot an entire season's worth in the British style with those fifty people: six hour-long episodes, with a dozen smaller, 20-minute shorts around them, filling in pieces of the background. We edited for days on end; Ibrahim and a team retrained a cheaper version of Minerva to do the first-pass editing; it would pick up the choicest cuts, and then I would carefully tease them together. I researched. I read. I called people. Parvati and the Nootonium injections kept me sane; I worked more, and harder than I ever had in my life. And as things inside NumberCorp got more and more frantic, I had the luxury of settling down on this one project. It would consume the next couple of years of my life, but it was my break: my magnum opus: my one big thing. Everyone has to have one.

Julius came to see me again on set, this time with a strange man in tow. I gestured for one of my assistants to see to them. We were wrapping up some replacement scenes and it was about twenty minutes before I could unplug myself and go see them.

"This is Heng," he said.

"Liu Heng," the man said, shaking my hand.

Heng was Chinese. The first thing that struck me was the similarity between the two men. Heng was tall, taller than all of us, but he had his hair cropped short, like Julius, and I almost thought he was Julius's Chinese twin. But the impression vanished the moment it formed. Julius wore his size like a shark, powerful and sharp. Heng stooped, bent slightly at the elbows. There was a strange light in his gaze, as if he was constantly looking at a piece of art, excited and respectful at the same time. He wore mostly white.

"Heng will probably be joining us soon," said Julius. "We were in college together, and we worked on the identity tech that the Number is built on. You could say he's the unofficial co-founder of NumberCorp."

"I did little," Heng said. His English was good, slightly British. "It was simply one small part of the system."

"You live in California?"

"Heng can't come into the US yet," Julius said. "It's a visa issue, something I'm working on. In the meantime, I'm showing them our operation. Pat, can you take them around, show them what you're working on?"

Them? Ah.

"I am ... an androgyne? In your terms," Heng said. "If it confuses you, you may use whatever pronoun is most convenient. I don't particularly care. A lot of people find it convenient to get this out of the way early."

I did so, confused and slightly irritated at being turned into a tour guide. Heng turned out to be hugely interested; the moment I started explaining the plots, it was as if a light snapped on inside, and the gently awed gaze became a focused laser. They picked through my drafts and diagrams and scripts.

"Interesting," they said, over and over again. "And when do you say this will be out?"

"Quarter one, next year?"

"I will be sure to watch it," they said solemnly.

I passed them on to Parvati for a tour of the set, and went back to Julius, who was watching us with a curious gaze.

"What do you think?"

"Unofficial co-founder of NumberCorp?" I said.

"Heng's actually done a whole lot more than he says," said Julius. We began walking in a general non-direction, around the set. "I think we're scaling to the point where I need more support on my level, on the architecture itself. Heng's one of the best in the world. I've been hunting them for a while, it's just this fucking Cold War situation we have going on. I can't bring him anywhere near the Valley. "

"Is he coming as CTO?"

Julius grimaced. "No, that'll eventually be Ibrahim's," he said. "We'll have to think of something official but out of the way . . . "

We watched the white-clad, monkish figure examining the big RED cameras with the curiosity of a little child.

"Heng's one of the smartest people I know," Julius said, as much to himself as to me. "We'll make this work."

When they were gone, and so much dust on the horizon, I turned back to my cameras and went back to shooting.

Success is a strange thing. It involves years of bending yourself to one single task, even at the expense of all others. Hobbies. Relationships. Side jobs. Friends. Most people just give up halfway. Those of us who do make it through to the end, by grit or by simple bull-headed stupidity, do it by losing ourselves in that tunnel, by wrapping our lives around a few things that really, really matter. And then, one day, you stand up to all the awards and the accolades and realize it was all worth it.

The days blurred together.

And then, one day, it was done. It was 2043. I remember signing the final copy, bringing it in myself to the studio - I refused to let anyone else touch it, and they let me, because they must have thought me crazy. I had a long beard wrapped in leather bands and a skullcut. My eyes, once brown, were now pale. shot through with spikes of black. Imager's eyes. Nootonium eyes. People moved away if I looked at them for too long.

I walked in the studio. Wurth, Julius, Ibrahim, a sea of others - I put the drive down, very carefully, and went and sat outside for the next two hours.

"Bloody hell, it's brilliant."

That was Wurth.

"You have a gift."

That was Ibrahim.

Others passed, murmuring words to my silence. And then the one I waited most for.

"It's perfect," said Julius. "It's everything I've ever dreamed about."

Eleven

The only memories I truly have of the next couple of months are snapshots of great clarity, like still frames stuck in a video. I remember Wurth shaking my hand: I remember the wine flowing, pale gold into glasses, and from glasses into us. I remember Parvati locked in someone else's embrace; I remember my name out there, on screens, on billboards, on the awards:

NUMBERCASTE
created by Patrick Udo.

I remember my team, splayed out in front of wallscreens on launch day, reading out the reviews as they came in, cheering with each one.

I remember my father calling, telling me he'd seen my name on a sign near the old apartment. Could I come talk to him? He coughed a little. Stage Four cancer, he said. Turns out there was no Stage Five.

I remember the world shifting and Julius putting his arms around me.

"I'm going to take that leave now," I told him.

I went home. Or rather, I tried.

Watching a parent die is a terrible task. My father, faced with something he could not talk down or browbeat into submission, spent his days with the bottle, as if he determined to drink himself to death, as if his alcohol could hold back the disease that swept through his brain.

In may ways, it was a strange world I came out to: after so long in the Valley, after so long in India, Chicago felt alien, like a rejected set from Blade Runner. There was the Gold Coast and Old Town with their glittering apartments and privatized schools; and the South Side threw at me its school dropouts playing basketball and selling drugs on the street corners; a fine line ran between the two, an unmarked yet very real divisor broken in places by subway and Airmail lines. Up North the police wore cloth uniforms and said sir! and ma'am. Five blocks south of our apartment they patrolled in units of three in riot exoskeletons and armor. The ATMs and card machines are down, they told me; the ones that work belonged to the hackers. I had Ecoin, but nobody wanted to buy. Hard cash or nothing.

I shut myself up in my room and read the news. Iran, Israel and Russia were duking it out in an unholy threesome of cybercrime. Some Nobel-prize winning economist wanted to resurrect the stock market. As if we hadn't had enough of Ai gaming the market. That was what had led to the market collapse in the first place, and with it the Depression we lived through. I scanned the rest of her thought-piece. Sure enough, she proposed limits on the number of traders and arming each trader with a certified Ai trading partner, bound by parameters. It would create a vehicle for funds, she said, and slow down the drain on the economy. I laughed. For an economist, she sure was stupid. Everyone was stupid back in those days. It was a terrible world.

I remember getting tired of the news one day and going to one of those North Side restaurants, watching them turn away people, one after the other, and I remember thinking this was not what Julius would have wanted.

I remember watching my father die, and I remember being tired, and at the end, I wanted him to go.

And meanwhile, my feed buzzed with NumberCorp this, NumberCorp that. Julius Common. Patrick Udo. Julius Patrick. Udo.

I was proud of myself. The series was snowballing beyond my wildest dreams – people talked about it; people wrote about it; and every one of those thousand faceless engineers who worked in that same building talked about it. Not only had I sold NumberCorp; I had also, completely by accident, given every employee of NumberCorp a reason to be proud of what they did.

When I was little, my mother, who believed in these things, used to tell me that I was born under a strange star; that I would be surrounded by change all my life, whether it came from me or from others. I used to believe it. In London, in Bombay, while watching all those thousands of people go about their lives, there came a point where I understood that she was wrong. We all are born under this star, one way or the other: all our lives are only chronicles of change.

When I joined, we had two hundred million users – a first generation that only adopted the NumberCorp because they had to. Now we had a billion second generation users: a teeming horde that knew how the Number worked and started changing how they behaved in order to game the Number. And the Number had changed, too: now it understood culture; now it understood careers and how they affected how people saw you.

The thing about being a successful tech company is that it's not enough to hit one out of the park. You have to hit and keep hitting; to keep pushing forward; to build on that tiny advantage and to sing your own praises until everyone else sings them for you. If you doubt my words, look at the empires of Facebook, of Amazon, of Apple, of Microsoft and of Alphabet. After a while you get to a point where you keep disrupting yourself, shedding fat without having a competitor cut it off you. Great companies are not built on one success. They're built on an entire pyramid of successes.

I read through the old pieces, one by one. NumberCorp was textbook. The ripple effects were everywhere. A thousand articles telling me how every upmarket bar, club and tourist destination had experienced an explosion of check-ins and geotags ever since the Number went online. Major newspapers displaying Numbers underneath their writers' bylines. Police departments firing low-Number officers and hiring community leaders with high Numbers instead. Julius's grand tour of support, assuring the public that the Number was infallible, pointing that it was leading the government to hire only the most respected; maybe it was the truth in his words, or the way he said them, but they believed him.

"NumberCorp commits to changing our Police," said headlines new and old, and the Guardian webcast spoke of how NumberCorp was, perhaps, the public's last true hope of technology keeping corrupt institutions in check. We had long since gone from hiding in the background: now we were holding democracy accountable, said Julius Common.

We were the good guys.

We were the future.

And, as India came online, those numbers tipped. One billion – one point five billion –

The numbers didn't even make sense anymore. I've heard it said that the first casualty of success is your perspective. To me a million people was an inconceivable horde: a billion was just digits on a screen; it seemed unthinkable that I had played any part in all this.

I sat by my father's bedside and watched the numbers pile up, reminiscing.

"What're you writing?" he would ask when he woke up, which wasn't all that often. I would show him, tell him the same words each time, and he would smile, proud of me even as his life drained away, and when he woke, he would ask the same question, again and again, his memory shredded by the disease that crawled through his brain. And my heart felt like it had burst and left behind only a shell of itself, like a star gone nova.

Wurth came to see me. So did the old Elkhead gang – Ibrahim, Aniston, a dozen others. Parvati did one better: she moved to an apartment close by. We looked at each other and knew there was some kind of reckoning coming, but for now it was easier to stow it at the back of my mind, to accept her hand on my shoulder.

One day there was a gentle ping on the door, and I opened it to find the man himself standing outside my little apartment.

"May I come in?" said Julius Common. He was alone.

I welcomed him in.

"How is he?"

"Doctors say another week."

"There's a company out in Black Rock," he said. "It does WBE – whole brain emulation," he added, seeing my look. "The scanning is still theoretical, but it's worked on animals, there's promise, there's a good to fair chance that –"

"We can't afford it, Jules."

"I own the company," he said. "Money is not a problem."

"No uploading," said my dad.

We turned to him. His eyes were bright, his face shriveled, but alert. "I don't want to be brought back," he said. "Not this way. Your offer's a few years too late, son."

Julius stood there with his head bowed.

"Thank you for coming," I said. It seemed oddly formal, but it also seemed like the release he needed. He nodded, clapped a hand on my shoulder, and left.

On the 1st of May, 2044, my father was pronounced officially dead. They took the life support away.

"What're you going to do?" Parvati asked of me a few days earlier. "Going back to work?"

I thought about it. My family, for all purposes, was gone. To say my career was thriving was an understatement; I was a microcelebrity online. LinkedIn showed me sixty jobs I could apply to and get; Facebook, Google, Anagram - even the Circle was hiring.

"Aha! The prodigal son returns!" Wurth exclaimed when he saw me walking into office the next day.

"I'm technically still on leave," I said. He must have seen the way I looked about, though, like a junkie looking for a fix.

"Drink?" he asked. I nodded, and we both drove out to Elkhead.

The bar had changed. While our 6th floor bar was still very much in place, the first few levels had lost their electropop and dance floors: now it was a library. Real paper, exorbitant fees, the kind of place only real bibliophiles went to.

All things change, even bars.

We were joined by a couple of others even before the seal on the vodka was broken. There was Ibrahim, the old dog; Alicia Random, who now was fairly high up in Algorithm; a few members of the production and promotion crew. The first few drinks were celebration. I knew my little webseries had worked, I just didn't realize how much until Wurth started putting the numbers down. 15 million unique views in the first month. 200 million the next. Close to 500 million before the quarter end – and still climbing. It was the most viral thing we had ever done.

They told me that Algorithm pored over each of those episodes to see how those new features could be built into NumberCorp itself. They told me bizdev was ringing up major businesses based purely on a few ideas I had penned down and fleshed out. And that explained the messages that I refused to check: the ones from awards committees, film academies, ad agencies, directors I'd never even heard of before.

"Not just India!" Alicia said. "You know the best part? I don't have to explain what I do for a living any more! I just say NumberCorp and everyone goes whoa."

"Perfect 5/7," Ibrahim said.

We laughed and drank to my health.

"How was Japan?" I asked.

"Don't get me started," Wurth said. "There isn't enough alcohol in this joint to talk about Japan."

There was a knock on the door and someone opened it to see

a giant of a man standing outside. He was tall and bald and looked a little lost. He scanned us up and down as if we were furniture.

"In here, Heng," said someone from the back.

"Oh," said Heng softly, and squeezed his bulk into the room. I noticed a few NumberCorp engineers stood up respectfully as he shuffled past.

"Remember the Chinese guy Jules was looking for a while back?" whispered Wurth. We turned to watch him. "That's Heng. Apparently he was uni with Julius."

"I met Heng," I said. "Julius brought him on the set while we were shooting." In the times to come I would get to know Heng better, of course, but for now I just stared at the large, dome-like head, the lost-looking eyes, and turned back to my drink. "By the way, anyone seen Jules recently?"

"Nah, he's too busy, man. Saw him with that Kissling woman recently, whatsherface, the famous one –"

"What, Anita Kissling? Doctor Kissling? Kissling Labs?"

"Yeah, yeah, I think we're building some kind of hardware . . ."

It felt good. And yet something had changed. Wurth was quieter, I think, and Ibrahim looked older than I'd ever seen him: they both looked like they were under a great deal of strain. Perhaps the others didn't notice, but I did.

"So ...what's next?" Wurth asked quietly as I knocked back my last drink and got up to leave. Buried in the question was another, unasked: when are you coming back?

"I don't know," I said.

And that was an honest answer.

"Staying nearby?"

"I've got a room at the Maverick," I said.

Wurth hesitated. "When you wake up tomorrow," he said. "Come see me at office? I've got something I want to show you."

Twelve

This is how things happened.

Sometime during the India campaign, while Aniston and I were trying to figure out how to sell to India, Julius and Wurth had apparently tried to figure out how to halt the wave of bad press coming our way. It had started with isolated incidents. Amali De Saram and Julius's string-pulling; the Hindu's critique of the Number and Wurth's response in a rival paper: things like that.

"Go on," I said, curious.

Wurth had a lovely office by that time: a stark polished wood floor met a faux-brick wall splattered with art. Dancing Man by Robert Jardin. There was a solid mahogany desk, well-used and carefully restored; in the four corners of the room were speakers that usually spoke in Ludovico Einaudi's music. Una Mattina, I think. He drew out two whiskey glasses and a bottle of vodka.

"And then we got hit again. The way we figured it, a couple of engineers who quit to form their own startup had talked about one of our updates. Some journalist had been listening in. The next day, RUMORS runs a minor piece about how NumberCorp was going to gamify life. You know that project that showed up on chat once, where Julius was talking about doing our own

SEO, recommendations thing?"

"Yeah?"

"We ran it from a place called Enfield, London. Apparently, and Julius won't confirm this, but the new guy, Heng, was involved. It shouldn't have gone anywhere, but someone shared it to Hackernews and someone shared it to Reddit and the comments sections started blowing up. And you know how shit like this completely breaks the business. I mean, we had customers up to here panicking.'

"What did you tell them?"

"Said it was a set for your web series, of course, special effects, and when that came out, it wasn't too much of a white lie. But then this happened."

He tossed me a datapad. There was an article on it. Milton Keynes News. I read through it, sipping the vodka. It was a strange - about a skunkworks unit inside NumberCorp called Crisis Response. CR, it said, was a strange project; ten people plugged into a Minerva extension, technically part of Communications. Their job, said the anchor, to bribe, threaten, sue, hack or otherwise shutdown any and all anti-Number sentiment on the web. Their source, they said, was someone inside NumberCorp.

I laughed. "I didn't know Milton Keynes did fiction."

Wurth was silent for a while. "I have a marketing budget of a billion Euro, Pat. You know what we spend most of it on? Making sure the news says only what they want them to say. You know what that much money can buy you? Right now the EU is hitting us for anti-privacy. Fucking Japan is protesting. Nobody hears about it. You write something about NumberCorp – I can buy your channel. I can buy your editor. I can find out who you are. I can call you and threaten to drop the Numbers of your entire family. Make sure your daughter never gets accepted to university. Make sure you never get a job. Screw you for life."

"Wait. You're telling me you blackmail journalists? Milton Keynes is right?"

"Spot on, actually. And it seems we have a mole in the company."

There is a wonderful word in the English language: flabbergasted. If you read it out aloud it feels like stunned surprise mixed with a keen sense of the ludicrous. That was exactly how I felt: flabbergasted. "Does Jules know?"

"It was his idea, his contacts. Remember Amali De Saram?"

I remembered Amali De Saram.

He nodded at the video. "Every so often, something slips through the cracks," he said. "Right now we're reaching out to the channel. Threatened to sue them if they don't give us the source. Minerva's tracking the last known locations of the people who broke the story and correlating that with the locations of anyone in the company who could have known this detail. There's not a lot. Clearly someone ratted out. We'll have the answer soon."

"The money alone," I said. "That's enough to buy a small country."

His desk lit up. "Speak of the devil," he murmured. "So the anchors say they don't have a clue, except it was by someone called Tobias Prophet. Prophet. Ever heard that name?"

I hadn't. Not then.

"Well, the video's offline," Wurth said, as if to himself. He turned off his desk and poured me another shot. "I'm sorry," he said. "This sucks."

"What the fuck, Wurth. What the actual fuck."

He drummed his fingers on the table. Another Common habit. "Remember the Department of Justice?" he said with mock cheer. "So, those guys reached out, wanting to increase the Number for all officers. They needed people to trust them, they said. Apparently, if you're an officer with a shitty Number, no-one listens to you."

"And?"

"And we agreed, of course. Actually, here's something Even better: I saw this piece on how the Number is so accurate that the US government uses it for visa grants. Big joke right there. We have an entirely different division in Houston that runs an entirely separate Number for visas. They're tracking people long before they even applied to enter the US. Guess who we're doing it with? The CIA. We've been hiring a lot of engineers and biz folks lately - official reason is they're for India. Between you and me, half of them don't go anywhere near India. We're pushing close to twenty billion dollars in revenue and half of that comes from governments."

He saw my expression.

"Don't. You want someone to blame, go talk to Jules. I'm just the guy hired to run the show. And he's right because he's got every three letter agency between here and Germany in his pocket."

We drank in silence. I was running this over and over in my mind.

It's not uncommon for corporations to keep secrets from most of their employees: even now, in the era of Trust and Transparency, companies regularly hide their darkest secrets from all but a very tight inner circle. That was what hurt the most. I thought I was part of that inner circle.

"So what are you going to do?" I asked.

"I'm on this train, no stops along the line." He suddenly looked ten years older. "Just letting you know, before you come back, what you'll be coming back to. If you don't believe me, just wait a bit."

''What are we waiting for?' I asked. It was a little past lunchtime.

"You'll see," he said.

Presently, there came a knock on the door. In walked a very tall, dark-skinned man. He wore very simple, very casual clothes, but from the cut and the fit it was clear that these were the kind of casual that cost almost as much as a suit. He looked paler than any man that color had a right to be and was shaking with either fear or anger. I recognized him.

"Nice Converse," said Wurth.

"Vintage 2004," said the deputy editor of Milton Keynes Media. "Let's get this over with."

Wurth opened a drawer and pulled out a slim, white package.

"This is everything?" said the man. He tore it open: there was a data slate inside. 'This isn't me,' he said, sounding puzzled and relieved at the same time. "Wait - is that Karen?"

"This is a teaser we have on every single one of you," said Wurth. His voice was suddenly flat, almost unrecognizable. "Yours is in the middle there somewhere. By the way, Smith - how old is that girl? Thirteen? Fourteen?"

The man's face split in an ugly sneer. "Enjoyed it, you fucking voyeur?" he said, the hint of a British accent limping into his voice.

"Hardly," said Wurth. "Disturbed, yes. Concerned, yes. Enough to alert the FBI agents sitting downstairs, well, maybe."

"What do you want?"

"I want Milton Keynes to forget Crisis Response,' Wurth said slowly. "In fact, I want you to denounce that rumor as a fraud. Maybe false data leaked by this Tobias Prophet guy. And from now on, everything that you write about the Number goes through me first. Prophet contacts you again, I want to know."

"I won't forget this."

"I'm sure the FBI won't forget your little videos, either," said Wurth. "Or your husband. Now here's the really interesting thing, Smith. I'm going to give the others the same package. Your stuff, their stuff, it's all in there. Prisoner's dilemma. Want to see who breaks first?"

The man looked like he was about to hit him. Then his nerve broke; he turned and fled through the door.

"What the fuck, Wurth," I said as the door slammed behind him.

"Oh, don't fucking look at me like that. You're still here, aren't you? You took Julius's dollar, just like me."

"Why are you even showing me this?"

Again that brief silence. "It's been a long time, Pat," he said. "I've always tried to keep this end of the business out of your way, because like I said, your work's been fantastic and Julius didn't want this messing with your head. But if you come back . . . this is what I need you to work on next. I need someone I can trust. Someone who's been here from the start, someone we all trust. This is the cost of keeping the empire alive."

That evening, I checked in to my hotel room. They offered me a complimentary bottle of wine. I swapped it out for cheap scotch.

"And what of the accusations by Mr. Tobias Prophet, that NumberCorp is under fire from hacktivists?" rumbled someone from the wall screen. "Given the level of access NumberCorp has into our lives, are we prepared to risk our data, our livelihoods, falling into the hands of the hackers and the pedophiles?"

"I would like to reassure Dr. Koenig that we are secure," said the voice of Julius Common. "In fact, Russell Wurth, our Vice President of Communications, and Senator Henry Caxton, one of our advisors, would now like to show everyone on this livestream a look at our secure data centres across the globe - and the political treaties we have with various governments to make sure our users' data is never exploited. We can't give away too many details, of course, but I hope this will put an end to the lies."

"Mr Common, regarding the Crisis Response allegations -"

"I'm sure a lot of your callers have questions regarding the so-called Crisis Response team that they say we're running. Firstly, I would also like to remind everyone this Tobias Prophet is a name on the Internet, and that these statements are completely fabricated. Right now the only weight behind this is a bunch of media outlets who want more views on their reports. I respect our media, and it's wonderful that we have a free press, but fact is fact and fiction is fiction. Once the FBI releases their report I expect all of these baseless allegations to be put to rest, thank you."

I felt dizzy.

I did the only thing I could: I went back the next morning, and as they say in Sri Lanka, I did the needful. I contacted Facebook, Google, Anagram, send them copies of the death certificate, asked them to take down my father's profiles. I paid for a funeral - not a burial in some compost-heap somewhere, but a pyre, in a wooden coffin, with his pen and papers around him.

"The carbon tax will be ten thousand dollars, sir," said the agent.

"Charge it," I said, tossing her my credit card. Ten thousand was nothing. While the payment processed - pyre funerals needed government sign-offs - I sent out emails to his colleagues. People I'd met only in passing, people that to me were only bylines in the news, but people that had to be there nonetheless. Because funerals, as my father once said, are for the living, not for the dead. I watched the storm clouds gathering outside my window and, for the first time, wished that I had never known Julius Common. Life would have been simpler.

And then I went back to NumberCorp. Wurth gave me a look of equal parts gratitude and pity, and together we went to see Julius in his office.

I have always disliked Julius's cavern at the Orthanc; it was a dimly lit place, built around a sleek, glistening glass-topped oval table. At some point he had laced reactive LEDs into the black walls; they responded to the mood in the room, and every single time I had been here- usually during war councils - they had glowed a dull crimson. Lots of people had been fired here. One corner of it was untouchable: that was his corner, the one with the high-backed leather chair and the real paper and the paperback books. I knew the titles by heart: *Cryptonomicon*; *Ready, Player One*; *The Circle*. No-one I knew had ever read those books, or dared to ask.

I moved past the table and the old books. At the far end of the room were two displays. One was the map I sought, crackling gently. The Americas were blue. Most of Asia was blue. Japan was a violent red. Europe looked like an invasion: the blue dots had taken Britain and France and Spain, but the rest flamed orange.

The other display was white. As I watched, the News logo wrote itself on top. Below it:

> PARLIAMENT REJECTS PETITION FOR NUMBERCORP INVESTIGATION
>
> By Ewan Sykes, PearceCast
>
> Corporate Watch threatens "civil investigation" citing alarms over NumberCorp's monopoly

TAGS: NEGATIVE, INVESTIGATION, POLITICS, UK, UNIDENTIFIED

> *EXCLUSIVE: OUR [ALGORITHMIC] OVERLORDS*
>
> *By Stephen Janus, Hatsuko Rees, Watchmen Press*
>
> *An inside look at the shadowy organization that's becoming part of every person's life.*

TAGS: NEGATIVE, INVESTIGATION, CORPORATE, USA, ANONYMOUS

> *THE LIFE AND LIES OF JULIUS COMMON*
>
> *By Julie Vidal, Libération*
>
> *Who is the man behind the numbers?*

TAGS: NEGATIVE, INVESTIGATION, PERSONAL, FRANCE, ROTHSCHILD

I watched the words write themselves, over and over again, on the white screen. Names changed; titles changed; organizations changed. With every report a thin set of lines would draw a tiny portion of the world. Ewan Sykes, it said, dropping a gentle pin just above Camden. Hatsuko Rees, it said, pinning a train moving across Germany. Julie Vidal, it said of a cafe in Paris.

Movement. I sensed it before the arm clutched my shoulder, an oversize contraction of steel and pressure. Kissing Labs, it said above the knuckles. I turned.

"Sir, you're not supposed to be here," said the guard with a polite smile. She didn't need to be rude - that arm could crush me like eggshells.

"Hey, we have authorization," Wurth said.

"I'm afraid I still have to ask you to leave, sir," she said, all pristine in her white Kissling armor.

Julius pushed his way through the door at that very moment.

"Patrick!" he boomed. The guard's grip jerked and fell away and she folded herself into the shadows. Julius came forward, looming in the darkness, and pulled me in a bear hug. Wurth he nodded to. We made brief chit-chat about how things were. "I'm sorry about your dad," said Julius, and he sounded genuinely sorry. He threw a questioning look at Wurth.

"I've briefed him," Wurth said tonelessly.

"Right," said Julius.

The job, as it turned out, was simple. For much of the next three weeks, I was Patrick Udo, NumberCorp's hottest ambassador, the temporary darling of both Hollywood and the advertising industry. I was to handle the public appearances - denying, at all possible points, that Crisis Response ever existed. Wurth, operating behind the scenes, would handle the rest.

"Don't worry about anything else," said Julius. "Look, Facebook will scrub all mention of Crisis Response from newsfeeds. Reddit gave us access to their moderator bots. Anagram and Totem folded without us even having to bother. In a year's time you won't find a single record of Crisis Response. Can you do it?"

For the next three weeks, I sunk back into the familiarity of NumberCorp, into the long-forgotten rhythms of this world. And in the background, we set up interviews, breaking news, thought leadership pieces tactically inserted and made to go viral. In swift strokes we reached almost every major media outlet across the world.

There was a term among magicians called sleight of hand; tricks you would use to convince an audience that the card was one hand when it is, in fact, in the other. What we did was sleight of hand on a grander scale. If someone ever tells you that big companies control the media, believe them. We don't control everything you read, but we control everything you don't see.

"If you repeat a lie often enough it becomes the truth," Wurth used to say, not without a hint of bitterness. I could appreciate the irony of his situation: he was terribly, terribly good at something he hated.

One evening I returned after a brisk jog to find a girl dressed in a rather vivid purple bodysuit sitting cross-legged from my desk.

"Hi," she said with a wide smile. "I'm Ana."

"I'm Pat."

"I know." The grin narrowed, became catlike. "Patrick Udo. You're a weird one, aren't you? You save too much. What're you going to do with all that money?"

It hit me. "You're Crisis Response?"

"Here to take all your problems away," she said, holding out a datapad. "Now, if you don't mind, check those names."

Her grin widened again. It seemed to be a permanent feature of her face. "Don't worry, I don't bite."

I took the pad gingerly and read the names. It was a list of senators who we'd heard were planning to lobby for a closer investigation into our business practices. I told Ana this.

"Not to worry, love, our problem now," she said, tucking it neatly away into a zipbag. "Now don't panic when you turn on your computer, everything's going to be a little wonky for, yeah, five minutes. Tell Wurth I said hi, will you?"

Wurth didn't show up all day; it was almost midnight when he finally called me. Via Secret, of all things. I picked up, fearing the worst.

"Pat, remember those three senators we had some trouble with? Did anyone from Crisis Response show up for them?"

I explained the girl in the purple bodysuit. Wurth cursed.

"Well, it's out of our hands now," he said, sounding resigned.

THREE US SENATORS GUNNED DOWN IN EMBASSY ROW, read the news a few days later.

Julius came to visit us. He brought with him a bottle of the finest Elit.

"That was well handled," he said. He looked proud.

"I don't want to ever do that again, Jules," said Wurth.

Julius looked at him for a long while. Eventually Wurth looked away.

"I have built a monument more lasting than bronze," Julius said softly. He raised a glass to us, downed it and went away.

As soon as he was out of the door, Wurth reached for the bottle. Neither of us said anything.

Three days later a group of twenty, perhaps thirty people, showed up outside NumberCorp's London gates. They wore Guy Fawkes masks and waved signs that flickered in and out with messaging.

FUCK THE NUMBER, they read. Police converged on them, sirens in their armor screaming, shocksticks raised.

There was the dull pop-pop-pop of anti-riot guns and dull thud that shook my eardrums. Someone had tried to drive a truck through the gate. All of London stood in stunned silence.

It was an omen of things to come.

PART IV

However, as the Church and the KGB give way to Google and Facebook, humanism loses its practical advantages. For we are now at the confluence of two scientific tidal waves. On the one hand, biologists are deciphering the mysteries of the human body and, in particular, of the brain and of human feelings. At the same time, computer scientists are giving us unprecedented data-processing power. When you put the two together, you get external systems that can monitor and understand my feelings much better than I can. Once Big Data systems know me better than I know myself, authority will shift from humans to algorithms. Big Data could then empower Big Brother.

In a Dataist society I will ask Google to choose. "Listen, Google," I will say, "both John and Paul are courting me. I like both of them, but in a different way, and it's so hard to make up my mind. Given everything you know, what do you advise me to do?"

And Google will answer: "Well, I know you from the day you were born. I have read all your emails, recorded all your phone calls, and know your favourite films, your

DNA and the entire biometric history of your heart. I have exact data about each date you went on, and I can show you second-by-second graphs of your heart rate, blood pressure and sugar levels whenever you went on a date with John or Paul. And, naturally enough, I know them as well as I know you. Based on all this information, on my superb algorithms and on decades' worth of statistics about millions of relationships — I advise you to go with John, with an 87 per cent probability of being more satisfied with him in the long run.

-*from* ***Yuval Noah Harari on big data, Google and the end of free will***
by **Yuval Noah Harari**, writing for FT.com

Thirteen

About three months later, I sat in a corner of Elkhead, sipping coffee and watching the big wallscreen.

It had been a very tough three months. I'm not entirely sure I can, or should describe exactly how that fiasco unfolded; some monsters are best left in the dark. But let me put it this way: at that time, there were perhaps twenty major news corporations in the country, and we had dirt on ten of them; five of the others didn't do tech, and the rest we simply kept in the dark. Every major journalist, news anchor and major editor was tracked; not just in America, but all across the globe. We had their data. NumberCorp knew where they ate; we knew what they spent their money on; we knew enough to know roughly where each of them would be on any given day at any given time. I played the good cop; Wurth played the bad cop; and, if we couldn't solve the problem, a little message from @CRISIS would arrive: want us to handle it?

No, we would reply in a panic. We sent them to the things we couldn't handle. The activists. The people in the Guy Fawkes masks. Nobody died, but the leadership of that little pocket of anarchy was located with all haste, and hunted down by the secret services and police of every country they scattered to. It wasn't many.

Whatever they did to them, we never found out.

They used to say that once something is on the Internet, you can never get rid of it. Not true; not anymore. Maybe that worked in the 90's, when the 'net was a sprawling warren only haphazardly linked by search spiders; maybe it was even true in 2010, when there were a few bastions that celebrated free speech in all its ugly glory.

But we live in a world where your thoughts are hosted on platforms owned by the one percent. Here, they say, is your free lunch: a space to host your thoughts, a community, buttons to show when people like you. There's one caveat: everything you put out into the void belongs to us.

You will not find a single record of Crisis Response now. All the journalists are gone, as are the activists. The only memories that do exist are this book and the videos I've released of these conversations. The end result is simple: Crisis Response simply vanished off the face of the earth. It didn't exist in search; it wasn't talked about in the news: it didn't exist. Julius's promise held true.

Only a handful of us remembered THREE US SENATORS GUNNED DOWN IN EMBASSY ROW.

Reading this, one might question why I went back in the first place, or why I even stayed.

The answer was simple. It paid well, and I was working a fraction of what I used to. Barring a crisis, I set my own hours, I worked from wherever I wanted. Most of my job boiled down to delegation; it was the dream state for anyone to get to with a salaried post - the point where you're more a consultant than an employee. My fame as a Valley celebrity filmmaker opened up all sorts of projects. I was setting up a partnership with an AR startup, for example, working on a spy game that layered right into the world. I was writing a book on marketing. Things with Parvati were simmering down: I was considering a long period of travel. My job was done from a series of cafes and at the point of a mobile phone. As long as things ran smoothly, Julius was happy to pay me well. If I wanted a reminder of what I would be without NumberCorp, I only had to step out, see the unems huddled up on the streets, freezing in the cold. And if that wasn't enough, I had enough memories of poverty from India to last a lifetime.

It's remarkable what you can get used to doing for a living when you know the alternative is to starve.

So I drank my coffee in ritual silence, figuring out my next steps in this sprawling warren of a company.

"Patrick Udo?" said someone.

I looked up. It was a thin, nervous-looking young woman. Blonde. She stuck out a hand. "Hi."

"Hi," I said.

"I'm Jana Butler, we spoke last week-"

If we did, I couldn't remember, so I started typing. "Jana, is it?" My screen lit up with her information. Ah, yes. Butler, UN-ID ftvN3pt4n724nw. Middle 2K Number. Education: Stanford Online. You can't get a Number that low with a Stanford education, especially if you're white.

Ah: jailed twice for DUI, resisting arrest and possession of class-C hallucinogenics.

"-this is about the job."

"I'm sorry," I said, trying not to sound rude. "We really can't hire someone with your Number."

"Please, if I -"

"I'm sorry," I said. "Policy is very clear."

Jana Butler hung her head. I waited for the inevitable to pass.

"Can I get you a cup of coffee?"

"No, no, that's okay, thanks," she said. She rubbed her eyes and attempted to smile. "My Number's pretty bad now, isn't it? Okay, then, Mr Udo. I'll- I'll figure out something."

"Good luck," I said, wishing I could do something for her. I watched her retreat slowly from the safety of the cafe and into the pitiless world outside.

My phone rang. It was Julius. I snatched it up instantly.

"Patrick, you around? Good, good. Can you come to my office?"

Walking into Julius Common's office was difficult: the last time I felt that same brittle hostility, the same pit in my stomach, I had been walking into a fight. Julius was sprawled across his chair; black on black in black. Amarasinghe, his face mottled from the Poulsen treatments, opened the door. He gave me a nod and what, from him, was supposed to be a smile. To me it looked sly and sneering. Then it was just me and Julius in the black room.

"Is everything okay at Coms?" he asked, watching me like a hawk.

"Everything's fine," I said. It was reflexive, and it was a lie. He must have seen through it right away, because he hesitated. I'm not one for overlong descriptions, but there was the weight of a lot of questions between us, ones that would not go away. "You wanted to ask me something, Jules?"

"I have a job for you, if you're up for it."

"What kind of job?" I asked warily.

"I need you to go to Beijing with Heng," he said. "It's the first part of a much longer project."

"I have work-"

"Which mostly consists of threatening people and writing PR," said Julius. "Good stuff, but I have something else in mind."

I think that was the first time I really dropped my guard. "What's your game?" I demanded. "What is it now? Are we killing more senators? Hushing up death squads?"

He surprised me. "No, no, nothing of that sort," he said, and for the first time in our long acquaintance, Julius Common looked ashamed. "If it's any help, it takes you as far away from CR as possible. I really need someone we can trust. Talk to Heng, think about it, let me know."

Which was how, a few days later, I ended up back at Elkhead, talking to Lui Heng. I had offered to meet Heng at his office, but no, Heng said, Elkhead was fine. He - I mentally corrected to they - walked in through the faux-wood door, looking a little lost. People got out of his way as he saw me, smiled gently, and came over in a curious, plodding gait.

"You can't search for me," they said without preamble, sitting down. "I have a really high Number, but no information will be revealed to you. If you want to know something, I'm afraid we'll have to do it the old-fashioned way: ask."

I was taken aback. "Why is that?"

"Asymmetry. It's a new update that I'm testing on myself. Society, human society, you see, is marked not just by social status, but also by the availability of information - coffee, please, thanks. The further up the hierarchy one goes, the more information is available. This difference is also a crucial part in how we interact with people . . . I'm trying to mirror that in the algorithm. It's just a patch. Let's see."

A short silence fell.

So," Heng said, "Patrick Udo."

"Hello," I said cautiously.

"You don't talk much, do you?"

"I prefer to observe," I said.

"Legolas, what do thy elf-eyes see?" Heng said. "Huge Lord of the Rings fan, I'm afraid. So, I'm going to Beijing soon. For me, technically, this is a vacation. For you, technically, this will be work. You know that China has its own system of what we have with the Number?"

I had heard about it. I knew that China had a system of scoring, that they'd had it for a long time - as far back as 2010, I think. Nobody knew what it did now, because of the Divide between us and the Bamboo Curtain, but every so often, while researching for the webseries, I would come across old articles hinting at it. It was supposed to be primitive, very much like what Experian and all the other credit agencies had had before we toppled them.

Heng made a sound that sounded like gwan shee. "Here is the shortest pitch, as Julius would say. Picture a state, or a dumb system, a set of protocols that spies on its people. Evaluates their actions - buying patterns, police interactions, public behavior, even - into a scoring mechanism. "

"Sounds exactly like us."

Heng fiddled with their coffee. "Yes, the fundamental premise was almost exactly what NumberCorp started out as," they said. "A single score for every human being. This implementation, however, is a bit more integrated than NumberCorp's . . . do you remember that epiphany you told me about when you started the web series: a girl giving up her seat to an old lady, and you could see her Number going right up? Thanks to surveillance covering every inch of every major city, that's actually possible here. Somewhere at the heart of every city is a . . . ministry where humans and pattern-recognition programs look at screens all day and add numbers to people's lives.

"The fundamental driving forces were simple: China's market economy was a colossal mess in those days. Unregulated, unregulatable. Also there was, you understand, generations of citizens who the Party needed aligned with their thought model. Political support for the Party was rewarded. Money and politics.

"It wasn't even the first time. In 2010, the State launched a pilot project that gave people points for what the Party called good behavior. Staying within the law, taking care of the elders, keep the streets clean, that sort of thing. They graded people; the highest received preferential treatment for everything - the lowest, they couldn't even get a job. The project was taken down after public outcry, but the data collection kept running until they had enough to build accurate behavior models. I don't think Julius likes mentioning it, but now the system is actually very thorough. Functionality-wise, it definitely does more than we do at NumberCorp."

That surprised me. "I thought we were the only ones in the world with all this stuff."

Heng looked mildly surprised. "James Watt patented the steam engine and kicked off the Industrial Revolution," they said."But two others built engines before him - four if you count Vitruvi and Hero of Alexandria. Most ideas are thought of long before we actually get around to making a business out of them.' For a second, a brief smile flitted across the large features. "Yes, probably everything. Have you ever read a novel called Nineteen Eighty Four?"

I hadn't, of course, back then.

"Pick it up sometime," said Heng. "It's an interesting book. Set in a country that was once England, a perfect surveillance state where the government knows almost everything about a person: they even have a saying for it - Big Brother is watching. The public is manipulated and held in line by a government that destroys individuality and even rewrites newspaper headlines to make sure that history is what this one state wants."

"I'm assuming that's China now?"

Heng smiled. "Every government manipulates, every news headline in this world is now rewritten," he said. "China is of course ahead of everything else because we've actually been doing this in public since the Cultural Revolution. But a surveillance state is a problem of technology . . . you know, when I was growing up, London was the most heavily surveilled state in the world? I always thought the Brits would reach their own dystopia first."

"How do you know so much about this?"

"Do you know how many people I've discussed this with and they've never once asked me that question? I'm afraid I worked on it. I also co-authored the initial math behind the Number. Julius would not welcome me without anything to back me up."

It isn't every day you hear something like that.

"I didn't build it," Heng said, seeing my response. "I was always more . . . a theoretical person. I improved the parts of it that Julius brought to me - at least, the scoring mechanisms. Others who could carry out my thoughts did the actual building."

Then Heng got distracted and held up one of my notebooks. "Paper? Real paper?"

It was one of the notebooks I carried with me wherever I went. "I like writing," I explained.

"Interesting," Heng said. "Where were we? Yes. This system I spoke of. Very much like ours, and like ours we will have to use it to get most things done. I want you to try and document it wherever you see it. It's work you're very familiar with. Can you do with me in China what you did for us in India? I can get one person into China, all expenses paid, and you'll have a week to build me the kinds of case studies you used to do."

I saw an opportunity. It was better than threatening people and writing PR, as Julius had put it. I could wash my hands of this Crisis Response mess for a while, get out the old camera, and get back to work that I loved doing. If they promoted someone into my spot, whoever took it might even have to own that part of the job permanently.

"Why not?" I said. "You'll have to give me some time to hand over my work, make sure everything happens properly. When do you want to leave?"

Fourteen

Traveling to China in those days was a lot more difficult than it is now. Even with Liu Heng's patronage, getting in was a bizarre and complicated process. First I went to the embassy, where I filled in a form - *name; parent's names and occupations; travel companion(s); purpose of visit; affiliated corporations; their contact details, mission statements, details of investment (leave blank if unknown).* They took my blood. Then a Chinese bot searched every single thing that it could access about me - apparently, on the way, it also knocked on the digital doors of the NSA, CIA and a whole bunch of other three-letter agencies, because someone from the CIA-affiliated side of NumberCorp dropped by for a chat one day. The bot must have been satisfied, because I was called in and given a list of flights that I was cleared to board with.

It was a surreal experience. I had spent all my life with the perks of being American: even during its slow decline, a citizen of the United States of America could walk into any airport, book a flight to almost anywhere in the world and, unless he was a criminal, he'd be on his way without any fuss at all. The United Nations Identity, built with the universal blockchain, had long since overcome the legal hurdles and bureaucracy of international travel. And here was one nation steadfastly refusing to change.

Beijing was perhaps the strangest landing I'd ever made. From the window of the plane I saw a sea of clouds, drawn in tufts across the sky, as if an Abrahamic God had decided to play with wool. Then we dipped; the tufts gave way to a riot of color that pulsed into the night. The color turned into streets; and before we knew it, the old Comac C919 had landed with a thud and a faint rattle.

They surrounded us the minute we got down from the airplane. Six large men, dressed very cleanly and formally; beneath their white shirts were chests that gleamed a strange metallic black. They looked like they wore gloves, but I had been around enough augmented people to know better. I knew that China took a very clear-cut approach to mechanical augmentation: only the military were allowed to supplement the human body, and even then only if paid for by the government.

The other passengers vanished, driven by that oldest of instincts.

"Ah! Liu Jianyu!" said Heng, apparently unfazed. "Aye! Nǐ chī le ma?"

One of them, flustered, began what seemed like a very formal apology. Despite his body, he stooped slightly before Heng, as if he was student before a teacher.

"Duì, duì," said Heng. The man, apparently relieved, nodded the others forward. "Patrick, these gentlemen will need to check our devices and record their device IDs. Can't be too careful with security these days, you know."

We'd prepared for this, so I handed my devices without a fuss. They were disposables - a Chromebook, a burner Android phone; any data I needed was on the cloud. They took us to a room, a lobby of sorts, and I spent an hour or so kicking my heels as Heng gently interrogated Liu Jianyu.

And then, just as suddenly, it was done.

"That was fortuitous," said Heng as we picked up our bags, re-packed our devices (which probably now had spyware installed) and made for the exit.

"Friend of yours?"

"Student."

Ah. My guess had been right. "He didn't seem too pleased to see you."

Heng looked up. "Few people are comfortable having their ungender teacher show up on their shift," they said. "Especially if that teacher is coming in from America."

I followed their gaze to one of the seemingly innocuous-looking chandeliers that adorned the vast space and received a rude shock. What I had taken for bulbs were actually large cluster arrays of cameras - what photographers called bug eyes.

"Liu Jianyu will probably be recalled to State tomorrow," Heng said.

"Is he in trouble?"

Heng shrugged. "They'll rap him on the knuckle for knowing me, but they've already spent enough on his body that he won't be decommissioned. There's no logic behind wasting a perfectly good supersoldier . . . now, am I the only one who's hungry? We can eat something while we wait for our car."

Alright, then.

Beijing hit me like a wave. A wall of noise rose in front of an endless background of gray glass and steel. Sixteen lanes of traffic swirled around us, performing an intricate dance that took them past us in a riot of color and advertising. Or was it propaganda? Half of it bore the five stars of the PRC flag.

Walkways looped the streets, looking for all the world like a giant metal spiderweb growing over the city. Two helicopters gently buzzed overhead at heights that would have been illegal anywhere else.

We walked for what (to me) seemed to be ages: it was only a kilometer or two from the hotel, but it seemed like we fought a whole horde of people to get there. People stared at me with what seemed to be barely disguised hostility. It was only much later that I realized it was just curiosity. Dark skin; they didn't see a lot of us over there.

My mission in China, outlined to me by Heng, was to observe. And to report. Just like I had in India; just like I had countless times. Liu Heng, as a Chinese citizen, had vouched for me, and under something like the Confucian system, I would be his responsibility. We had seven days in China; three to spend wandering the city, and three to spend around Tsinghua, the university Common and Liu Heng went to, where the Heng family exerted considerable influence, and I could be freer with my questions.

"You want me to record everything?" I said, already thinking of buying a camera, or maybe a field recorder.

"Keep it to conversation," Heng said. "Many people will not talk if you record them. I'd rather you collected notes."

The car rolled up outside the cafe.

"Go on," Heng said. "I have to meet some old friends now. I'll meet you tomorrow at breakfast."

I stood up, shook Heng's hand and got in the black taxi, feeling suddenly alone. I checked my phone. Three messages from Julius; one apology from Wurth; one from Parvati asking why I hadn't called her in a while. Was I okay? The taxi took me away to a hotel, which mercifully turned out to be from a chain I was rather familiar with.

@JULIUS: How's China?

New, I replied. *Strange.*

I think my first real shock came at Tsinghua University.

American universities trend towards one of two extremes: they're either interconnected, upper-class social hubs, or they're digital accreditation platforms. Tsinghua was an old-school university - a vast area of land with student housing and microcampuses and laboratories scattered across a densely packed space. A subway line ran through that: we took a car that seemed almost empty, save for a neatly dressed Chinese woman who had the tell-tale marks of a drone photographer around her eyes.

This time I noticed the cameras. Curiosity overtook me: I tried to imagine what they saw.

Nothing here: nothing out of the ordinary. Neat crowds of students flowing around teachers and staff like rivers of human flesh. They were not alike, nor did they dress alike, but there was a sameness there; they gave off the impression that if their clothes could have been the same color, they would have been.

Liu Heng, it seemed, was a bit of a celebrity here. People, after staring at me for a while, automatically assumed I was his aide; I was introduced to face after face, professors, star students. Most of it made no sense. I had a translation bud that supported Mandarin, but what they spoke was dialect all their own.

I watched them. They were, by and large, good people. Perhaps they took a lot more selfies than I was comfortable with. Everything was a bit more ritualised than I'd expected.

But then again, this is how we treat strangers: we go through all the motions until we know what sticks. It was only much later that I discovered that there were entire schools that taught people how to behave, especially in front of a state camera; how to smile, how to greet someone, how to cross your legs. Children are sent to these schools for a year after puberty; adults often opt to go again. Later I learned how travel, especially to other countries, was a privilege reserved for a rare few. No wonder Liu Heng seemed like a celebrity: the very fact that he had crossed a sea was special to them. Two billion people, living entirely in a loop of their own.

While waiting on Heng once, I caught a whiff of perfume. An extraordinary tall and pretty girl stood behind me; she looked like a student.

"Mister Patrick Udo?" she said with a thick accent.

I can't remember her name, but she was arguably one of the most beautiful women I'd ever met. Nor do I remember the conversation. But I was fascinated. She sat down right next to me in the reception, and, while we waited for Heng, we spoke about life in the Valley, about what I did, about NumberCorp-

"Having a good chat?" said Heng, startling us both. They nodded to the girl. "You can go now."

She stood up, bowed and left. "She was interesting," I said.

"She is a student with a future," said Heng. It was the first time I'd seen Heng angry. It came off them in waves. "A system far beyond her control has turned her into a plaything for people like you and me. She cannot resist: none of them can. Not if they want to keep their education, get a job, or ever travel outside these borders. It is crude to keep her, Patrick."

It took a moment to digest this.

Our next stop was a cafe with a surprisingly Silicon Valley

aesthetic. Two waitresses bustled over. They seemed to know Heng.

"You seem popular."

"My family is . . . well connected," said Heng. "Or maybe they've just been alerted to our presence. It's hard to tell with the State. My Number is at the point where it would hurt them not to pay attention to me."

Consensual slavery? I wrote.

"Once, China produced over half the world's electronics," Heng said, as we stripped open the packs of sugar for our coffee. "Everything from cell phones to computer parts to vibrators were made here."

I knew this already, but I noted it down. "What happened?"

"The people who invented capitalism began to understand how capitalism worked when they were on the losing side," Heng said. "While American companies controlled the means of production, everyone was happy. But things took their logical course, and once they realized that the free markets that they trumpeted let other nations compete far better than they could, they tried halting the process. Remember the old 'Bring Back Our Jobs' campaign? When I first heard of it I thought they wanted to resurrect Steve Jobs, but instead, America went back to being a manufacturing nation."

Well, China certainly didn't seem hurt. "What happened?"

Heng smiled. "What else would happen? The manufacturers always end up being owned. Like their American counterparts a century ago, Chinese businesses had far too much economic power to be stopped. Products that once said 'designed in California, made in China' now read 'designed in China, made in California'. The cycle reverses. Fifty years down the line the manufacturers will switch again. And again. Economics gives us the cyclical nature of the world."

The coffee went. The food arrived.

"Julius and I, we had an accord," Heng said, as we began to eat. "We would both, independently try to create this massive vision that we worked on together: a model where software would pave the way for ... well, absolute trust and a perfect understanding of the worth of a human being.

"We both succeeded, in our ways. And for a time, this was mine - I would perhaps not have left China if my system hadn't been turned into one more means for the politicians to rule this world. The idea was to transcend politics, not to die crushed under its boot heel. And on that aspect, I did fail.

"You see, when Julius asked me to come back, it was like being given a second shot at a failed exam. The Number is better than this thing that runs here, algorithmically and ethically. For one it's a lot more complex, because we have to deal with so many different contexts. Even better - we don't enforce political belief. We rely on different services using it to surround a user with touchpoints to the point where we have all the data - and we let those services decide what they are going to offer. A more democratic system. A more beautiful system, one that expands faster, more creatively, than either Julius or I could have ever imagined."

There is a photo I have of the journey: a gleaming black spire of a building, something that looked like a shard of glass dropped down from the sky. A high, graffitied wall loomed in front of it: on the front, in blazing red letters, was scrawled *THEY'RE ALWAYS WATCHING* in Mandarin. Two guards stood outside. Unlike the variety that had accosted us, these were, very conspicuously, military creatures: they wore hulking grey metal suits that I could only think of as power armor. They could have given the Ultramarines a run for their money.

Us, across the street, sipping our wine, right at the heart of the city.

THEY'RE ALWAYS WATCHING, screamed the wall in a language I didn't understand.

Heng called for wine.

"But we control the algorithms," I noted. "Someone controls everything."

"The rationale is that at NumberCorp, we are the good guys," Heng said. "Which I'm sure every dictator in existence has told himself, so it's hardly a valid rationale. But NumberCorp has principles. Publicly published principles. It's not a government. The whole system relies on so many companies knitted into it: if we were to flout our principles...they'd leave. We've built a web that holds us in check. These people, Patrick - for them that was never the case.

"It's actually a fascinating problem, if you look at it from the other end. What the Number is, from a technical and political perspective, is a distributed system. Every single bank, restaurant, apartment complex, brothel - whatever integrates the Number automatically became a stakeholder, sharing the Number with both its clientele and its competition; and as a result, every single ecosystem eventually becomes part of Julius's giant web. Here in China, it's one central entity. Easy to impose, but as you can see, it takes remarkable effort - right down to cameras in every public space - to really make this work."

"So what are we trying to do?" I asked. "Build this? This level of system? Cameras on the streets, the works?"

Heng was silent again. "Some of what NumberCorp is going to do next may seem this way," they said slowly. "But Julius's real genius was to realize that the market would be more self-sustaining than a government. All of us could die right now and the Number would exist in the background of humanity for as long as western civilization exists. You built that visionary web series, Patrick . . . did you never stop to think what it might mean if it all came true?"

I had a sudden, mental vision of the world, gripped by a vast hand in the NumberCorp colors. "Do you think that's what it'll come to?"

"What do you think?"

I remembered something Wurth had told me the day I joined. "I believe we'll change the world," I said.

"I believe we already have," said Heng. "And when you get back, you'll understand why." They raised their wineglass. "To Julius and his vision, and to yours."

"To Julius," I echoed, eying my notepad, where, outlined in red, was *CONSENSUAL SLAVERY*?

I've since had the great fortune to travel to China several times - not just with Heng, but once I lived and worked there as the China correspondent for Singularity magazine. Singularity, always a very well-funded revolt against the cheap standards of modern journalism, gave me access to almost every single tech hub in mainland China .. . enough perspective to explain to you what I saw then.

Imagine a city of nothing but tech companies. Not the mini-villages of the Valley; imagine an artificially constructed city, with every building designed and planned by the government, with each building leased out.

Thousands of these are startups, manned by people reared in an ultra-competitive system where the second and third best, fleeing in shame to other countries, would become the CEOs of Fortune 500 companies.

If no-one hears of the thousands of geniuses in this place, it is probably because a handful shined so bright they made a permanent mark on history and stole everyone else's thunder. If you've studied your Renaissance history, here's a parallel: Boticelli's name outshone that of Andrea del Castagno in much the same way. Picture sprawling postmodernist empires of malls and technology, home to tens of thousands of coders generating billions of dollars in revenue, inhabited by geniuses left, right and center. It was a world of extreme innovation, even by Valley standards.

The Chinese called these zones 'tech parks'. Any other country would have called them provinces. Or states.

There is a saying in Sri Lanka: '*godayata magic*'. Common, who taught me the term, told me that it was slang for when some yokel from the village sees a cool piece of tech for the first time. China was magic, and the first time there, I was the *godaya.* I, being accustomed to the Valley, was ushered into a world ten times larger than anything I'd ever dreamed of.

But let me flip that coin.

That glittering city is one among a thousand; set in a world where a Ministry of Propaganda decides what is true and false; where a Great Firewall spies on every single word that you type online; where journalists, once an exotic breed, are now extinct, and all news is distributed by automated services, rewritten by a few low-wage college students, and sent out into the world. China was never big on robots or AI, because they had a ready supply of people and a need of jobs; and so the lowest on the scale - taxi drivers, the laborers, the waitresses - mastered the art of turning themselves into robots, perfectly compliant, in case their Numbers dropped the next day and they lost their jobs.

It was a world of both extreme civility and terrible abuse. I once saw a waitress being molested, in public, in a packed restaurant, by someone who was clearly a high-ranker; no-one in the entire restaurant so much as looked at her. "The State will judge him," said the girl who served me my coffee, although she did not seem to be hopeful. Heng, when I narrated this to him over our daily catch-up, was extremely disturbed.

That man - I later learned through Heng - was arrested a day later, demoted, stripped of all rank and privilege, and assigned to work repairing potholes. The next day he was run over - apparently by some joyriders. There were no penalties for that: he was too unimportant for the system to care about.

My notes from that first trip are scattered now, but some remain. *Transparency metrics for public servants, search by name, department or ID*, says one. *Number banding*, says another. *Jobs selected by govt for each score tier. Middle class job options index listed.*

Fringe, low-score communities turning into game parks for rich people, read another. Activists forced into mental hospitals.

And that last, most damning note, this time circled, highlighted and underlined:

SLAVERY.

Fifteen

When I got back home, I took a shower. I changed. And I headed right back out into the city. I drove the rental and stopped in San Jose, more by accident than by design; and then I parked the car and walked, soaking in the people that swirled around me. There was some sort of university party going on, or maybe it was the younger crowd at one of the big tech giants; shirtless men and girls in fishnets ducked in and out of bars, spilling light, noise and heat out onto the streets. People in costumes ran amok. A Batman high-fived me as I walked past.

And here were college students, unhindered, unfettered, not turned into playthings by a nameless state. Here were people who lived as humans should - free, happy, slightly worried, and terribly drunk.

My phone started ringing, but I ignored it. I just sat there, soaking it in, sipping my alcohol, letting China out of my system, letting the glow and the haze restore me to normality. I have no memory of getting back home - I think Parvati picked me up when my phone detected my alcohol level and autodialed her - but I woke up in her arms, with a hangover the size of the continent. No state-sponsored algorithmic cruelty in sight.

All was as it should be. I locked myself in my office and began to write about China. Julius had once again instructed me to keep it offline; once again, I put everything else out of my mind and wrote.

Julius read my report with a frown. "That bad?"

"That bad."

"I thought Heng was exaggerating," he said, almost to himself. "This would never work, not here."

He put the report down. "Alright," he said. "Up for some more travel?"

"Where are we going?"

"Enfield," he said. "We're going to the UK."

Twelve hours later, glass of wine in hand, I was approaching a white bus parked just outside Heathrow. It was entirely white and had a look about it that screamed armor. London airports are famous for being congested with traffic, but even taxicabs avoided it.

Milling around were a dozen engineers. Some of them I knew from India. Ramesh Nagata and John Holden from Research. Abdul Kamal, Blockchain. Yannika Burton, Social Psych. NumberCorp's superstars. Combined IQ of a small continent.

And here was Wurth, looking like he'd just stepped off a plane.

He had. "What's happening?" he said as soon as I sat down next to him.

"Just as clueless as you are," I said. "Japan doing good?"

"Don't get me started," Wurth said.

There was a knock on the door. It was Heng. They nodded to me as they went past, slightly stooped, and sat in the front with Julius.

"Everybody rested?" asked Julius.

Nods, yeahs, a couple of enthusiastic thumbs-ups, a low cough from Wurth.

"What I'm going to show you is completely and utterly top secret, you understand? Any word of this gets out, we know where you live."

The grins faded. Julius laughed.

"Only a joke, people," he said.

Somehow it didn't sound like he was joking.

The bus took off. In the distance, London turned slowly, looking for all the world like a cluster of lights huddled up against the river.

London had always been a bit of a strange place. I remember this moment, back in my Koenig days: stepping out at night, getting out of the taxi, and seeing a family of unems. Mother, father, a little girl. Huddled in a bare canvas wrap over a barrel fire, watching the lights glow across the Thames. I remember stepping over homeless people sprawled out on the pavements, watching with vacant eyes as we cut through them without even seeing them, talking acquisitions, parties, nights out, spending on coffee what they could have survived on for a day.

It took me a while to piece this together properly; weeks of back-and-forth, but the general gist of it was this: back when the UK's tech bubble crashed - and I mean, really crashed - Julius launched an insane new project: we would build housing, not just for their employees, but for anyone who wanted a home. The only condition: that they sign up as experimental users - for life. It wasn't that strange an idea - after all, Facebook had a village of sorts clustered around its campus in the Valley; Google already had entire apartment complexes built for people who worked there; and all the rich bio-tech companies - ExMed, AmGen, Gilead - they took it to the next level, running private police and all the works. It was simply that we would be doing this to the public. In Enfield, a largely burned-out part of London.

Like many things that happened over my stay in NumberCorp, this turned out to be the seed of something much, much larger. Number Village was, from the start, meant to be a community that ran the Number in totality. That meant the full package. NumberCorp Credit handled everyone's financial scores, advised them on how to improve, from the moment they were sixteen to the day they died. Records kept tabs on everyone's government and employment records - everything from birth certificates to performance evaluations. Influence lived in everyone's phone and in every public camera, analyzing how people met, who they met, where, what ideas spread the most, who spread them - you get the picture. Of course, people didn't need to know all of this; all they knew was that Number was one app on their phones, and this one little app told you how popular you were, what you were popular for, what was happening in the city, who was going to what. If you wanted to keep your apartment, you used it daily. Religiously. And that was that.

Like the others, I'd heard only the vaguest of rumors about this; it was completely outside my jurisdiction and almost completely disconnected from the main inner workings of the company; when Wurth had first mentioned it to me, he had described it more or less as a research project, little more. I didn't realize the 'project' was actually a thousand people living in a village that we had built for them.

It made sense, in a perverted way. This kind of thing was only really possible in two places: China and in the UK. The UK government, by law, had so much data access it made the CIA look weak. Three-letter agencies tracked every website someone visited, their call data, and even the apps they used on their phones: they'd been doing this almost since 2020. I'm not entirely sure how Julius got the government to agree, but I can hazard a few guesses: the sterling pound was at an all-time low. People everywhere were struggling to make ends meet; and here was a rich tech startup solving the problem wholesale.

So step right in, the government had said, and NumberCorp had marched in wholesale, using Aaron Kotalawala's construction contracts and his billions. They might have even laughed at this crazy Valley company solving their problems.

So picture row after row of Edmonton houses, all glass and warm wood and cut cement. Picture ten thousand people living NumberCorp lives. Sharing. Oversharing. Paying their bills with NumberCorp-issued cred cards. Shopping at ShopShare. With their credit limits tied to how popular they were in the neighborhood and on social media. With advertisers able to tap into them anytime, almost anywhere.

Village 0, said a sign reaching for the sky.

Into my mind, unbidden, came something Ibrahim Monard told me, not so long ago: I have seen the future.

"What do you see?" said Julius.

It looked quite ordinary to me.

Julius pointed at a building nearby, a peculiar castle-like structure.

"NumberCorp PS 101," he said proudly. "One of the best schools in the country. Experimental syllabus. Proper education in everything from the classics to the STEM fields. We track every single student score, every test result, every track and field performance, even fights. A high Number, fresh out of school means they made all the right choices. Means they networked ahead. Talent and influence. Exactly what we want to hire for. I've already got some of the most powerful companies on the planet already committed to hiring these guys. And people pay us to advertise to these people who we know will be high performers in the future. We invest that back into the next generation. And so on. And so on. We've already got some incredible results."

The pointing finger turned. Our heads swiveled with it. "We reworked the Number incentives with a much more extensive ruleset," Julius said, talking faster. "It's not just things work and connections anymore. Have a hobby or a business on the side. Write poetry. Do gardening. Maybe even be paid in Number for being a good parent. Every single action that they can take, every single thing they can do with their lives, has been graded, Numbered, and built right into the app. None of it takes away from their happiness, because with the ad money we're giving them universal basic income. For life. As long as they're good to themselves and the others, they can do whatever the hell they want. UN goals: end poverty. We've made it work at this scale."

"Holy shit," someone muttered.

"We haven't needed police," Julius said. "We've barely needed civil services. Everything's self-organizing. If we think we need traffic control, one ping and the system picks someone out. They get their Number. If we need someone to host an arts exhibition, one ping and we can get a few people with spare time together. They get their Number. Look at them. They're happy. They're living good lives. They're working together. And these are the people they left behind. If we can make this work for them, we can make it work for anyone."

"Some of this is still manual," Heng interjected at that point, almost apologetically. "Someday Ezra and the Algorithm team will take over and Ibrahim and the Product team will be fleshing out this code properly. The predictions engine, that is running only on basic templates-"

"Point is, this is what we're building up to," Julius said. "The point is for the first time in human history we have the technology - and now thanks to the UN and our own Research folk we have the data we need to make this work. Everything else is just application.

"Holy shit," Wurth said again.

My phone vibrated. Tags. Social media. People all around us were taking photos, tagging themselves in pictures with the great Julius Common and his employees.

Julius Common stretched out his arms to encompass the whole village, pride written in bold strokes on every inch of his body. "We're going to have so many problems once we scale, but if things go right we'll be rolling out in three years. The big one. The Society update. We'll roll it out after Inequality. Has a good ring to it, doesn't it? Well? What do you think?"

"It has a certain touch," said Heng.

"Yes, yes it does,"said Julius, grinning. "So this, people. Heng and I figured out how to build the damn thing. That stuff you're writing, Pat? It's not just a pipe dream. It's real."

Wurth and I stood stunned. I'm sure the others felt the same. And all I could think was that Beijing had followed me home.

It was quite late when we got back to the office. The windows looked out over London, dreary London with its iron skies; the Eye turned gently in the distance, one of the few things that stood out in that curiously flat landscape. Julius called for a late lunch and sat with us, leaving the engineers to Heng.

"If you're up for it, I want you attached to the team running the Village," he said quietly, as the wine arrived. "Basic reinforcement learning. You first define a goal. You don't tell the system what the goal is, because it doesn't understand jack, but you define a series of rewards for actions that'll take the system to that goal. You want to teach it to run? You'll reward it when it learns to stand. When it takes the first step. When it begins to understand direction. And so on."

I understood.

"Well, that's how people work, too," he said. "That's how society works. You set up a series of socioeconomic rewards and people get in line. They self-organize. That's what a government does, right? That's how it's all held together."

We clinked glasses.

"The Village, even though the tech works, hasn't figured out its reward schema yet," said Julius. "You saw China. You saw Beijing - Rus, remind me to send you that report. Here's how it goes. Either we create the wrong set of rewards and the whole thing becomes completely ineffective. Just another social network. Or, we create another wrong set of rewards and we end up with a totalitarian state. Fucking 1984. Here's what we're trying to do here: we're trying to use the Village to figure out what those rewards should be. Control the system. Experiment with how many points you should get for going to school every day. See how people react. Use human intuition to guide it; it'll learn. We're trying to build a pattern, a stable machine learned model, that we can apply to the rest of the world."

"That's ambitious," said Wurth. "Jules, that's a hella big job."

"Well, someone has to do it, right?" said Julius. "Our governments are fucked. Our leaders are imbeciles. Democracy? Even in the state where it was invented, Athenian democracy collapsed every two hundred years. And it collapses now. Communism? Failed. Having human monarchs? Doesn't work. One queen might be the ideal ruler and the next one might be a complete jackass. Have you guys read Plato's Republic?"

Neither of us had.

"Well, here's how one part of it goes," said Julius. "Plato asked a simple question. If you were stranded on a ship at sea, and the captain just died, would you hold a vote on which direction to turn the ship, or would you find the most experienced sailor among you and put him in charge? Which one? A or B?"

"Of course, the sailor," I said.

"Obviously, B. So democracy is out. Governing is something that requires expertise. But nobody in their right minds wants monarchs, other than the Brits, and they're using that family as a tourist trap. When you become king, that's a lot of power, and human social dynamics kicks in and eventually everything goes to hell. Freedom of speech? No. Madness? Eventually. Right?"

"So this is the solution?"

"This is the only solution," Julius Common said, staring out of the window. "In ten thousand years of human civilization this might be the only real solution we've ever found. Build a system that spans the world. Something that hooks into every single aspect of your life; something that can be both carrot and stick depending on where you stand. Train that system. Show it the lines in the sand. Fuck the governments and the United Nations and all that bullshit people get up to. "

"Jesus Harry Christ, Jules," said Wurth into the silence that followed. "I've always said you were ambitious, but -"

Julius grinned, the old shark. "Too far?"

"Way out there," said Wurth. "How long have you been working on this?"

The food arrived, a momentary distraction.

"No chance that you might have been inspired by the web-series?" I offered jokingly as plates were set down in front of me.

"Everything I've done, everything I've dreamed of, was for this," he said as we sat there, our faces lit by the half-light of the London sky. "It's not as fancy as what you guys put on screen, Pat . . . but I think you'll be surprised at how close the tech is right now. Decades of building the Number. All those billions. And this is where it all comes together. Just imagine reaching into the world and ripping out all the rot and the bullshit and the politics.

"I need your help. I've sent the two of you all over the world. Between the two of you you've sold the future to almost the entire world. You've seen what the Number does. You know what works, what doesn't, what we need to avoid. We own the markets. Which means we own humanity. And if we can sell this dream, guys, if we can do that, one final push, and we can make everything better. This is our chance. Right here."

He smiled, as if struck by something. "You know, if it makes sense, go ahead, spin it, say we built this after what we kicked up for India. I don't care who gets the credit. Pan narrans, not homo sapiens. All that matters is how we sell this story."

What is that word for being so awestruck you forget to be afraid?

"I'm in," I said.

Sixteen

That was many, many years ago.

If, when I had started out on this journey, you had told me that I'd eventually end up where I was, I'd have laughed in your face. And yet I now looked out at the madding crowd and raised my glass to myself.

That point came to me again while writing this book. I am forever jumping from one point of change to the other, and this is how we tell our stories.

The end began with a headline.

NUMBERCORP'S HEAD OF INTEGRATION COMMITS SUICIDE.

It was a writeup by some small, hack magazine. Ibrahim Monard, 45, it said, was found dead in his quarters. Ibrahim, who lived in New York with no family, was considered one of the finest data scientists in the country and was one of NumberCorp's highest-ranking officers, with many internal sources placing him in command positions of a sizable portion of the company. Coroner's analysis, it said, showed something shocking: Ibrahim was the product of extensive gene-engineering, possibly one of the last, illegal children of the splice. There were photos linked in an untraceable cache. The source, an eyewitness, wished to remain anonymous.

Within hours the news was everywhere. I sat there in Enfield, in a dark corner of the cafe, clutching my coffee and watching the news explode slowly across the Internet, like some rotting creature that had finally unfurled its wings. It sparked a minor media firestorm as journalists all over the world, biting at Wurth's leash, seized on the news with glee. Suddenly there were a hundred, no, a thousand voices pointing out that Liu Heng, NumberCorp's CTO, had just left for China. What was that about? Data theft? Corporate espionage? Meanwhile, what of the mutated freak?

The world howled. Overhead, the sky broke open and rain began pouring down in earnest. The Center For Disease Control was called in. I watched my screens pile up with news, statuses, opinions and a statement from NumberCorp.

Pending the autopsy, it said, Ibrahim Monard was indeed confirmed to be gene-engineered. However, it was far from the perfection that the term implied: while gifted, Monard's augmentation had left him with a series of cancers in his body. It was tragic, terribly tragic. NumberCorp will, of course, fight the state and the government to ensure that he was given an honorable, human burial, and not dissected and cast aside.

> It doesn't matter what we are born as, *said the press release.* That is not something we get to choose. What matters is that we choose who we become. Ibrahim died on his own terms, a productive human being with a Number well over 12K. His work changed the lives of millions. We will honor him in death.
>
> Signed,
> CEO, NumberCorp,
> Julius Common.

And to us, to those who worked for him:

> In light of recent incidents, we will be invoking the Employer Rights Act of 2020 to declare the following:
>
> 0) All employees of immediate extraction from China or its allies, or having family within those countries, are required to report to HR immediately.
>
> 1) All employee clearance, barring the heads of departments, is now reduced to Level 1 privileges. Over the next week, we will begin the process of rebuilding access on a strict need-to-know basis.
>
> 2) All employees are required to allow the company to access their phones, social media accounts, personal computers and any applications with messaging functionality. To ensure privacy these accounts will only be accessed by MINERVA for the explicit cause of detecting possible information risks, and will not go under human scrutiny.
>
> 3) All augmented employees will be required to undergo summary scanning for any systems that may compromise our cause. We will be working with our partners at Kissling Labs for this.
>
> *I personally realize that these measures look and sound draconian. We have always run NumberCorp as an open ship. Despite our extremely valuable intellectual property, NumberCorp strives to hire people of all walks, ethnicities and augmentative status, because intelligence and a propensity for hard work have never been confined to one race or one country. I have no doubt that when the press gets hold of this, as they will, there will be many who are happy to accuse us of being*

fascists.

However, we do what we do not in isolation, as we once could have done, but with a complex web of partners and allies who we must at times please regardless of whether we, as individuals, agree with them or not. Our lives are (sometimes) not our own. From womb to tomb we are bound to others.

Julius Common,
Founder, Chief Architect, NumberCorp

Several days later, Julius called me from his office. Not the London one, but from the NumberCorp HQ itself.

"How soon can you get here?' he said without preamble.

"On my way," I said. It was early; outside my window was a city that had yet to wake. I made myself some coffee while my phone assistant looked up flights. It was practically a knee-jerk response now. Ring the bell, and instead of salivating like Pavlov's dogs, I'd start booking flights. The London Eye hung gently in the background, lit up by the soft gold of the sunrise against the gray emptiness of London fog.

Hours later I was rolling into San Francisco again; and then the Valley. Alicia Random met me at the gate.

I could tell something was wrong, because Random looked like she'd seen an entire army of ghosts. "You need to come with me," she said urgently, dragging me off in the direction of Orthanc, the lone black tower that Algorithm operated out of.

"What's happening?"

"Can't explain to you now," she said, words spilling out like bullets. "Let's get this over with."

The tower loomed above us, black and forbidding in the evening light. A single guard stood outside, augmentations gleaming in the Kissling white. Next to him, lounging casually, was a woman with dark hair and dark clothes. I don't remember a lot of what she looked like, but I do remember feeling real fear. I'd say it was something in her eyes, but honestly, outside of novels, eyes have very little to do with this sort of feeling: they're just orbs stuck in a mask of skin. It was the rest of her: the way she stood, the way her neck pivoted at odd angles, the way she kept her hands hidden out of sight.

The Kissling guard put out a hand. I felt the brief tickle of a scan. Then I was in; the woman was leading me up unfamiliar paths to a conference room. She walked with a low, ranging gait, like an animal poised to pounce. For all of my wanderings in NumberCorp premises, Orthanc was the one place I'd never been into. Algorithm was kept locked away behind the strongest security measures; whether it was for protection or prevention was something that was always up for debate.

A clunky 2020's-era airlock rolled ponderously away. Inside was Julius . . . and some others. I looked over the faces. They were inscrutable. Natalie Durand of Bizdev. Maria Kovacs. John Piper. All new people.

"Don't let the CIA lady spook you," said Julius. He looked like he hadn't slept for a while.

There was a half-hearted titter from those behind him.

"I'm supposed to give this to you in official lingo, so let's get this over quickly. You're required to ingest a drug that will, for the next three hours, block most of your ability to lie. You'll also be wearing an fMRI device that'll tell us if you are lying."

Someone handed me the pills. Another guided me to a chair and fitted a slim metal band around my head. I was terrified. I tried to get up, and hands pushed me down, hard.

"Don't fight it, Pat," said Julius. "It's not going to hurt."

What followed then only exists as a hazy hole in my memory. I remember Julius asking me about my work here. What I had done. Whether I was happy.

I told them what I had done.

What did I like about NumberCorp, what did I dislike?

I thought about this for a long time, and answered at length.

Then there were questions about messaging editors from the press, clandestine things that had not been logged. I remember explaining our blackmail scheme in great detail.

And then the question that really stands out in my memory: did I know who Tobias Prophet was?

By this time the drugs really had a hold of me. I don't remember who asked this, but I'm sure it wasn't Julius: it was a sharper voice, somehow, more suspicious. Then blackness.

When I woke, or at least when I remember waking, Julius's face floated in front of me. The gray eyes searched my face.

"He's alright," he said to someone behind me. "Pat, drink this."

Water was thrust at me. I drank, greedily, and tried to ask what happened. The same sharp voice said something from behind me.

That darkness fell again.

When I came to again, it was to the sound of my phone ringing.

It was evening, or at least, it looked like evening. My wallscreen saw fit to show me a forest of gentle green lit around the edges by a setting sun; artificial rays lit up the faux brick room, turning my vision into a soft sea of green, gold and brown.

Except it wasn't my wallscreen. It wasn't even my room. I looked around at NumberCorp's hospital wing. There was an autodoc vein running into my arm.

My phone vibrated on a tray next to me.

Disoriented, I picked up. It was Wurth.

"You awake?"

My eyes were blurry; out of reflex, I set my optics on record.

In the movies, they show lines of text flashing in front of your eyes. Operation successful. Things like that. In reality, it's much more subtle. It's very much like flexing a finger. You barely think about it: either your hand works, or it doesn't. It just happens.

Nothing.

Almost fully awake now, I stumbled out of bed. There was a moment of disorientation. The ground tilted, and then I crashed to the floor.

"Pat?" said Wurth's voice over the phone. "Pat, you alright? Pat, I'm sorry."

His voice, and the room, faded away.

When I came to again, Julius was sitting next to me. His voice echoed loudly. Things shifted in and out of focus. There was a vague roaring noise outside and a pounding headache in my skull.

"My eyes aren't working," I blurted out the moment I saw him. "What the fuck did you do to me?"

The roaring noise resolved itself into the sound of rain.

"I'm sorry," Julius said to me. He had a look about him like a dog who'd been kicked too many times. "We overreacted very badly."

I tried to sit up. I found this rather bizarre. "What the fuck?"

"Overreacted," Julius repeated. "Can you read?"

He held out his phone. I reached for it.

"This is a leak posted anonymously to Wikileaks and to torrent networks everywhere about three days ago," Julius said slowly. "It . . .well, it leaked a lot of shit, Pat. Village. Algorithms. Crisis Response stuff. And you know what? It came from your user ID."

I was stunned. I flipped through the phone. There it was, out to the damning public; text files; documents describing the inner workings of our algorithms; a whole dossier

"You see why we had to call you in?"

"What did you do?"

"We . . . tapped into your neural shunt," said Julius. "Your recording functions have been shut down for a while. At least three days, they tell me."

I was stunned. "You're fucking joking, right?"

Julius held out a glass of water. I took it, hauling myself up. The place was empty, except for the two of us - and another bundle of clothes maybe three beds down from mine. Julius watched me drink.

"We thought you were Tobias Prophet," he said. "Minerva showed a whole bunch of discrepancies - messages going from you to addresses we couldn't trace. Phone records with numbers that came up unregistered. Suspicious searches on your work accounts. Coinciding perfectly with every single Tobias Prophet data leak we've ever faced."

"That's insane," I protested.

"So you told us," he said. "So we looked again. We have access to everyone's comms now, so we did find our guy."

The headache throbbed, intensified. "Who?"

Julius said nothing, but nodded sadly at the person a few beds down from mine. The small bundle stirred, moaned, as if in pain, and shifted. The cloth fell away from the face.

A small face, used to smiling. A very familiar one.

"Wurth?"

"He's sedated," Julius said. "They're going to take him away soon."

In those moments I could have written pages about how I felt; now all that remains is a dull spark of anger. When I had calmed down, Julius was bleeding from the lip. He wiped it off and looked at the blood on his hand, as if in disbelief.

"You have to understand," he said, and his voice trembled a bit. "These are serious people we're dealing with here, Pat. CIA. Mi5. I couldn't."

"I want out of here," I all but snarled at him.

Julius rubbed his eyes with his thumbs, the first time I had ever seen him do that.

"We're putting together a conference," he said at last, almost to himself. "One more Utopia Con. If you're leaving, I'd like you to do it after. Three months, Patrick. I need you on my side for this."

He gestured. One of his extraordinarily well-dressed aides stepped into view.

"You're now assigned to Mr Udo here," he told her. "Anything he asks of you, do it."

"Sir?"

He turned to me, ignoring the dumbstruck attendant standing there.

"I'll see you around," he said, a little sadly.

The big man left the room noiselessly. Utterly spent, I fell back into restless sleep.

When I next came to, Wurth was next to me. His face was bruised and he had a split lip. In the simulated sunlight he looked old, far older than I had ever seen him to be: there were lines on his face that I couldn't remember.

Again, instinctively, I tried to switch to recording. Again, nothing.

He handed me a flask. It was coffee, laced with Nootonium. It was disorienting to be back on my feet, but the coffee worked; Wurth waved the assistant away and guided me towards the balcony. I noticed he had manacles on his feet and wrists, things that weren't connected to each other.

"You fucking idiot," I said the moment I could.

"I can't believe he let you hit him," he said.

There was silence.

"Listen," he said. 'I'm sorry about what happened, I really am. I know this wasn't our deal. But what we're building here is changing the world. I know a lot of people like the idea. Ezra loves the idea. She used to say that the Number's more accurate and better than politicians and all the human scum we put in charge. Agreed. Humans make terrible choices. We make friends with bad influences. We marry people we shouldn't. Every presidential term we go to the polls and vote in idiots and charlatans. But I always believed that it was our right to make these stupid choices. All our stupid choices have led us to make the world what it is to day. It's how we progress. You put a machine in charge and you give people the right answers to every question, we're going to lose what makes us human. I did my best to make sure Julius's systems are as fair as possible, but you know, who guards the guardians? Who watches the watchmen?"

"How long, Wurth?" I demanded.

"All this time," he said.

"And all this time you and CR were just chasing your own goddamn tail?"

"I'm sorry, Pat."

I remember Julius once telling me about trust. Trust, he said, is how well you can predict another person's response in any given situation. It might be a conversation, it might be a fire - as long as you have an internal mental model of how that person will react, then there's trust. Even if you're trusting them to do the wrong thing.

"You're dead," I said.

"I did give the CR people a good run though," Wurth said.

"Why?"

"I'm not some grand villain with a master plan, Pat," he said, with a touch of sadness in his voice. "All I wanted to do was make the media understand what's at play here. Someone had to push them. If Crisis Response wants to clock me out, well -"

We left it at that; we left it unsaid.

"Are you mad?" said Wurth anxiously. "Listen, it's just ... shit happens, right? No permanent damage, no harm done, just a little bit of panic over some super-sensitive stuff. And Pat, you got to punch Julius."

I laughed shakily, and that dispelled the tension. We talked; we chatted, as we do, about older days and happier times, when the world had been a simpler place. And when they came, when it was time for Wurth to leave, I took slow, faltering steps with him to the door.

Three days later, the CIA spook came to see me. She took one look at me.

"Common says you're free to go," she said. Her voice was harsh and oddly metallic. "We'll be keeping an eye on you."

Physically, I was fine, but anything involving recording implants leaves you disoriented for weeks because of all the connections to the optic nerve and the brain. That's the first thing you learn the hard way when you graduate and buy your first set of implants. It took me a few hours before I could function well enough to take a shuttle to the campus entrance. The guard there gave me a hard stare, but he let me through: soon I was outside the Wall.

My phone buzzed. It was Wurth. I didn't pick up.

WHAT'S YOUR NUMBER? screamed the wall.

I tapped through every place I could go to: every place I had to go to. Clearly some semblance of work had continued in my absence. There were meetings booked on every floor that day, even one at Julius's house that night. There were calls and messages. Most of them from Wurth. All a couple of days old.

I swiped them away. "Elkhead," I said, picking the one place that nobody was going to.

Elkhead was full of people keeping three feet from each other at all times: loners, like myself, with a slight buzz of conversation among them. A few heads swiveled around to look at me. I ignored them and went through my routine almost on autopilot: ordered my coffee, picked up my epaper, and settled down in my corner. Elkhead's epapers were one of the few publications that didn't rely on News: instead, they read feeds off a wide variety of open directories. It was nice, every now and then, to read the far-left conspiracy theories and the half-baked theories that we wouldn't cover.

NUMBERCORP TOP EXEC ARRESTED, said the front page. There was a photo of Russell Wurth smiling, his hands outstretched to an audience I couldn't see.

Julius called me before I got to the Wall.

"I'll make sure your salary goes on," he said. "Call it a pension. Breathe a word to anyone and Crisis Response comes for you. No police. No lawsuits."

I couldn't resist: I was still angry. "Standard offer, then?"

If there was an apology due, he didn't make it.

"Goodbye, Patrick," he said. "I hope the world treats you well."

That was the last time I spoke to him in person.

And thus we come to this moment.

I stood outside the Wall. It was the 13th of November, 2046, and I had come a long way. *WHAT'S YOUR NUMBER?* screamed the Wall, just like it had all those years ago when I first joined Society. In the years since we had all changed; we had changed the world; the only thing that we never bothered about was this wall.

Memento Mori, I said to the Wall, driven by a brief gust of memory. Old Latin. Remember that you, too, must die.

In the distance, NumberCorp Village Beta rose, a tangled maze of skeleton houses and builder bots. A large signboard read *HELM'S DEEP* - one of my lasting contributions to the great machine. *ATLANTIS ALPHA*, read another, rising into the sky from another empty patch of land.

My attendant (who, among other things, turned out to have an augmented spine) helped me limp to the taxi. Later I learned that her name was Media, that she was born to trailer trash parents and had run off to the Valley to look for a job; that NumberCorp had picked a whole lot of them up for cheap, because their Numbers made sure nobody would ever employ them. But all that came later. For now we eased ourselves into the glass cage of the taxi. It took us past the strange company-fortress-villages of the Valley, past the glamour, past the glory, past the dreams of Julius Common.

It was not the way I'd wanted to go at all.

PART V

Just watching Facebook's F8 Day two keynote and it's all about the future.

On one side of things, Facebook is truly the generous inventor. Open sourcing telco level infrastructure that will make tech driven cities of the future possible.

On the other side, there's a dystopian picture of sorts forming when Facebook shows its ability to look at a video and in real time, process what it's seeing and hearing and understand what actions people are taking, and then translate languages real time.

I suddenly picture a city where Facebook constantly processes all the moments being added to its network. A parade happens downtown and as people live stream it and Facebook detects more and more devices crowding the area. It reaches out to others who might be interested and dictates what the best plan for the day might be. To those less interested, it spins the wheels of its ad networks and tells us which restaurant we should get food from today since our preferred location is more crowded. As the parade goes on and more media comes in, Facebook recognizes faces and records who was where and who was with who. Quietly, it correlates interactions on its networks and every time each person's paths crossed each other and the giant AI nods its head. Some people's relationships are indeed more serious than others. Even if they don't know it. And one day, when they make it official on Facebook, the AI will know which moments to serve up as an album of time together.

And while all this happens on the ground, over our heads, wings spread wide, Facebook's aircraft beam down Internet to all of us, their presence serving as a silent reminder of who is watching us each moment of the day.

- **Adnan Issadeen**, Systems Developer at Buffer, 4/20/2017

COMMON: A HISTORY

Watchmen Press Archives

Content type: raw text

Channel: N/A

Warning: 302; contains errors and possibly unverifiable attribution sources. Hold publication until confirmed.

COMMON: A HISTORY
by Patrick Audomir Udo

Julius Common was born on the 3rd of September, 2000.

It was a historic year. In France, the marvelously iconic Concorde crashed for the first and last time, leading to the death of commercial supersonic air travel for the next two decades. The Tagish Lake meteorite hit the earth and was forgotten. The first artificial heart started beating. Israeli troops withdrew from Lebanon after 22 years of haunting its battlegrounds. The NASDAQ market, peaking at 5132.52, signaled the beginning of the end for the famous dot-com bubble.

In Old Québec, Canada, Noel Gunasekara, a Sri Lankan immigrant, and Seraphine Common, a native of Québec, discovered that it was, indeed, a boy.

Noel, a tall, brooding man, had arrived in Canada some years ago, fleeing Sri Lanka's JVP insurrection. Seraphine, a diminutive schoolteacher with a fiery temper, had been through a tumultuous first marriage that had left her with a house, a dog and a sea of debt. He was a thin, dark firebrand who had trouble holding down jobs. She was willowy, with a heart-shaped face and angry eyes. A few photos of them exist online.

Those who knew them describe their marriage as an unhappy one. "They loved each other, but some people just aren't the type to, you know, be together," said Angela Common, Seraphine's sister, who succumbed to leukemia shortly after she told me this. "When the boy came, we thought it would do them good. Make them a bit happier."

For a time, it did. Joshua Julius Gunasekara was a healthy child, and by all accounts, rabidly curious. Over the period of time that I've known the man, we've discussed our childhoods at length – usually when there was a bit too much wine around. Young Julius, it appears, was smart, and he remembers Canada fondly. He remembers Seraphine's old, rambling house: he remembers scoring well in class: he remembers Noel, no stranger to hard work, slowly settling their debts, making sure his family had enough to go on.

The house is now gone, of course: when I traveled there for our Canada launch, that entire block had been turned into a

SynthMeat factory. Common stayed in the car, a strange look on his face. It was the first time I had ever seen him look sad.

If there was one thing that held the young Julius captivated, it was the computer. Julius was a third-generation geek – far too young for stories of mainframes and even dot-com fortunes, but part of a generation that saw the rise of the Social Web. He grew up with the rise of Facebook, Twitter and Reddit, of Flickr and TinyChat. Going over the old Internet archives, I can only imagine what it must have been like to grow up in that era. The first two decades of the 2000s was a curious marriage of prosperity, fear, discovery and innovation; news reports alternated schizophrenically between reports of war and reports of new companies claiming to revolutionize lives. And it was a strange world: a world that worshipped different heroes: men like Elon Musk, who dreamed of travelling the Red Planet; women like Angela Merkel, almost single-handedly holding together the economy of a coalition of countries that had spent most of civilization fighting each other; girls like Malala Yousafzai, who stood up for terrorism and took a bullet to the head. Social networks were popping up everywhere, startups in the Valley were clocking insane valuations, and everywhere you looked there was an almost desperate urge for entrepreneurship. "Do your own thing!" was the calling card of those times. To me, it looks like a world falling out of love with religion, out of love with democracy, looking for new hope among despair.

These were the times Julius lived in. From what I've gathered, his father played a key role in these early years: Noel Gunasekara, the unsatisfied rebel, would force the boy to watch the news, and sometimes he would drop by the public library on his way home: and for weeks at a time father and son would pore over the teachings of John Locke, Zeno and Descartes – physical books, rented out before the Kindle and the iPads disrupted that industry. People who knew Julius when he was young – and there are always a surprising number of these once a man becomes famous – tell me he would often hang around for his father at the gate of their little three-bedroom house, looking for all the world like an eager puppy.

This is only the backstory, though. Our tale really begins in June, 2013, when something called the Snowden Incident happened. A whistleblower by the name of Edward Snowden leaked confidential material regarding the United States intelligence, detailing a devastatingly powerful surveillance program called PRISM. Two old-school news sites, the Guardian and the Washington Post published the devastating disclosures. Much detail is irrelevant, except that which hit the common man the hardest: the leak fingered Facebook and Google as being participants in the PRISM program, sharing data with the US government.

The world was in uproar for a while. Not only did the leak throw violent light on the peace-through-control stratagem pursued by the United States at the time: it also raised questions about what democracy and government control meant in those times. It also brought to many a harsh truth: since the turn of the century, people had been putting up their faces, thoughts, religions, work woes and daily routines up for public scrutiny; Facebook, Twitter, Orkut, Google Plus - all of these had only made it easier, expanding this sharing of identity to a billion people in just a decade. Social media knew more about a person than anyone else in the world – and now that information belonged to a shadowy agency under the United

States government.

More than anything, the PRISM disclosure was what nurtured Julius's obsession with computers and social networks. From the little I gathered over the years, he became obsessed with it. Anna Krismathy, who schooled with him, remembers Common as he was then: "He'd go into this distracted funk. I swear he'd actually forget stuff," one told me. "It was like restocking your library. You toss out old books to make room for the new. There was no point talking to him when he was in one of these moods, no point at all, unless it was social media algorithms or stuff like that. If you actually knew anything about that he'd talk to you for hours."

It marked a definite turning point. Years later, in one of our conversations, he opened up a page he'd saved and kept for years: a thread on ReadTorrent, the open-source Reddit clone that ran on P2P Bittorrent networks. Someone started a discussion on PRISM. Someone else came and floated PRISM 2.0: it would be, they said a network that existed not just in mobile phones and web browsers, but everywhere; a network that would monitor everything you did and have it on record. POLICE STATE POLICE STATE, someone screamed in reply.

Someone else came along and said, well, if you're monitoring people, why not go all 1984 on them? Why not measure their impact on the world and people and use that as the basis for a social network? After all, that's how real-life worked – the more influence you had, the more important you were thought to be. It wasn't a question of talent.

After a hundred trolls had died down, the first poster came back and said thoughtfully, of course, if you could integrate certain social values and behavior norms into the system, and reward people for obeying them . . . the 'good guys' would rise to the top and social pressure would make the others follow . . . at the right scale, you could enforce good social values, good cultural values . . . it'd be like the law, except it would enforced by the whole of human society instead of a few lawmakers.

Let the people police their own actions to rise up this social ladder.

Why not?

The question hung around for years. Why not?

It was a thought experiment that lived quietly, being kicked around by the Internet literati, curled up amongst the forums and the nepotism, waiting for reality. Waiting, I suppose, for Julius Common.

Common himself had an interesting way of explaining this.

"Do you know what trust is?" he asked me once. "What is trust between two humans?"

I thought about it and bumbled through the Oxford dictionary explanation. Common smirked and shook his head.

"No," he said. "Trust is how well you can predict another person's response in any given situation. It might be a conversation, it might be a fire - as long as you have an internal mental model of how that person will react, and if that model is accurate, then there's trust.

"So what do you need for that model? You need data. You need information. Thus to trust someone, you first have to know about them. The more information you have on a person, the better your model. If I can represent you, as a human being, in this society, in a way that makes meaning to someone else, and if I can make that available, then I've just created more trust in you." He spread his arms, sweeping over Silicon Valley in one grand flourish. "And that, Patrick, is what we're really doing here. We're creating trust in a world that's forgotten how to do it. Isn't that poetic?"

Then there came a time when Gunasekaras were doing well – at least on paper. We have to shift away from the son to the father. Noel Gunasekara was successful: working in public transport, he'd spent years sketching and designing a new generation of hybrid, automated Tramcars – yes, the same ones that run on our streets today.

Few records of Gunasekara exist, but by all accounts, he was a driven man, passionate almost to the point of bitterness.

"Noel? Good friend, bit of a madman," said Dr Ahamed Thawfeek, the celebrated climate change campaigner who now sets climate control policy for Britain. "I knew the guy when we were at Westons. He'd get this glint in his eye and next thing I know he'd be pitching half a dozen people his latest idea. Nevermind that he was basically a research assistant without a degree. Firebrand too, pissed people off all the time. "Have to say this, though – that man taught himself more stuff than most of us learn in PhD programs, and he's the reason we have working transport, eh? Talk about underestimating a man, eh?"

Noel sold the initial design of his Tramcar to Transport for London, which subsequently started contracting it out. It would be fifteen years before the old red buses were swapped out, but that doesn't matter to the story: the Gunasekaras were suddenly rich. Or at least, modestly well-off.

But all was not well at home.

Firstly, Noel was apparently a bit disappointed in his son. Julius was barely a shadow of the firebrand his father was. His school friends - 'associates' he calls them, never friends -

describe him as aloof. 'Weird guy,' said one. "Just not one of us," said the other. "Argued a lot, like a lot, especially with the teachers," the third told me. "The teachers liked him too, but they also hated him a bit, I think. There were days when we'd wish he'd just shut up."

All of this completely failed to impress Noel. "My father," mused Common to me, "wasn't stupid, but he was from an old generation. As far as he was concerned, you lived and died hauling freight and playing cricket and all that stuff. He became a brilliant engineer, but he never understood why I wasn't more like him."

"I think mine's pretty disappointed in me, too," I said.

Common shrugged. "Have you ever read a book called the The Rule of Four?"

I hadn't, of course.

"A son is a promise that time makes to a man, the guarantee every father receives that whatever he holds dear will someday be considered foolish, and that person he loves best in the world will misunderstand him," quoted Common. "That's just how it is, and how it always was, and how it should be."

Disappointment in his son was not the only plight that Noel faced. The marriage was falling apart. The details are scant, but I know that they argued. About what, Julius never told me, but he once did share a surprisingly intimate detail: After every argument, Noel would usually go off by himself until Seraphine cooled down, and in the morning Julius would tiptoe downstairs, picking up books and little ornaments as he went. Sometimes, if it was a particularly bad fight, they would have little pieces of tape on them, and if books, tear-drops where Seraphine had tried to glue them back together. Eventually, these fights would come to consume their relationship with each other, by Julius's account, spreading like wildfire to everything. Seraphine Common, from what I know, became and remained a bitter figure, deeply affectionate and remote at the same time, ready to lash out at the slightest provocation.

After years of argument, Noel made a sudden decision: to relocate to Dulwich, England, yanking his family out of Canada. Seraphine's protest was overruled, and Julius found himself staring at an unfamiliar house in an unfamiliar street.

On paper, Dulwich was a decent place to live. Low crime, a bit of history, and not a few famous names floating in and out through it; Dulwich Village, despite all modernization, still clung on to the image of the quaint English town. It was also, Julius points out, 'stupidly expensive' but it gave Noel one last shot at 'fixing' his son by sending him to 'a proper' school. Perhaps Noel hoped for some measure of peace and reconciliation there.

This was not to happen. Seraphine disliked England with a passion. In Quebec she had family, people who knew (and respected) her; Dulwich was new to her and alien. She held a succession of jobs; once as a supervisor at an apparel chain; once as a human resources manager at Ess 3, a failing custom smartphone business. In between she tried to get Noel off the whiskey.

Nothing worked. Noel, having, put his son into boarding school, seemed to abandon his familial concerns; he began to spend his evenings locked away in his study with a bottle of whiskey.

Over the years, as his consumption increased, she became harsher and less forgiving, and the strain on their relationship increased. Barely a year into their life in England the shouting matches intensified. Sometimes loud curses and weeping and the sound of things shattering would pierce the night; this would be followed by one or both parents being absent for the best part of a month.

Common was fifteen at the time - old enough to understand. He blames his father.

"All he had to do was pay her more attention," he points out. "My mother was used to people around her. He took her away from everything she had."

And what of Common himself?

Unbeknownst to his parents, young Julius sold drugs. Not in the traditional sense: he played to his skills. These sales were online, run through some of the Internet's hidden underground drug markets. Every so often, Julius would buy large doses of drugs in bulk, using Bitcoin stashes mixed multiple times for anonymity. These shipments were broken up into 'safe' doses and shipped, not to him, but to the house of Micheal 'Wavey' Raman, a 20-year-old skinhead who lived three streets down. Wavey would pay Julius via proxy, in cash, and Julius would reinvest that money in Bitcoin.

As a side perk, Julius Gunsekara got protection: no-one in school would touch him. The Gunasekaras - when they were home - would often open the door to tough-looking young men who would shuffle around awkwardly until Julius emerged to greet them. Money would change hands.

Raman, who was busted seven years later for multiple counts of drug abuse and assault, would ramble at length about his admiration for Julius back then. 'Kid was smart,' he said to the Times years later, once all the fuss had died down. 'We never did coke, no heroin, nothing the sniffers could pick up. I wonder if he's still interested, eh?'

Julius readily admits to this part of his life. "It's fair to say I was pushed into it. Ironically, though," he told the world once, in an interview with the Tanner Report. "All this stuff about entrepreneurship you see online? Get out there, start a business, make it sustainable, so and so forth? That's spot on if you're a drug dealer."

I still have that recording. The voices are still crystal clear.

"Much of what I became later was based on those years," Common continued, speaking of his eventual re-emergence as the founder of the ubiquitous Number. "Somewhere down the line, I started teaching myself history with the computing. Then I realized that the history of the world is largely a history of sustainable systems. Every so often a system comes along that completely changes the world. People never notice these systems until they're right there in their faces and all the alarm bells are going off. Agriculture. Christianity. Guns. The Industrial Age economy. P2P networks. Take any major event in history and I'll show you a system behind it.

"Consider Bitcoin. Monetary revolution. A chance to break out of a rigged system. P2P and the pirate sites? Copyright, theft, yes, but they also moved American culture around the world without bottleneck of price or service availability. American movies, American TV shows now projected American dreams and nightmares onto the rest of the world. Every great system had a far more powerful effect hidden beneath this obvious layer of icing.

"Just like agriculture for humans, all of these systems have repercussions far beyond the first few decades of their existence. The trick is that these systems have to be sustainable. There has to be enough incentive, on a human level, to keep them running. If there is - well, there you go: that's your history-maker right there."

A pause. "I imagine that right now, you're feeling a bit like Alice. Hmm? Tumbling down the rabbit hole?"

Then there's the anchor of the Tanner Report, assuring him that they knew what he was talking about.

I can almost picture that cocky grin of Common's intensifying.

"Well," he resumes. "It took me a long time getting there, but I knew what I wanted to do. These systems - so powerful, so . . . intrinsically part of our lives, that it just blew your mind when you looked down and realized how far the ripple effects went. I wanted to be the one building those systems. I wanted to be the change."

"So tell me," asks the anchor after a long pause, "How does a rookie drug dealer get to where you are now?"

Which brings us to the second part of the puzzle: Arab Spring.

Let me give some context here. The Arab Spring uprising, now barely mentioned in the chronicles, was a chaotic war that unfolded in the Middle East: most people only heard of it because it was one of the first wartime incidents where citizens used social media to outflank the newscorps. Certain events triggered a brutally violent government crackdown in a little country called Syria (which doesn't exist now). In retaliation, people took up arms and started back. Soon a full-scale civil war began.

History tells us it was chaos. In desperation, Syrian civilians began fleeing - to neighboring Iraq, to Turkey, to Greece, anywhere they could.

Arab Spring brought an interesting technical problem to the table: by the time the media got ahold of the photo of a boy washed up on the beach, over four million refugees were awaiting UN registration. Now there was the question on identifying these people. Many of the refugees had lost all forms of identification; no country wanted to extend their ID to them for fear of legitimizing terrorists (and there were those among the refugees) or setting up a colossal immigration precedent.

The problem of ID had been faced decades prior to this by computer scientists, and the answer was public-key: an algorithm generates two sets of numbers: one long, called the private key, and one short - the public key. The private key is used to encrypt data, and this encryption can only be reversed with a public key. Everyone knows a user's public key, so it was easy to verify a user - apply their public key, and if the program didn't spit out gibberish, that was their data. Even better: to securely send a message to that user, sign it with their public key, and only the private key can unlock the message.

You wouldn't have expected this kind of tech to hold up to quantum computing and all of these other breakthroughs we've had, but it did: the moment we got better at cracking these codes, we also got better at making them. A drunk statistician in a bar once joked to me that a million monkeys banging away on a million typewriters would probably churn out the collected works of Shakespeare long before you hacked one person this way. I took a course online where a sober statistician said pretty much the same thing.

Back in 2015, a volunteer group called Bitnation set up something called the Blockchain Emergency ID. There's not a lot of data on the project now, BE-ID - used public-key cryptography to generate unique IDs for people without their documents. People could verify their relations, that these people belonged to their family, and so on. It was a very modern way of maintaining an ID; secure, fast, and easy to use. Using the Bitcoin blockchain, the group published all these IDs on to a globally distributed public ledger, spread across the computers of every single Bitcoin user online - hundreds of thousands of users, in those times. Once published, no government could undo it; the identities would float around in the recesses of the Internet. As long as the network remained alive, every person's identity would remain intact, forever floating as bits and bytes between the nations: no single country, government or company could ever deny them this.

"That was, and I don't say this often, the fucking bomb," said Common,

In one fell swoop, identities were taken outside government control. BE-ID, progressing in stages, became the refugees' gateway to social assistance and financial services. First it became compliant with UN guidelines. Then it was linked to a VISA card. And thus out of the Syrian war was something that looked like it could solve global identification forever. Experts wrote on its potential. No more passports. No more national IDs.

Sounds familiar? Yes, that's the United Nations Identity in a nutshell. Julius Common's first hit - the global identity revolution that he sold first to the UN, and then to almost every government in the world - was conceived of when he was a teenager. A young Common, bored, highly skilled and hungry for success, pounced on it. Here, at last, was a chance. A potential for a system. Something with ripple effects powerful enough to be, as he calls it, 'a history-maker'. Perhaps he saw a chance to impress Noel.

"I think I forgot everything else for a while," he told me, and with a strange mix of awkward humility: "I started playing with it, of course. Then I went home at term end and showed it to my father, and he took one look at it, and started making suggestions. Could I change this? Could we have a GUI? I thought, 'fuck it, why not ?'"

He did exactly that, tweaking the system layer by layer until his father stopped making suggestions and started getting excited. It was his first serious project.

"One night, Noel called," said Dr Thawfeek. Thawfeek, who was almost seventy when he gave me that interview, was incidentally also a resident of Durham. "He tells me his kid wants to start a company. Now Noel - nice guy, but to be honest, pushy character when he wasn't up to his nose in the drink. I told him well, if your kid wants to get into business, talk to a businessman. No, no, he insists. He says the kid's got something related to tech. He wants me to take a look at it."

Thawfeek was wizened, almost shrunk, with a reportedly fearsome intelligence that breaks the bounds of social convention every so often. A brief grin broke the otherwise unsmiling face.

"I have to hand it to Julius. I never knew the kid was into tech, but he definitely was. He'd taken this identity solution the UN was using for the Syrian refugees and tuned it - to the point where you could basically take it, click around, and set up this very secure, almost unhackable ID system in seconds. Of course it'd still use the same cards and bollocks, but you know, the tech was very back-end, such that you didn't really have to spend on expensive servers and crap - just keep adding home PCs to the lot and you could end up with like a million people on record dirt cheap. You could run the damn thing off a potato, that's how light it was.

"Of course, I told him it was more a product than a company, but Noel was convinced they could make money off it and went ahead with the business anyway. Set himself up as the CEO, called himself an entrepreneur and so on. The kid wasn't too happy about it, but he went along."

It was a bomb - and not in the sense that Common meant it to be. Nobody even remotely connected to Government would listen to Noel and Thawfeek. A Sri Lankan immigrant from Canada trying to sell something to the British? Laughable. The elder Gunasekara would stand, hat in hand, waiting for minor Ministers to give him five minutes in the room. The younger would pace around the room, almost completely disinterested. On the table between them would be untouched cups of tea, gently cooling. Sometimes there was a secretary around; Julius would demand to see what software she was using.

It didn't work. Gunasekara's habit of pushing his son as a child prodigy fell flat. Thawfeek's name didn't impress, either - the doctor was not in good standing with those in power. Desperately, Gunasekara tried selling it to commercial companies, but they simply laughed him out. In the first of many setbacks to come, Julius Gunasekara's identity solution was shuttered away, and he was indeed sent back to school.

But that identity solution of Julius's - exponentially improved, but built upon the same framework - showed up decades later at the United Nations. The UN-ID was adopted by almost every single country worth its salt. And when the Number launched, it suddenly had a ready-made ID system to tap into - and not just any ID system, but the ID system, one already inextricably linked to every single aspect of government and travel - a system that tracks billions of people across the globe and has survived everything from the riots to all-out cyberwar. This failed teenage experiment became the beating heart of NumberCorp. And to this date, Arab Spring is still in Common's head: the first time he pitched NumberCorp News, he used Arab Spring as an example.

I don't know if Julius Common had all this in his head in 2015: all I know is that he was fascinated. I know chaos theory says otherwise, but I'll stake my money on that Chinese proverb anyway: if not for PRISM, and then Arab Spring, and Noel Gunasekara, we may not have had Common - and the Number would be just a pipe dream on a forum somewhere.

Two years later, Julius's parents divorced.

"I didn't see it coming," said a grown-up Julius Common to me, over three decades later. "Apparently everyone else did. And they expected me to. Of course, I thought they were getting bored. Trying out new things, that kinda stuff. I wanted it to be over quickly - but Murphy's Law, of course."

Murphy's Law: Anything that can go wrong, will go wrong.

Of course.

The divorce was far from the quick, clean break Julius hoped for. Over the years, his parents had only grown further and further apart; Noel Gunasekara's aloof drunkenness had often driven Seraphine Common to find solace in other partners. Noel himself was not innocent: there had been what the neighbors called 'indiscretions' - the most notable involving a young girl from the neighborhood. When the volcano erupted, Young Julius was in the center of the firestorm. The divorce was punctuated with drunken fights, a lengthy legal battle, and lastly, a fit in which Noel Gunasekara disavowed his son.

"You ever had your father tell you you're not his son?" he asked me once.

"No, not really."

"Tell me about him. Your father."

He listened - and drank copious amounts of cider - as I talked about my father, a beat journalist with a short fuse and a great aptitude for the indoors. He listened for a long time. "My father was nothing like that," he said at last. "My father was smart, but angry all the time. The anger drove the smarts. Eventually he burned out. The anger turned on us instead."

He looked out of the window again. We were at Common's famously eccentric aeroplane of a house in Sri Lanka,

"You know what's funny?" he said, and I remember this as if it was only yesterday. "Life was good. We had money. We had income. We were middle-class people with middle-class ambitions and everything was just fucking perfect on paper. A few more years and I'd have made it to Oxford, maybe met a girl, made my money, settled down ... white picket fence, 2.5 kids, the works. My kids would have gone to private school and run businesses. The grandkids would have been spoiled millionaires. Blown all the money so it could start all over again.

"The cycle. Everything was perfectly on track. Our lives were sorted. But then people are people. They're never satisfied. It's never enough."

He drained his glass. Outside, the sun was setting, the last rays coating the green hills of the Kandyan landscape with gold. A lone six-lane highway cut across the view, emerging from this sea of orange and pink, only to sink back into it again. A uniformed aide appeared and gently took the glass out of his hand.

"Mr Common is done for the day," she told us.

COMMON: A HISTORY - II

Watchmen Press Archives

Content type: raw text

Channel: N/A

Warning: 302; contains errors and possibly unverifiable attribution sources. Hold publication until confirmed.

COMMON: A HISTORY - PART TWO
by Patrick Audomir Udo

It would be normal, and indeed cliche, to say at this point that adversity builds character; indeed, it would be a beautiful story if the loss of his father defined the life of Julius Gunasekara, and thus brought about the revolution. Life, however, has a way of disappointing storytellers.

Seraphine weathered the changes well. By all accounts she found solace in the church; by the time Julius returned from school for the holidays, his mother had wrapped up the legalities. She had even arranged for his name to be changed; he went along with it.

Thus, that summer, Julius Gunasekara became Julius Common. Noel would continue paying for his son, but would no longer see him; the last conversation the two ever had in person was when Julius had his father sign over ownership of the company they'd set up to peddle the identity solution.

It was a cold and rather brief end. If anything, it led to precisely the opposite of one might have hoped for in Julius. Noel was the entrepreneur. Julius was not. In the company of his mother, life became a series of simple milestones - passing exams, putting together the makings of a corporate career.

Common does not readily talk about this period of his life. Nor are there photos or old associates willing to discuss it. As we tread the halls of Kandy's famous Golden Temple, our conversation carrying over the ancient poetry of Buddhist chants and incense, he told me, in halting steps, what had happened.

The Bitcoin exchange stuff stopped. The philosophy books took a back seat. He slowly become more social; and at the same time, he started fading from the world he lived in - a world of ideas and code. Seraphine's dutiful brand of parenting pushed her son away from the computer and into a more acceptable world - her world, the world of attractive resumes and corporate ladders.

Common's school reports - saved in the annals of an archaic database, retrieved, printed, signed and presented to me - show consistent A's in History, Maths, Science, Computer Studies. Enough to get into university, though he never made it to Oxford, the one that he so prized. That part would elude him forever.

What of the systems? Once, in Sri Lanka, on a pilgrimage, I brought up the subject of his own company - and his prodigious tech talents.

"There's a lot of thought about overturning the system, doing it on your own, breaking free, the whole do-your-own-thing startup pep talk stuff," Common said calmly. "But to do that you need a vision. Rebels without causes end up dying broke and unhappy. At that stage in life, I was thinking - here's a track, the only track I can really see, I'll take it to the top, and when I get there in five, ten years, then I'll look around and see what I can do. Let's be realistic - only a rich or a really stupid kid could have made a business really run at that age. I wasn't that rich kid. I wasn't stupid, either. I had doubts.

"So I took the safe road. I kept my expenses low. Saved money. Studied. People I knew were busy getting laid or wasted or both. I worked. And one thing I learned on the way is that you shouldn't show people how smart you really are. That freaks them out. Always dumb yourself down a bit, be relatable, be predictable. You know. Ace the test when it matters, but outside, be a bit stupid, take a joke, whine a bit. Human stuff: it gets you places."

In 2018, Noel Gunasekara was arrested for assault and battery on his ex-wife. He was brought in by his son. Seraphine Common received treatment for two cracked ribs and trauma to the head. A doctor who remembered the case told me how a thin, looming man came to visit the ward one day - a man with angry red eyes and tears running down his face. How the woman's son - shorter, whiter, with a manic look about him

- leaped for his father's throat and was beaten savagely, then and there, to within an inch of his life. The police came and took the man away.

They put the son in a bed next to his mother.

Common told me nothing of this. And as it happened, one day, I let it slip.

"Where did you hear about this?" he asked.

I told him.

"How did you find this doctor?"

Number Search, of course. He was silent for a moment.

"That'll be all for today, Pat," he said at last. "Let's pick this up after your next assignment, shall we?" A faraway look had come into his eyes.

The next time I tried to search the Number for Noel Gunasekara, it came up empty.

I don't know what it's like to have an abusive childhood. My family didn't work that way. But I do know a few people who have, and one thing they all seem to share is a relentless, burning anger, simmering beneath the surface. Not the kind that inspires people to be hard men; just a low acid that pushes them into scrapes and makes others keep their distance. Common has it at times. I can almost picture him as he must have been at seventeen; young, brooding, a ghost haunting the house of his parents.

Then the penny dropped.

"So one day, my mother starts to vomit," he told me once, as we discussed our parents. "She's been feeling off for a long while, so we didn't really think much of it. Anyway. Took her to the hospital. Know what they found?"

"No," I said truthfully.

"Leukaemia," said Common. "Doctor wasn't sure how to break it to us, but he came up and said 'It's stage four.' There is no Stage five. The best they could do, he said, was help her live out her last days in happiness."

Eighteen years is a lot of time. Enough for a wife to be estranged from her husband; enough for a son to grow up not really knowing or caring what his parents went through in their lives. I believe Julius had distanced himself from his mother quite a bit. For instance, he cannot remember what she liked and disliked, except for her rigorousness in paying the bills. He does not remember what she wore or what she did in her spare time. He does not know what made her happy. Like many other children growing up, Julius had relegated his mother to being just the source of the food and the clean clothes - just background noise. The catch is that most of us have a second chance - perhaps to return from college and see our parents for who they are.

Noel made very little fuss. By then he had realized that he could no longer help his wife; that incident in 2018 had changed many things. He took off on long business trips. And so his son was suddenly left to deal with this dying stranger who happened to be his mother.

That's the gist of it. I suspect there's more, but that's all I'll ever get.

"I tried," Common told me. "I stayed with her. I took care of her. I tried to make it better. I failed, of course."

Of course he did. Leukaemia is a terrible disease. Those affected by it suffer as cancerous white blood cells attack and their bodies destroy themselves from the inside out. The medicine hurts just as much, destroying figures and ravaging faces, throwing the body into endless pain.

Towards the end, when it got really bad, Common took to mixing sleeping pills with his mother's tea. And then he could have some silence; for a while, he didn't have to hear her crying anymore. He would slip out of the room to his computer, and put his headphones on.

"One day, my father came home," he said. "He'd been away for a month, I don't know where. He looked at me and said you look like hell, get up. And he took me out to McDonalds. I hadn't been out of the house for months except to buy supplies. The next day a caretaker arrived - you know, one of those people you hire when you don't want to look at your parents dying anymore."

Seraphine died as she had lived: bitter and unhappy. Noel was the first to throw earth on her coffin. Julius was moved to an apartment four blocks north; the house went up for rent.

Something snapped inside Julius the day Seraphine died. He piled everything he had of his mother - her clothes, her documents, even her medical records - into their cramped Peugeot. In the back was 'two litres of kerosene, one bag of chips and one bottle of dark red rum.' He drove for a long time. Then, just past midnight, he parked in the darkness. Common got out, methodically smashed the windows open and doused the seats - and his mother's belongings - with the kerosene. Then he lit a match.

"The stupid part was that I kept waking up and expecting my jeans and T-shirt laid out for me, you know," he told me. We were on pilgrimage; again, in Sri Lanka; in Kandy, to be precise. He was the pilgrim; I, the follower, chronicling it. We spoke as we walked. "She used to do that. It took a lot longer than it had to for me to start making my own tea and fixing myself breakfast. It didn't hurt. It just felt like what you feel when you misjudge a step - you feel this microsecond of surprise, that little 'oh' moment, before you correct yourself. My mornings for the next six months were basically those microseconds piled up on top of each other. Every day felt like a mistake."

I watched a present-day Julius Common bow and present flowers to the stone Buddha that waited, unmoved, and asked my next question.

"Regret? Not really," he said, carefully arranging frangipani in a circle around the other offerings. "What happened, happened. It could not have happened any other way."

"How do you say that?"

Julius Common looked at me quizzically, and gestures, his arms encompassing a hundred other residents of this temple. "We're here, aren't we?"

It was 2019, and Julius Common was drifting.

At first getting out of Dulwich sufficed: he drifted to London, then to Bristol, then to York, tracing a meandering route across England. Noel tried getting in touch, but to no avail: Julius knew how to hide from the system. There are photos of him in this period – mostly with his father. His face would look slightly worried, if not for the eyes - thin, squinting eyes that sparkle with anger or concentration. They were both known figures and the news services ran a short piece on them.

One day, in one of the many, many pubs he happened across on his journey – Julius has no recollection of where exactly this incident happened, but believes it might be Edinburgh - he spotted a Chinese student sitting in a corner. Common, drunk, walked up to student and bought him a beer, and the two started talking. In the early half of the 2000's,

Chinese students would migrate en masse to the West for an education; often hard-working, and more dedicated than their counterparts, most of them ended up being scientists, researchers, software engineers. By 2019, the tables were slowly reversing. Julius's new bar buddy was one of the generation caught in the middle, graduating into a world where foreign labor was no longer as welcome as it used to be, and faced with returning to a country where their Western education was no longer a badge of honor.

Common went back home to his father and told him he wanted to go to China. Things were cold between father and son, but Julius found a bed to sleep in and the proverbial place by the hearth still open. I suppose a man can only stand to lose so much. Noel Gunasekara only laid down one last law: his son had to go to university in England.

"He had this thing for England," Common explained to me. "He wanted me to get into Cambridge, or Oxford, or any of those universities whose name makes you feel like it's been there since King Arthur. A place with history, you know. Standing."

"Why didn't you go?"

He shrugged. "History is written by those who look at the future, not the past," he said. "Cambridge was good if you were the son of a rich businessman and wanted an MBA. Or an artist. I didn't care about that bullshit. If I was going to go to university, I wanted tech, and there were always only two places that did tech the best - the US of A and China. So I applied for scholarships."

It doesn't make sense now, but it makes sense in the context of those times. Picture the world as it was in 2019.

It was, in many ways an unstable world. The US-jihadist

wars were dying down - they were not completely dead, but ISIS / ISIL had provoked international witch hunts that left all but the most fanatical behind bars or beneath ten feet of dirt. The Unicorn Bubble of Silicon Valley had blown billions out of the water, but to the rest of the world these were trivial issues. Germany was in trouble; protectionist markets and ever-increasing exports from India hamstrung its economy, causing vast stockpiles of exports to build up unsold and unconsumed. The Eurozone was slowly but steadily collapsing. Russia had Belarus and Ukraine, had proven their military might in Syria, and now Central Europe was inching towards the East again. Politicians prayed for the best. Analysts feared for the worst.

Then there was China. In the early 2000s, a few people predicted that China might actually become the next superpower. By 2012, this prediction bore the mark of prophecy. There was hardly a product you could flip over without seeing the "made in China" mark in a discreet corner somewhere. It was assumed that China would soon be calling the shots on the world's financial system - and that the Chinese renminbi soon replace the dollar.

By 2015, the IMF had added the renminbi as a reserve currency alongside the dollar. The prophecy came true. Matters came to a head in 2018, when China shot down three US fighters flying over the South China Sea and threatened World War III. The US responded by launching two aircraft carriers. Things would have come to a head if Russia, backed by the EU, hadn't threatened nuclear annihilation to both parties if they didn't step down and resolve their differences quietly.

That year was when the world looked at the most powerful nation and realized that it was not the most powerful – hadn't been for quite a while, in fact. The man on the throne was no longer Uncle Sam but the Dragon playing chess with the Russian Bear. China was suddenly no longer the emerging superpower. It was emerged. England, in contrast, might as well have been the Bermuda Triangle.

"My father wasn't too happy about it, of course," said Common as we discussed the world as it was back then. "But that bastard was never happy about anything. I told him if he wanted me out of his house he'd have to ship me over the ocean. We had a bit of a row over that."

"What happened?"

"We had a bit of a row," he repeated.

When the letter came from Tsinghua University, in Beijing, China, Julius accepted it. It was his ticket away from his father. Two months later, he flew out, taking very few things with him - his favorite Star Wars Tshirt, an old, battered ebook reader – and, almost as an afterthought, his laptop. Containing all his grand plans for identity, and every other half-decent idea he had ever had.

"He wanted legacy," said Common, telling me this tale decades later. "The Gunasekara family name and all that. I wasn't going to give it to him. I wasn't going to leave anything behind."

"That sounds harsh," I said.

Common's eyes flashed. "Harsh?" he barked. "You can take your judgement and go to hell with it." Then, a moment later, as I expected: "Sorry, Pat."

"I understand."

"You don't," he said. "You never will."

SOURCEBOT WARNING: UNVERIFIED SOURCES OR SOURCES OF QUESTIONABLE QUALITY. ARTICLE INTEGRITY HAPHAZARD.

Perhaps Noel was not as distant as Julius made him out to be, for somewhere along the line he had set up a small but active series of fixed deposits, stock options and bonds for his son. Common, landing in China, was significantly richer than most people his age. And while Tsinghua would consume the bulk of his account balance, he did have money in the bank - enough to live a decent life in China, if he wanted to. So, to be fair to Noel Gunasekara, I'd say he did what he could for his son.

Common, in telling me this story, left out one detail. And that was a very, very important detail, one I discovered much later. You see, when Common left, China had just begun a controversial new project. The idea was to provide a publicly accessible credit score to each and every citizen. If BE-ID was the unwilling prototype for the UN-ID, then Social Credit, as this new project was called, can be called the forerunner of NumberCorp. And that, as it turned out, was a whole other can of worms.

I remember asking Common what China was like. "What was it like? That's an odd question. It was like China, of course," he smirked. He was in a good mood. "Oh, you meant for me."

Tsinghua University, which Common attended, was home to 50,000 of the nation's best and brightest. Next door was Peking University; these two, with five others, fed a sprawling estate of malls and tech companies. Hundreds of these were in research, fighting each other at the very bleeding edge of science; their competitors were literally a stone's throw away, attending the same schools, sitting at the same restaurants, shopping at the same malls.

"The first day I landed, I stayed at the fanciest hotel I could afford," Common told me. "Hotels around the world are pretty much the same. There's you, there's the staff, THEN the outside world. It's a good place to get that first peek and run back to.

"The second day, I had breakfast, went out and started walking. I suppose I was heading for the uni. I walked, and walked, and walked, and walked. There were faces all around me. Sometimes someone would look at my face and you'd see their eyes go 'Oh, foreigner. Ignore' and they'd snap back. The air stank.

"Eventually they all started looking the same, these millions and millions of faces. And the only thing they had in common was that none of them cared what happened to me, and the only thing I had in common with them was the fact that I was there on the same soil they were on. I thought to myself, 16 million people in Beijing and nobody gives a damn if I live or die. It was the loneliest I had ever felt. And now that I was here, I couldn't go back. There was no way out."

The melancholy could not last. Common had set the wheels in motion: soon he was being ushered into the coordinator's office. Hands were shaken. Schedules were made clear. He needed accommodation.

For this he enlisted the aid of an unlikely ally: a young economist-in-the-making called Aaron Kotalawala. This is where the man who runs Atlantis finally comes into the story. Kotalawala was a lean, tall and ruggedly impeccable senior, a year ahead of Common. Every morning he would be found doing his usual two mile run at the crack of dawn.

Aaron Kotalawala came to China in a rather haphazard manner: he'd attacked someone in a nightclub in Colombo. In a very Sri Lankan fashion, that someone had turned out to be the son of a particularly wayward minister. Aaron's father, the real estate mogul Reinzy Kotalawala, had packed him off to China before the minster's goons could get to him. The local students liked him: despite the playboy air, Aaron was a brilliant study. He spoke Mandarin like a native, and was very generous with his money.

Of course, Aaron Kotalawala would grow up to be NumberCorp's infamous Vice President of Business Development, creator of the world's most exclusive real estate.

Life at Tsinghua must have been rigorous. The Chinese education system is known for their experimental teaching techniques. Right now, it's neural downloads. In Common's time, it was an alternating pattern of hypnosis-aided study and self-exploration. The program Julius's scholarship was attached to was called "Deep End". It threw students together in a series of challenges – mostly involving actual government research. Students were exposed to a broad spectrum of subjects – a heady mix of computer science, physics, mathematics, sociology, economics – and assigned to prominent researchers as apprentices. The researchers had complete control over how long the student spent studying under them – and what their final qualification would be when they got out.

Here Common met another link in the story, a person who supplied most of the hard detail around this piece: Liu Heng.

Heng was the product of three generations of Chinese academics. Heng was - and still is - a very large man, almost uncomfortably tall, a giant from a land unaccustomed to giants.

They have been described as being aloof, almost monastic, a reputation added to by his being gender-neutral. He spoke then as he does now - quietly, carefully, with great weight and a slight stutter.

As the story goes, the two sat at a table at a little restaurant called the Slow Boat one Friday, slightly drunk and deep in thought.

Picture them. Common, dressed in his uniform black Tshirt and jeans ("Style follows practicality. Black was easy to clean"). Tsinghua had weeded out some of the Common that landed in Beijing; his hair was neat, his nails not bitten to the quick, and he actually wore shoes. Heng wore loose-fitting white, the very antithesis of Julius - black, white, short, tall; chaotic, composed.

The waitress approached. Three shots of neat rum for the black-clad foreigner; a glass of wine for the tall Chinese. Unknown to the her, the two had a real problem: submission time was coming, and neither of them had a project to submit. All they'd decided on was that they'd work on it together, whatever it was.

SOURCEBOT WARNING: UNVERIFIED SOURCES OR SOURCES OF QUESTIONABLE QUALITY. ARTICLE INTEGRITY HAPHAZARD.

Time was short. Tsinghua would not settle for cheap derivative papers - they had tried. And the legions of students in situ had decimated the topics they could work with. Desperation was setting in. Each would suggest a topic and the other would shoot it down. This I have from Heng himself. Like I said, I got to know Heng well over the years.

The last idea was simple: dig out the old blockchain identity project - and do it right this time.

The Bitcoin blockchain is an old project, and if I haven't properly explained how it works, it's only in sticking to my premise of not explaining the technology. Bitcoin itself was the world's first revolutionary currency that wasn't quite revolutionary; designed by the elusive Satoshi Nakamoto (who was never identified), Bitcoin brimmed with possibilities that threatened entire governments - tax-free international transfers, fund transfers that no bank or government could halt, and so on - but it never found enough users to actually bring about a financial revolution. That success was relegated to later derivatives, and by that time, with banks funding the development processes, the old controls were firmly in check.

Nevertheless, they all relied on what was called the blockchain: a linear, chain-like log of transactions.

Consider a credit card company; the transaction history of a card is stored within that company, and usually available only to them. If they're breached, and the records altered, that's it for that card. Bitcoin solved this problem by taking those transactions and handing out a copy to every single user around.

Every user on the network would store a copy of the entire history of every transaction that ever took place, and a user could only be part of that network if they constantly compared their history with everyone else's and maintained an identical record. If they forked - if their records were changed, or they refused to accept the global consensus - they were cast out. End of story. Any hacker trying to breach this system had not just one system to break into; they needed to simultaneously break into hundreds of thousands of computers. And, since it was stored in a linear fashion, one transaction stacked on top of the other, reversing an older transaction was nightmarish - almost impossible, one would say. It was consensus. It was, to put a political spin on things, democratic.

Over the years, many had figured out ways of using this system for public IDs - even Common, as detailed in the first article in this series, had dabbled in it. Common chose to redesign this system. With Heng, Common designed a network stored names, passport numbers, addresses and email addresses. To protect privacy he encrypted user records; if someone else wanted to see your ID, they would digitally generate a signed request to view an unencrypted copy of your data; if you countersigned that request, they'd be shown your ID and you'd be shown theirs.

And that's still how the Number works: the encryption's gotten better, and the signing processes hidden beneath cards and smartphone apps and simple button presses, but under the hood, it's still the same. I'm pretty sure Common was thinking of a police officer pulling someone over and asking to see their ID. "I'll show you mine if you show me yours," he says when describing this system to his students at Berkeley. It usually gets a laugh out of them.

A year and a half later, they were done. All three graduated well. Aaron Kotalawala returned to Sri Lanka. Heng peeled off too; Tsinghua has offered him a shot at a PhD. To them it was an interesting project; it was done, that was it. But not to Common - Common, who, burning with the possibilities, took his code to the United Nations and built a company with it.

The rest, as they say, is history.

COMMON: A HISTORY - III

Watchmen Press Archives

Content type: raw text

Channel: N/A

Warning: 302; contains errors and possibly unverifiable attribution sources. Hold publication until confirmed.

COMMON: A HISTORY - PART THREE
by Patrick Audomir Udo

That's the official story - the one that's right up there in the tech bible next to the stories of Bill Gates, Steve Jobs, Elon Musk and Mark Zuckerberg. It's simple. Clear, and it makes sure Julius Common gets the credit. That's a good story.

We tend to turn our heroes into myths, and we like our myths simple. Nobody cares if King Arthur got bored with his knights or what Arwen did to pass the time. All we care about is one good story, one rational narrative, one clear signal calling through the noise.

But there was always one more side to this story. After many years of deliberation, I'm compelled to tell it.

I began this series of articles during my tenure at Number-Corp. The Watchmen Press does not accept advertorial content, and to make this story worthy of submission I have had to dig further and deeper into Common's story than anyone had ever done before. I have done this with Common's fullest co-operation and perhaps a light touch of embellishment.

We must now talk about China.

By 2015, while Common was discovering Arab Spring and the wonders of Bitcoin Identity, the Chinese government had begun what was known to the West as the Social Credit project. Nobody really knows why they started it, but the way they spun it got the press drums beating. "To promote social trust and transparency between buyers and sellers" became "China introduces social scoring for complete transparency" and "Incentivizing social trust?"

Eventually, the press forgot it and stampeded over to coo about Uber and the tech bubble in Silicon Valley. And when China half-heartedly threatened war, men and women who had hitherto only written about dating apps suddenly started writing expert reviews on Chinese military tech.

Nevertheless, the Social Credit project continued. Drained of funds and attention, it was moved to cramped, squared-off section of a refurbished warehouse and turned over to Dr Wu Xin, who lectured at Tsinghua University. Twenty people crouched over laptops and tabs. The air conditioning rattled. Often, researchers would just get fed up and cycle out for the relative comfort of a nearby coffeeshop.

Dr Wu Xin herself was a brash genius, with a certain ruthless streak that saw her through two marriages, six companies and a sizeable chunk of political power. Nobody really understood why she had taken on the Social project; perhaps, some whispered, the powers that be wanted her out of the way. Those who know her often mention two things - her smoker's cough and a steady stream of complaints about the stupidity of the world at large.

I don't know the how or the why or the when; I suppose these things will never be found out. What I do know is something Liu Heng told me in passing: somewhere down the line, Social Credit took on Julius.

I suppose the reasons are simple. The project was understaffed, they needed a decent identity, and this undergraduate system looked just fine on paper - good enough that Wu Xin offered to get Common directly into their Masters program (another tidbit from Heng). "Bright. Can be useful. Talks too much. Needs focus," she is said to have noted after meeting Julius for the first time.

Heng, when he told me this, chuckled at the 'can be useful'. "That's high praise coming from my mother," he told me softly. "People to her were either useful or not."

Xin promptly hired her son and his new friend. The friend brought Aaron Kotalawala along. She hired him, too. But there is ample evidence to indicate that Wu Xin did not hire Common for the reasons Heng gave me. In her court records in 2040, she confessed to having recruited three young students from Tsinghua - including her own son - to carry out corporate espionage. The other two, though never named in her transcripts, were probably Julius Common and Aaron Kotalawala.

Is this difficult to imagine? Again, recall China in the decade before the Truce of 2030. "War footing" was not an exaggeration. South China Sea tensions were at an all-time high, and, if history is not mistaken, it was a situation not unlike the days of the Cold War and the Iron Curtain. The Chinese economy was straining prodigiously for three things - to exceed the United States' military capability on the oceans; to win the Mars race; and to become the economic center of the world. All three were well underway.

Older readers might also recall the case of the Eagle Watcher's Club, the innocuous-sounding agency that broke into both the Pentagon and the NSA. That was also China. We'll probably never know the full details, but we do know that one of the biggest state-sponsored electronic warfare efforts in history was also in the works.

In this context, it must have been pretty difficult for Xin to study the world of credit scoring as much as she liked - especially since holy trinity of Experian, Equifax and Callcredi, believed to have some of the finest systems in the world, were English. When Common presented himself (and presented Aaron Kotalawala, with his political connections), it must have been an amazing stroke of luck. Here was a Canadian with a UK citizenship and a Sri Lankan with enough political connections to get into any part of the West without anyone batting an eyelid.

Perfect.

If she sent her son along, it was only to watch over them.

This is the view held by the remnants of the Social Credit project - those researchers who actually worked with Wu Xin. Out of the original fifty-three, there are twelve still willing to tell this version of the tale. In their webcast The Great Firewall

And Other Histories, Dr Brian Zhou and Alana DeRisse describe the Social Credit days in great detail.

SOURCEBOT WARNING: UNVERIFIED SOURCES OR SOURCES OF QUESTIONABLE QUALITY. ARTICLE INTEGRITY CHECK FAIL.

One of the things they touched on was Common - viewed very much as a hired investigator or a data hound within the project, with little actual contribution to the codebase or the project strategy. According to them, the story of the student project is 'a believable myth'; Dr Wu Xin, they say, was the one who initiated contact. Not because they were special, but because they were the easiest to reach and the most malleable. The rest was mostly logic.

Zhou and DeRisse do point out that Wu Xin had Common sit in on all the in-house strategy meetings, and wonder whether this was the catalyst that inspired Common. Zhou, writing on the future founder of NumberCorp, saw as a "rather bright but unfocused person, too argumentative and brusque in his views; indeed, I avoided him often as not, not wanting to be drawn into an argument with someone of lesser knowledge."

In hindsight, perhaps Zhou should have argued a bit more with Julius Common. As he himself notes, it might have saved him from obscurity.

However, one does not simply turn undergraduate interns into spies.

At first the Social Credit project began to pipe-feed them secondhand data - demographics, anonymized credit score information, datasets from private companies already operational in China. Dr Wu Xin would handle the Tsinghua authorities. Julius, Heng and Aaron were to be given carte blanche to work on the project as they saw fit. It was a rare exception, but it was managed.

Julius and Heng began the laborious process of poring over the data, looking for something they could work on. Almost for the fun of it, Julius would run complex pattern-matching algorithms on the datasets, looking for something to work on. Heng, who seemed to know what he was looking for, would sift through ideas one by one, testing them against random samples.

No doubt there was real legwork, because they were not sent out into the field from the get-go. To test them, Wu Xin had them concoct and conduct elaborate analyses on existing data. What they got done were mostly trivial calculations - a set of graphs showing the credit score gap fluctuating across microgenerations wound up on Common's blog and made a bit of a splash; Heng followed through with a cultural inquiry, pointing out that the changes were tied to shifting attitudes towards consumerism in the media.

In times like these, Aaron, quietly and without fuss, would arrange for whatever they needed - processing power, cloud subscriptions, even first-years for data entry. The room he shared with Julius became a confused maze of computer parts, discarded food wrappers and people sitting in silence with their headphones in their ears. The arguments continued.

Initially, however, Aaron and Lui Heng were quite wary of each other. Though they'd crossed paths many times often, their ideas ran completely counter to one another, even on the most trivial of things, and Julius's irritation was quick to build.

"Heng and Aaron really did not get on when we met," said

Common once with a grin. "Polar opposites, right? Playboy businessman versus academic. We had this argument where Heng was like, "Why the fuck do we want a rich stoner on the project? I've heard of bacteria that are smarter." And I'm like, "Just try it for a week, okay, he's a lot smarter than he looks. And -" he shrugs, "well, it worked, didn't it?"

Indeed: as NumberCorp's history will show, Kotalawala worked better than anyone expected. But back to the story. They argued often. Or rather, Heng and Aaron argued; Julius, when irritated, would simply leave.

"Sometimes they would argue," recalled Common, a vague smile playing upon his features. "Not on the project itself, but around it, with their ideals, their beliefs - you know. Working on a dataset that large is like looking at the ocean: you can't help but look for things you want to see in there." The smile deepens. "Even Heng. He hated arguing, but get him started and he'll give you a good run for your money."

"And what would you do when they did argue?"

Common shrugged. "Let them fight it out. Let the better idea win."

Shades of Rand there. Nevertheless, this curious philosophy works. In fact, it seems to have been the direct predecessor of NumberCorp's notoriously combative, argumentative culture, where "May the best man win" is scrawled in ten-foot letters inside NumberCorp's headquarters; except the artist has crossed out the word "man" and replaced it with "idea" scrawled above. The famous art critic Ivan Pavlonsky wrote that this embodies the retirement of the concept of a man as a unit of labour, and his subsequent replacement, in modern society, with an infinitely more valuable unit: the idea.

But I chose to believe that it embodies Common's ethos in

the realm of ideas: let them clash, and execute on the one that wins.

In NumberCorp this motto led to a fiercely innovative culture that zigs, zags and continues to innovate at an incredible pace. Something like this must have fostered in that small apartment back in Common's past, fermenting and boiling over into genius, because before long, the Common-Heng-Kotalawala trio became known faces around campus.

Part of it was because of Wu Xin's project. By now, the first phase of the Credit project – a national credit-scoring system – was well under way and in use. It was a hot topic of discussion, especially in the slightly more liberal atmosphere of Zongguancun; anyone associated with it was identified very fast. Soon, Common and Kotalawala were being invited to speak at events about its progress.

But most of it was because of the sudden, explosive amount of work that they produced. A brief summary of their publications is enough to see why. In just under two years, the three turned out a fantastic amount of literature and analyses, some of which are studied to this date: Credit is the New Caste, The Economy versus the Spending Patterns of the Rich and the Poor and The Ones in the Middle all became landmark papers, and not just because they burned through quite a sizeable chunk of the personal finance landscape in the process.

Credit is the New Caste is particularly interesting, because Common's voice seems strongest there. An almost dreamy postulate, it explores the concept of applying a roughly Hindu-esque caste system based on net worth. Only those with true economic smarts, it says, can rise to the top in such a system, and by dint of that, economic collapse would be made almost impossible. It sparked wild, global debate at the time, not all of it positive. Common began to build up a reputation outside of China. Those were good papers.

What of the Credit project itself? Doubtless there were rumblings of the information leaks, but Wu Xin, locked away with her cigarettes, squashed them. The interns were right on target. No doubt it made the task of using them as spies much easier if they were already known for their research.

And Julius, much to his resentful happiness, went from being an unknown stranger to being . . . someone.

"It was a good time," acknowledged a modern-day Liu Heng, from his glass-and-concrete office in New York, present to me only as a photo and a chatbox.

"A simpler time," said Aaron Kotalawala, in his wood-and-leather study in his California mansion. There is a tinge of regret in his eyes.

"Best time ever," said Julius Common, in his eccentric aircraft of a home. "But of course, such things never last, do they?"

It has to be accepted that we will never, with absolute precision, be able to pinpoint what happened next. According to Zhou and DeRisse (and those that remain of Wu Xin's Team 39) say that one fine day in May, Julius Common, Liu Heng and Aaron Kotalawala were summoned to Wu Xin's office. In attendance was the Dean of Tsinghua and the lecturers mentoring the three. It was exactly one year and six months since Julius and Heng had sat at the Slow Boat and drunkenly wondered what they were going to do with their lives.

SOURCEBOT WARNING: UNVERIFIED SOURCES OR SOURCES OF QUESTIONABLE QUALITY. ARTICLE INTEGRITY HAPHAZARD.

The conversation that ensued was never recorded, but it was heated. Several witnesses heard Kotalawala, now fluent in Mandarin, lapse into a stream of swear-words in English. The Dean, a ponderous man with a big belly, shuffled out with sweat on his bald forehead. The lecturers followed, escorted by three women. One of them had a red lens in place of her left eye.

"Technical Surveillance Department of the PLA," writes Zhou. "I was disturbed, to say the least, and we were all very frightened. "Technical Surveillance is like American NSA, except more secretive and vastly more powerful in those days. Because of the work we did they always had a presence around the Project, but we had never seen them before. One did not talk about Technical Surveillance."

The three were led out by more Surveillance staff. Only Liu Heng looked calm. Julius Common looked stunned and Aaron Kotalawala looked livid.

"This isn't what we signed up for, goddammit!" he shouted.

"You'll live," said Wu Xin allegedly said. "Go get me what I want."

Four months later, Julius, Aaron and Heng boarded a flight from Beijing to Heathrow, London. Rumor is that they were taken by Surveillance for espionage training; a rumor only, but underscored by the fact that the three were never seen on Tsinghua again.

Tensions were high. Julius and Aaron walked ahead. Heng followed. Two Technical Surveillance agents – this time without the conspicuous lens-eyes – escorted them through security. The three followed and were soon lost in the crowd.

Obviously, Liu Heng would later deny having said anything of the kind. There are no records of any actual espionage that took place - both sides would have been far too clever for that. And here, regretfully, is where I lose detail and venture back into the domain of public knowledge.

Julius, having been indicted into the Social Credit program, graduated in record time. He then transfered across the world to Stanford to pursue a PhD in – of all things – economics - while mysteriously earning a collaborative spot with the United Nations. Liu Heng stays in China. Aaron Kotalawala goes back home to Sri Lanka. The trail goes cold.

But there are remnants of the story of the Social Credit project. The Great Firewall And Other Histories is still online. A 2026 paper titled Scoring Credit: Algorithmic Approaches, Pitfalls and Hypotheses describes eighteen different credit scoring algorithms in minute detail - mechanisms which were later found to have actually been in commercial use at the time. A couple of websites leaked internal accuracy tests versus simulations of the systems at Experian and a dozen other companies.

And of course, today, we have Society, the giant system that runs the People's Republic of China. To China, Society was the definition of the Confucian "guanxi" (): a complex idea of social connections and relationships, of associating oneself with others in a hierarchical manner to maintain social and economic order - and the idea of "face" () - a complex blend of social status, propriety and prestige. The idea of enforcing this with software fit like a glove. It has even been argued that Society, realistically, could never have been fully conceived of anywhere else, purely because nowhere else was such a depth of technical expertise and a culture so willing to receive it. What was a terrifying infringement of rights to the West was, to the Chinese, a better implementation of social concepts that had been around for thousands of years.

Nobody can and will ever confirm this, of course. But consider this: Wu Xin confessed to corporate espionage in a UN court in Vienna, accepting responsibility instead of letting her son go under.

Shortly after that, the Chinese government demanded the source code for the Number - ID, Credit, Records, Influence, all of it, on grounds that the root of it was the intellectual property of the government of the People's Republic of China.

There is a saying: a lie can go around the world before the truth has time to put its boots on.

I like that saying. There's a lot of truth in it. Especially because part of the story is something that has been lied about many, many times. Even my version of it is not complete: there are gaps I can't bridge, but I'll be honest about them. And by the time you read it, this will probably be the only record of what really happened in China. Remember that Julius Common and the Chinese government, between them, control virtually all of the world's publicly accessible information supply. Remember that stories, like coins, have two sides. I have spent a lifetime preaching one side; and now I cross to the other.

SOURCEBOT WARNING: UNVERIFIED SOURCES OR SOURCES OF QUESTIONABLE QUALITY. ARTICLE INTEGRITY HAPHAZARD.

Epilogue

Epilogue

Have I done justice here?

I wanted to give you some idea of what they were like, Russell Wurth, Aniston, Ibrahim, Julius Common, even Liu Heng: I want there to be some memory of not just what they did, but how they did it, and what they were like as people. So many of us have been crushed under Julius's unstoppable march towards godhood. It is the least I can do to remember some of them.

And yet NumberCorp was - is - such a vast and complicated beast. So many wheels turning; so many lives on so many lines. Have I, in wasting time on the bits of conversation that I recall, done them a disservice? Every time I go over what I have written it feels as if there is so much more to write.

At the end, I must believe that I have told the story as best as I could, as keep moving on.

Russell Wurth, as far as I know, was taken in again for questioning. He was tried for data theft and the selling of state secrets to the Chinese under the alias Tobias Prophet. He was incarcerated for a year in Fort Wintermute, a high security facility near Cahaba, Alabama, designed for housing the most hardened cybercriminals.

Years after his release another inmate published a video series describing in explicit detail the brutal regime of hallucinogenic torture and sexual abuse that Wintermute systematically applied to every inmate who was held there. The reveal only hardened Wurth's reputation.

Liu Heng, to the best of my knowledge, lived and died a devoted intellectual. I came in touch with him briefly during my later career. Heng eventually came to be something of an intellectual hero in both China and the West, and his publications eventually became the basis for reforms on free education throughout the world.

And I?

When I left NumberCorp, I was all of 35. Like many others of my generation, I dreaded waking up and seeing my face, now lined and bony, in the mirror. We had grown up believing that life ended at 30.

I was surprised when it didn't. Life, as it turns out, goes on, and the only thing that makes it end is when you believe it does.

I took to the road. It was a strange itch; and I told myself I was safer away from NumberCorp anyway. The shadow of Crisis Response still loomed over me. I went to Russia; from Russia to India. Arundhati Khatri and Nassim Khalil, who'd worked on my webseries, remembered me there. Old ghosts.

It was they who got me to teach. Soon, moving halfway across the world, I was teaching. I taught photographers how to do old-fashioned photography -no light fields, just prime lenses. I taught film students what moments to capture and what to leave behind. Teaching resonated with me. They say the ultimate purpose of all life, from a bacterium to a human, is to pass on information. I'm sure this was initially meant genetically, but the way I see it, we pass on information much faster than genes ever could. I was speeding the process. It felt good.

I never expected to run into Julius again, even though he lived in my life in a thousand ways. Every morning I'd check Number News on my phone. Tap, tap. There, just above the news and the social gossip and the who-checked-in-wheres, was my Score. My Score was critical. It got me the best tables at restaurants I went to, all simple but pricey affairs. It got me into the VIP section of any club when I wanted to party. It got me first-class tickets on the airplanes. When Atlantis opened up in the UK, it got me my penthouse suite at a fraction of the actual price: the management was just happy to have me there, knowing that over time, everyone's Scores would rise simply because I was around. People were nice to me on principle. That's how good it was.

And it was a reminder. Of Julius, of NumberCorp, of what we'd built. Ten years ago half these people wouldn't have given two hoots about me. I didn't have to drive a Lamborghini, hang out at expensive clubs, Instagram the rich life, and all that. In a way, the Number was liberating: I could live my life the way I wanted, and as long as my work was relevant, I didn't need the facade.

One fine day in November, I woke up, brushed the face, washed the teeth, to borrow a phrase, and got on with life. The sun rose, the Perpetual Cherry in the courtyard shed soft red leaves, like it always did, and I drove off to the airport to pick up Corky.

Hatsuko Ida, or Corky, as I called her, was my obsession. She was smart, funny, intelligent - you know, all the phrases people use to describe the people they're infatuated with. And she was a spectacular mix of African-French and Japanese; unconventional, but ... some people draw us like moths to a flame; Corky could have been dead broke (in fact, she was, back then) and wearing rags and people would still have been drawn to her. Corky had a tough childhood. Her actual body was minus one arm and half a leg: what she wore was mecha. It always got her into trouble at airports. Today she leads Overwatch, the UN special agency that actively hunts child abusers. Some day, if she ever reveals the full extent of what was done to her, you'll understand.

They had her in an airport detention area, all concrete and metal rails. I stopped the officer outside. "What's the charge?"

"We can't let her in without a resident signing for her, sir," he said. I must have frowned, because he looked apologetic. It looked odd, because he was wearing full tac armor, and you don't see many apologetic faces on the north end of a hardsuit. "Zone law, sir, sorry about that. Nobody with a Number below 10K gets in, that's what we're told."

I signed. Atlantis law. The place was built as a VIP zone, but the requirements had risen. "What's hers?"

"8K, sir," said the apologetic officer.

"Bit black and white, isn't it?"' Two years ago 8K would have entitled her to live here - apartment, car, the works.

"Company rules, sir," he said, letting Corky out of the detention room. Corky smiled when she saw me. We hugged.

"Your boys are being a bit unfriendly, yeah," she said.

The officer pretended not to have heard.

"Oy," she said, turning to the officer. "What's your Number?"

"Tell her," I told the officer, knowing he'd never respond

otherwise.

"3.5K, ma'am," he said stiffly.

Corky was outraged. "Three thousand five hundred and you're bloody keeping me out, running security for a place like this in bloody riot armor? That's not enough to be barmaid! How much do they pay your arse?"

The officer gave me a pleading look. She had a point, but he probably needed that job; I led her away.

"You rich people have shitty rules, you know that"' she grumbled.

No we don't. Mostly we have excellent rules. But that was an interesting insight, the first of that day. As we drove, we discussed that officer. Corky soon calmed down enough to start asking the kind of questions I loved hearing from her. How did he feel, looking out over the dwellings of the rich and the powerful every day, knowing he'd never be able to live in Atlantis? Knowing that, if it weren't for that job, he wouldn't even have been allowed close enough to see it? After all, a 3.5K Score is abysmal; poverty, a short stint in prison, debt - that's 3.5K.

"He's probably just happy to have a job in the first place," decided Corky. Her phone pinged; she checked it, and looked stunned. "Damn, Pat," she said slowly. "The combined Score of this place is in the billions. You could do. . . well, damn, anything!"

"How'd you know?''

She showed me. It was a clever app, layered on top of Google Maps; it pinged people in an area and mapped out their Numbers. We were surrounded by a sea of numbers.

"Now you're part of it, too," I said. "Welcome to the one percent."

Corky had never been to my part of Atlantis before, so I gave her the full tour. Despite the name, Geneva Tower is in Edo, a very Japanese zone, all hillocks and forests and faux-wooden bridges. Perpetual Cherry trees, the products of decades of commercial GMO, weep red leaves into an artificial river. Buildings the color of stone, wood and old ivory are placed with great care, designed for fine views. Drones don't work here. Planes can't fly above us. It's a wonderful place, and like most wonderful places, it's exorbitantly expensive.

"Would you like to live here?" I asked as we leaned over a bridge, hoping she'd get the hint.

"On my salary?" Corky said. Her laugh reflected in the water below. Then she got it. "Oh. Nah, Patrick. This isn't my thing."

"What isn't? Me?"

"Oh no, no, not you," she said quickly. "I meant this. Atlantis. Reclaimed theme-park island for rich folks and celebrities, yeah? I'm from London, Pat, across the Bridge. I don't belong here."

"That can't be the problem," I said. "The whole point of this place is that you can do whatever you want. Look around, Corky. Open space. Legroom. Fresh air to breathe. It's not a polluted hell-hole like London."

"I like that hell-hole, thank you very much, I live there."

"Why?"

Silence. "I don't know," she said at last. "Look, there's more life there, yeah? Yeah, it's crowded, yeah, the Tube's always fucking broken and the traffic's terrible, but it's life. You've got rich folks, poor folks every type of folks in between. And I need that, Pat. That's what my art works with. This place, it's nice, Pat. Calm. But it's boring. It's flat. The people here are all the same. Black, white, they're all rich people, they all think the same and act the same and tell themselves they're special. Present company excluded, of course."

"Flattered, I'm sure," I said dryly.

She hugged me. "Don't be mad," she said. "I like this place. It's quiet. Maybe someday I'll get tired of everything and want to come here and be with you. But we'll let that happen later, yeah? For now, I don't want this quiet. I want people, I need to be around people. Real people."

"Real people," I echoed.

"You know what I meant."

"No doubt," I lied, changing gears. The bridge suddenly felt like the wrong place to be. "So. Shall we, then?"

I kept running that phrase over and over in my head as we left. Real people. As if all the rich and the powerful and the high Scorers were somehow fake. But why? If anything it was everyone else that was fake; all those teeming millions of people that had barely distinguished them from the muck. And Corky, Corky was no real person herself. Her 8K score made sure of that.

I think I convinced myself that it was her insecurities, that she liked it outside, where 8K was celebrity, as opposed to here, where that Number meant detention in a shitty airport cell. I told myself she wanted attention. And then I think I forgot it, because Corky had a good time. We went racing on the kart track, whizzing by in old petrol cars with the basic suspensions. It was pleasantly nostalgic. We had tea in Helion; she stared out over the mountains, wrapped in thought, while I fielded calls. Then, because we were both tired, we came back to my place. I took a nap while she jacked in, bouncing around the Internet in her own private reality.

When I woke up, the first of our guests had arrived. I'm never good with one person for the whole day; I like to shut off during the evenings. Corky, unfortunately, was the polar opposite, so I'd put together a good list for her. The Sakhalins, curators of the famous Volds Digital Art Gallery; Tekka Innaryut, one of the last true Medieval history scholars (though I doubt he ever made money - there's not much value to knowing your history when Google knows everything). Hari Gnanaprasand of the Global Weather Shapers Hub.

And a few others. Corky's kind of people: artists and do-gooders and people gushing about humanity even in this age of machines. I spent the evening walking around with champagne at the ready, letting their conversation wash over me.

"So I heard Narya is running for President this year?"

"Narya?"

''-did you see?"

"Floods in the Maldives, just terrible. You know, we might need the Chinese to come rebuild that place."

"Another island? We just finished building Atlantis-"

"Oh, amazing, just amazing. The way she extracts the idea, you know, the very essence - they're calling her the second Yeats -"

"Of course, we have to consider ocean currents and shipping lanes; the sea might actually be better with the Maldives out of the way-"

"How can you say that? We're talking about an entire culture!"

I smiled. I was used to people like this. As long as the world existed, so would they, hatching plans for the rest of the world over caviar and truffles. Never mind that the actual power lay elsewhere. No, people like these would form committees, speak at meaningless conferences and pat themselves on the back when someone actually did make a change. It's human to pretend you're in power.

Real people, a voice inside me said testily.

"You know, for a host, you're not looking particularly interested in your guests," said a familiar voice behind me.

I turned. There, standing in my little lobby, was Russell Wurth.

"Bloody hell," I said.

Wurth looked old. When I had last seen him, he was still a young man; clean shaven, with flawless skin, he'd always looked too young to be drinking. The Wurth standing before me had stubble and wrinkles around his eyes. His blond hair was carefully combed, but it was longer and tied down to his shoulders. He wore a neat black shirt and white pants. It made him look like a European hitman.

"Elkhead," he said, no doubt guessing exactly what was running through my mind right then. "Er. Minerva. That Indian chick you were dating. Parvati. It's me."

"I see you lost the glasses," I said, extending a hand.

Wurth shook it. "New eyes altogether."

"You're fucking kidding me."

He grinned. Corky caught my eye and started to make her way towards us; I waved her off. Later, I promised. She nodded and beamed at someone else instead.

I turned back to Wurth. "Don't worry about the crowd. Drink?"

The grin vanished. "We're long overdue for one," he said, looking uncomfortable. "But no, I was just, ah, passing by. Just saw a lot of activity around your pad, and I sort of knew Corky, and figured I'd drop by and see if you were alive and all that."

We studied each other.

"You look good," he said at last. I swear he sounded jealous.

"You look like hell," I said.

"Yeah, well," he said. "Julius's big conference is tonight."

"You want to stay for dinner? Let's watch it on the big screen over a drink."

There were two wallscreens in my apartment: the one downstairs, which was public, and the other one upstairs.

The one upstairs was a NumberCorp tracker, and it was buzzing. The first big Number conference in years, trumpeted the media. Utopia. Speculation ran wild. Corky and her circles paid no attention to it, and didn't probably even see it, but it was all anyone on my feeds had talked about for a month.

We clinked bottles and, as if by unspoken covenant, spoke only of trivial things. The weather. Atlantis. The Germans, who had figured out how to 3D-print a full, adult human body in less than a week, and what that meant for us. The Speakers for the Dead, who were now offering to revive your loved ones as perfect android replicas, and how the UN was banning them. What might it mean to live in a truly legal, post-death world.

NumberCorp we left for the last. There are some things you don't talk about until you have the excuse of being drunk.

"You know I don't exist on the Number anymore?" he said suddenly. "Run a search."

I did. Nothing came up.

"No Number, no records, no nothing," he said, a trifle bitterly. "Julius's way of punishing me, you see. I don't exist on the system anymore. I'm untraceable. Ironically the hackers all think I'm a genius because I've managed to go off the grid.

They're doing it to themselves now."

"How'd you get in here?"

"Turns out there are other ways of making money," Wurth said. "Couple of operations out here that need good hacker services. I call up the boys in the cloud, they deliver, I take my cut and make sure everyone gets paid what they're due. And your boys outside the gate, they think I'm super-VIP because they can't read my Score." He downed another shot, and looked confused for a moment. "You don't mind drinking with a convict?"

"Only if you can't hold your alcohol," I said. "So what do you think he's going to talk about?"

"Well, he's giving the damn thing from the United Nations, so I don't know, but it better be a bombshell. Why are you here, anyway? No invites to the big conference?"

I shrugged. Truth be told I had, like all ex-employees, gotten event invites months ahead of schedule. I simply never went anymore.

"You've changed," I told him.

Wurth shrugged. "Everything changes," he said.

We drank in silence until the conference began.

The conference is a special thing in the tech world. A few minutes of carefully orchestrated stage time have turned old men into legends and flipped company reputations around. A lot of work goes into the magic of setting things up just so that you don't see the moving parts. Done properly, a conference is magic; a few delays here and there and that godlike keynote becomes little more than a corporate presentation.

Wurth and I, we knew what NumberCorp could do. We knew exactly how mesmerizing Julius could be when he spoke. I personally had no idea what the conference might announce, but I expected the usual trappings: glamour, glitz, a show of social force.

Instead, the camera cut to a single shot of Julius Common in front of a podium. He was dressed in his trademark black - a shirt and a suit of severe cut and color. His face hovered above it, a thick triangle, now topped by salt-and-pepper stubble.

"Julius Common, Founder and Chief Architect of Number, live from New York City,' said a disembodied voice. There was equally disembodied applause. The camera pulled back, and I suddenly understood the reason for the stillness and the suit. Julius stood at a single central podium carved with the laurel wreath and the globe; around him, in circles, sat the members of United Nations.

Julius looked directly into the camera and began to speak. His face betrayed no emotion.

"Madam President; Mr. Secretary General; delegates of the United Nations; ladies and gentlemen. On behalf of all of NumberCorp, I would first like to thank you for inviting me to speak here today.

"As you know, we have a long history with the United Nations. In fact, I believe this partnership really began when we decided to adopt the blockchain technology that my first company, Tenjin, developed. With our technology, and the political and social power present in these halls, we were able to give the world, for the first time, a global, distributed identity system that complied with the standards set by the Geneva Human Movement. Not only did we overhaul an old system and remove so many inconveniences; we also made it possible for people to move from nation to nation as true, global citizens, and for countries to enable immigration and travel policies with much greater precision than ever thought possible.

"The UN identity blockchain was an incredible achievement. Yet some of us, while working on it, saw ways in which we could use that same technology to improve other parts the human condition. Thus, we began work on the Number.

"Today, the Number touches 4 billion lives. Together, we have changed so much. We have fought the forces of materialism and wasted consumerism that threatened to erode our civilisations, to turn our democracies into shallow voter pools, and with great effort we have truly harnessed technology for transparency. We have given, to people, for the first time in the history of humanity, a measure of themselves; tangible, understandable, a system that accurately reflects all the nuances and complexities in how we humans actually work together. The repercussions of the Number have since spread long beyond the technological framework that we set out to build. In this time of great financial, spiritual and political turmoil, we have brought trust back into a world which forgot how to trust. By reacting to social context, we have reduced racial, gender and mechanical inequality. In an age of chaos and unrest, we have made the world greater than it was.

"This is important work. It has made a real difference in the lives of our people. And it could not have happened had we not worked together.

"And yet, we remain, as humans, in a vicious cycle. We, rob, steal, cheat, kill each other, and we blame it on our government, and we say it's alright. We say it's fine. We say my country is not your country because of this imaginary line in the sand. And thus we fabricate conflict and we kill in the names of gods."

He paused to sip from a glass.

"On my way here, to this institution, I began re-reading

the history of the United Nations. After the first World War - which happily none of us remember - we created the League of Nations, and we said, well, perhaps this instrument will help everyone work together and preserve peace. That failed. After the second World War, we created the United Nations. We haven't failed, but neither have we succeeded. We are, on reflection, fraught with politics and ego and all manner of useless causes - the very things that make us human. Some tell me that our dream of a unified world has always only ever been a fool's hope.

"Now at NumberCorp, I find myself in a unique position: for the first time in human history, we make that dream come true, not with fallible humans and with politicians, but with precise, fair and just algorithms. We can do it without violence, without bloody revolution. Thanks to the Number, ladies and gentlemen, we are now sufficiently integrated into every single economy that we can judge our politicians and our leadership and hold them accountable to the cause of global peace. For the first time in human history, we can tap into both public sentiment and all of our frameworks of global regulations and agreements to allow for a stable, global political climate."

Did my eyes deceive me, or did Julius look tired?

"In fact, the next set of updates, which my team and I have been working on for the past five years, will bring precisely this capability to the NumberCorp network. No more tyrants; no more errant ministers. We will not need embargoes. We will not need political tribunals. We will have governance, led not by human egos, but by goal-oriented algorithms."

There was a swell of noise that almost threatened to drown him out.

"And I have the great pleasure of announcing that every

single one of our major partners and most of the political leadership of the United Nations have agreed to this. I see this not as a replacement for the work you do here, but I see us as an extension; perhaps a spiritual successor. Of course, some parts of the United Nations may become redundant -"

He held up his hands for silence.

"May be redundant," he repeated. "Don't get me wrong: I fully expect this to come as a shock. But this is how we progress as humans. We went from horseless carriages to self-driving, self-organizing transport in a hundred and fifty years. We went from powered flight to putting a man on the moon in sixty years. We've always progressed in leaps and bounds. It is our ability, no, our duty, to do what is efficient, and to do what is best, to evolve not just our vehicles and our cities and our homes, but also the social structures that hold us back."

Julius Common had just told the UN that he was replacing them.

"Jesus," whispered Wurth.

On the screen, Julius continued.

"And there are a couple more updates, and ironically this is still related to the subject. Despite all the division and discord in the world, there have always been movements that transcended geography and politics and taught people how to live well. Jesus, the Buddha, Mohammed, they all created philosophies that promoted stability; that have said to people thou shalt not kill, thou shalt not steal - and set a code of ethics for people to live by.

"Over the years, in our search for truth, we studied all of these religions and distilled what we found there into what we call the Guidance Update. We believe - no, we know - that these truths are timeless; they are universal; and every single ruleset that we have built inevitably leads us to a certain set of behaviors. We will not kill; we will not steal; we shall not covet what is not ours. At NumberCorp, we took a look at what we planned to do - to set rules down and enforce them - and realized, looking at the old religions, that if we can't actively tell you how to live within those rules, how to live better lives through them, then that just makes us tyrants.

"So, members of the United Nations: I'd like to introduce Guidance," said the voice of Julius Common, broadcast to billions of us in the world outside. "Guidance will remember everywhere you go, everything you do, and it will suggest to you how you can do better - and where, and why. It allows you to access the billions of factors and data points that we compute, and it can use that to show you who should be friends with, and who to avoid, where the best place to work will be for you - and a thousand other decisions that we can help you with. It is a next-generation distributed intelligence that lives in your phone, your watch, your home. Every day, Guidance will be at your beck and call, helping you get better. We've created the ultimate social companion."

And he smiled. It wasn't the old shark grin; this was something altogether more sober, something more restrained, but it was a smile nonetheless.

"I have no better way of putting this than to say this," he said. "The Buddha, Christ and Mohammed had to rely on God and karma and human priests for judgement; we don't. We have data. We have algorithms. We have Guidance. God is now available as an application, on your mobile phone or in the cloud, twenty four seven, three sixty five. It's our way of making the world a better place."

We sat in stunned silence, watching as, on the screen, some

of the world's most powerful leaders rose in a standing ovation to Julius Common. They knew when they were beat.

When it was all over, Wurth stood up. He looked like I felt: dazed. It all felt terribly surreal.

Corky called out to us as we headed downstairs again. The party, having drunk their way through our wine, was now winding down. "You're staying for dinner, of course? You two look like you've seen a ghost."

"No, I need to go," said Wurth. "Late for another appointment."

Wurth's car sat outside my gate, a squat McLaren that shone an ominously white color. For some reason it reminded me of bones. It opened up neatly as he approached. He stood in front, as if he had forgotten what it was.

At the gate, just before he vanished into the night, he grabbed my shoulder.

"He said God."

"I heard him," I said.

"When I was a kid, there was a light in our backyard," he said. "When we turned it on in the evening, these little insects would flock to it, drawn to the light. They would buzz and circle around it in a frenzy until their wings gave out and they fell to the ground and died." In the darkness he suddenly seemed small. "Listen, I know those creatures were the result of millions of years of evolution. Time and genetics told them to seek the light. Maybe a response to the sun. Then we humans came and broke all of that in a few centuries. Some guy invented the electric bulb and behold! In every nation, on every continent, confused insects would buzz around these new . . . suns . . . and die. You know what that reminds me of?

Every time Jules changes his mind, a thousand, ten thousand, a million of us buzz and die. We're the insects, aren't we?"

"I understand why you don't like him," I told him. "But you have to admit, he's going to make it work. You know he will."

"Always an idiot, you were," said Wurth sadly. "What was that saying Julius used to have on his hand? Memento? Something to do with a slave telling the Roman general not to get too cocky?"

Memento Mori. Of course I remembered. "Something of the sort, yes."

Wurth nodded. "You were Julius's," he said. He stuck out a hand. "It was good seeing you, Patrick."

Author's Note

This book is not meant to be a moral lesson, nor is it a particularly wild feat of imagination. I wrote Numbercaste simply as an extension of trends that I already saw in our society - from algorithmically created social bubbles to fake news. Many sources quoted before the time of writing is real; some are fabricated. China's social scoring project does exist as of the time of writing, although most of what's in the story is pure imagination on my part. Conjecture about Facebook, Google, Twitter and SpaceX are also feats of extrapolation on my part and not indicative of how things might actually turn out.

If you enjoyed it, please review it on Amazon; a rating and couple of words about what you thought of it go a long way towards showing the author where their work stands. It also helps potential readers decide whether or not to buy this book. I hope you had as much fun reading it as I had writing it.

Dedication

It's traditional to write a dedication at the front of a book and acknowledge people at the back of it.

But this book has been a long and very personal journey, and the people who helped me along this road mean a lot to me: I want to dedicate Numbercaste it to all of them.

Firstly, to those extraordinary friends of mine who, who, with both the velvet glove of friendship and the iron hand of critical analysis, looked at my ideas, dissected my writing, and helped me polish a raw Numbercaste into what it is today.

To Aisha Nazim, who sent me forty pages of notes listing every spelling mistake and grammatical flaw. To Nisansa Dilushan de Silva, who examined at the economics and politics represented in the book, and stress-tested every detail ("What's with this population drop?"). To CD Athuraliya, who pushed me to do my best work, who taught me that the world of bleeding-edge technology often far outstripped my own predictions. If they're not too ashamed of being called the editors of this book, I'd say that's a very accurate description.

To Sharon Dinasha Stephen and Dilina Pathirage, who showed me where I am as a writer, and where I should aim to be.

To Adnan Issadeen, who is quoted in this book, and to Lasantha David, for their unfailing ability to cut down my bullshit where they see it, and for thousands of insights into technology, life, and 18-hit combos in Mortal Kombat.

They say a human is the sum of their friends. I can only look at these people and say that I am less than the sum of them put together. I blame almost all of this on the bad influence that my cat has on me.

Secondly, to two writers I greatly admire: Nayomi Munaweera and Navin Weeraratne.

Navin, at one spectacularly windy evening at the Station (Geek Meet, early 2015), gave me the first two pieces of advice a writer should ever get: to show, not tell, and to protect my time, and to pour everything I could spare into my work.

Nayomi taught me everything else I know about being a writer. She's been a mentor from afar ever since a friend dragged me to a meeting with her at Barefoot. Over many, many conversations, she taught me to be patient, to keep going, one word at a time, and to look back every so often and kill my darlings (not the people, I mean, the writing. The people are in short supply and tend to frown upon being killed).

Thirdly, to the good people of Reedsy (fantastic tooling, folks) and to the indie authors who have spent their time helping new wordsmiths. I'm talking about Hugh Howey, Mark Dawson, and the amazing people of the 20books group - Michael Anderle, Kevin McLaughlin, JR Handley and others. People like this, people who like seeing other people succeed, who spend their time and energy nurturing others wherever they can, are rare gems.

But most importantly, this book is dedicated to my mother,

Padminie Hettithanthri. She's an extraordinary woman who saw me as a writer long before I saw it in myself. There's a story about how the principal called my parents once and asked if I was alright in the head, because something about a seven year old writing about a dying, diseased stray dog freaked them all out.

My mother's fond of that story. Every so often she dredges it up, asks how the writing is going, reminds me that I don't eat enough, and tells me that I should have studied writing, not Physics, at school. And every so often when I look up from the computer there's a hot mug of coffee waiting outside.

That's the best thing in the world.

Made in the USA
Monee, IL
24 July 2022

10266604R00177